When Tharguen and his team travel to Dûnelor in an attempt to secure an alliance with the desert dwellers, they discover a sinister plot, and some of the most dangerous Morkans are behind it.

Tharguen is forced to face the darkness of his past, Niome must unlock more of her newfound powers in order to protect her kingdom, and Bahvley is shaken by truths uncovered when Teloria is faced with a deadly and undefeatable new foe.

Also by Celinka Serre

Stardust Destinies I Variate Facing
(the first installment of the series)

Stardust Destinies Short Stories
(found at www.medium.com/stardust-destinies)

Various Fiction Short Stories
(found at www.medium.com/@BinkyInkWriting)

Stardust Destinies

II

THE DROUGHT

by

CELINKA SERRE

Edited by Cleo Miele

Cover Art by Sophie Brunet

Binky Ink
A division of Binky Productions

www.binkyproductions.com/stardustdestinies

Published by Binky Ink
Edited by Cleo Miele
Cover Art by Sophie Brunet

ISBN: 978-0-9919965-5-1

Dedicated to
The book's biggest fan, my Mom.

<h1 style="text-align:center">ACKNOWLEDGEMENTS</h1>

As this is the second book of the series, it is exciting for me to embark once more on this journey with the Five of the Star and all their close friends whom they cherish. There are many friends whom *I* cherish who throughout every step encouraged me, inspired me, helped me develop an idea, or provided insight that allowed me to further develop my characters.

Many such friends will find their likeness in some characters, fearless warriors who join the Five to fight "For the Freedom of Life!" To respect their privacy, I will not mention names, but as I promised I would write: "See, now it's in print, so you can never be forgotten." This friend from long ago will know which character she inspired me to write.

In addition, I must give acknowledgement to my close family and my husband, whose words of encouragement continually help me refocus on the things that matter most to me.

Moreover, it has been a tremendous joy working with Cleo Miele who edited this book. She was able to suggest changes that at the same time retained my voice as the writer and also enhanced the narrative just that little bit that made all the difference.

Last but not least, I must give thanks to my cover artist, and friend, Sophie Brunet, who once again, has brought a scene from the book to life in the form of a gorgeous painting. The scene on the front cover and back depict two incidents that are connected, and I can't wait for you to meet this new kind of foe.

So without further ado, thank you to all who have helped and continue to help with promoting this book, and to all who have become devoted readers as they, as you, continue this journey with me and the Five of the Star.

Table of Contents

Recap On What Happened Last

When the Great Wizardess Elina died, she uttered her last words to her apprentice, Niome, who then secretly left Teloria to find out what lay at the Great Rock. Meanwhile, Meysah gathered a small team of Jimmy, Vigh and Boreth to go after his sister. After many days of travel, they found Niome and reached the Old Grey House where Drúgan lived. His secret apothecary was inside the Great Rock, and that was where Niome would discover the house, advice, and a potion that would later save Jimmy's life.

At this point, the five Telorians realised that their mission was more complicated and more dangerous than they had anticipated. They now had to travel to Mork to retrieve the *Book of Enchantment* stolen by Mirauk, who was constantly searching for the *Complement Book,* for he wished to pass through the Portal at the Dragon's Lair, thus gaining ultimate power over all the lands.

They were the only ones who could stop it all, but they only first discovered it in Firlan, where the people referred to them as the Five of the Star.

They set off for Mork, but Niome was soon captured by Morkans and separated from the others. The other four were befriended and taken in by the Dalvarans. Niome was held captive at the Morkan caves where she was watched over very closely by Gowtch, a polc who helped her escape one night and revealed his true identity as a Telorian – a long-lost friend of hers, Tharguen. He had once been Bahvley's best friend, and he declared that Bahvley was alive, though no one knew where he was or had been for the past fifty polken years. They found the others at the Dalvaran secret hideout, and the six Telorians and a great many Dalvarans set out disguised as Morkans.

It was on their way to Mork that they encountered an army incidentally belonging to Bahvley, who was also in disguise with a new people, the Kikies. The larger group went to Mork together, where Niome succeeded in retrieving the *Book of Enchantment.* However, it cost her a painful encounter with Mirauk. She looked into his evil gaze and suffered several of his immense powers, one of which involved Mirauk probing her mind and retrieving valuable information. The others worried she would die in the struggle.

Mirauk had cast spells on the Five to test them and exploit their weaknesses, which they experienced on their way to the Portal: Niome fought illness, waking up to prove herself indeed stronger than Mirauk; Vigh had to save Bahvley's life and his own from death by suffocation when rocks tumbled down, entrapping them; Boreth had to find his peace of heart when he found out that not only had his master died in Teloria but that many of his close friends and family had as well; Meysah had to confront a dragon and conquer it without slaying it; and Jimmy had to face death and remember the potion to prove his will, which he did just as they stepped out of Darakön.

At the Portal, Niome came to understand that no one should pass through it when the dragons burnt the two books containing the key spell to enter it. Now, Mirauk would no longer be able to steal any books or ever gain power over all the lands. At last, the Telorians could go home.

However, the war wasn't over yet; in fact, they had merely begun their journey towards victory. Still, when they arrived home, they were honoured and awarded with many gifts. Bahvley became King, Tharguen became Captain, Boreth and Vigh became Lords, Jimmy was recognised as an apprentice knight, and Meysah was partnered with him. Niome was named the Great Wizardess of Teloria, recognised as the one most powerful wizardesses in Kaulchèc History.

Filling In The Blanks

*I*n the six years that passed in Teloria, Niome wrote the new *Spell Book*. Vigh and Boreth got more in touch with their magical side while training Jimmy and Meysah, who became quite skilful; everyone was amazed by how quickly they learnt, and especially by their skill in the advanced techniques. Niome grew in power, though she didn't realise it yet, and it would take some time before others became aware of her progress. She created her own crystal orb as well as a new wand.

Together, the Five created a special spell to call out to each other when they were apart, for they couldn't always be by each other's side. The spell sent the feelings and state of being of the sender so that whether they were in trouble or simply relaxing, the others would easily know.

Niome made a few trips to Mistoff to give news to the Pleessies and learn a few secrets on how to create a magical shield for Teloria, which would take a while for her to learn – more than six years, for much was involved, including learning the proper pronunciation of the Pleessy language. Boreth spent much time at the Old Grey House with Clahria. None of the Five had ventured very far, though, save for when they paid a visit to their Dalvaran friends. Bahvley and Tharguen had at last seen the statues of themselves at Dalvar Fortress. *'What a sight!'* they marvelled, eyes wide.

The reconstruction of the wall around Teloria proper was completed, and the Telorians began building a double wall in certain areas for reinforcement. Selemil personally oversaw this project. Bahvley was starting to get the hang of being King with the guidance and aid of Selemil, Henker and Nsarmön, who acted as his advisors. Tharguen established his 'small army', as he liked to call them, with twenty Telorians of various ages at his command. Teloria was certainly not in short supply of brave and skilled knights – not in Tharguen's team, anyway – and Tharguen trained with them every week.

Phynd decided to take most of his Kikies back home with him, travelling the very long distance by sea to report back to the Kikies in Kikiland, as those who now knew the ways of the polcs needed to pass on their knowledge and new talents. He promised to return to Teloria with many more Kikies than ever before. In the land of the Kikies, they only had smaller ships for travel; they had never needed warships before. Seldom had wars ever occurred in all of Kiki history thus far. Now, using their knowledge of battleships gained in Teloria, they were planning to build a grand armada, and those who knew how to build would go home. Phynd would have stayed, but he was their Captain, and so ten Kikies stayed and became part of Tharguen's team. Among them were Celor, Mië, Tithil, Forthil, Dessimë, and a few others with whom the Telorians had become close.

Tharguen and his team decided to travel to the Desert of Dûnelor to ally themselves with the people who dwelt there, for Teloria would need their help in the coming war.

Timeline Review

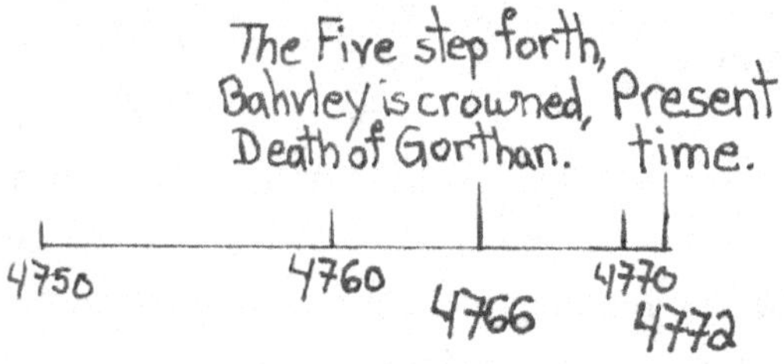

CHAPTER ONE:
An Unfortunate Misunderstanding

Tharguen and his small army journeyed through the desert. The air was still, the weather was dry, and the sky was clear. They had been walking through the desert for three days already, and no one had come to welcome them yet. They had waited at the gates of the rocky wall that surrounded this vast and magical desert, but no one had come then either. It was quiet; only the birds of the sandy sea could be heard.

Tharguen turned to face his team. 'We'll need to be on our best behaviour; the Dûnelorians are a proud people and deserve our respect. Their ancestors come from a great and distant land. The Dûnelorians have seldom explored outside their magical desert and usually keep to themselves. Sure, there has been the odd Dûnelorian-Telorian union in marriage, but they've been few and sparse. And in recent centuries' – Tharguen looked across the dunes – 'since Mirauk's rise to power, the Dûnelorians have not ventured outside their desert at all, except when threatened.' He turned back to his team. 'We're going to need to earn their trust.'

'Best we shrink to our fairy size, then,' said Celor. 'We don't want our numbers to seem too imposing.' Tharguen nodded, and with that, the ten Kikies vanished from sight.

Tharguen looked around again. 'Perhaps they are watching from afar and waiting for us to make the first move. Let us show them a sign of friendship.'

'How are we to show them a sign of friendship if we have nothing with which to show them?' asked Ihal, a young girl. Ihal Nim was tall, red-haired, eighty-nine polken years of age and very skilled in the arts of knighthood.

'We'll figure something out,' answered Tharguen.

'You ask too many questions,' Lóim said to Ihal. He was Jimmy's age, dark-haired, and reputed to be stubborn.

'Well, it's for a better understanding,' retorted Ihal. 'At least I'm not arrogant like you are.'

'Hey! I'm less arrogant than I was before I ever had anything to be arrogant about.' Lóim thought for a moment, wondering if his retort had made sense.

'Just ignore him,' said another girl who stood shorter than Ihal. She had hazelnut hair, and she was ninety-one. This was one of Ihal's best friends, Mittah Riverdam.

'It doesn't matter, Mittah. He's just jealous that I'm better than him.'

'Why must you always compete with me?' asked Lóim.

Ihal and Mittah walked away without answering.

'I think the question is why do *you* always compete with her?' said Hûcklo, his companion, from behind.

'Huck, don't you know, I compete with everyone!' Lóim smiled at his friend.

'I wish I could remember some of my family's long-lost customs,' said Malcolm, coming to stand beside Tharguen. 'Our Dûnelorian ancestry comes from long ago on my mother's side. They've all been living in Teloria for millennia.' The young polc shrugged. 'At least I get to visit the place where my ancestors come from. Perhaps I'll even discover a long-lost cousin.' He suddenly perked up.

'I'm sure any family you have here will be happy to be acquainted with you, Malcolm,' said Tharguen.

'Thanks, Captain.'

'Captain,' said Lóim, his tone urgent. His eyes narrowed on something far in the distance. Tharguen arrived beside him. 'Look, I believe those are Dûnelorians coming our way.'

'I believe so too,' said Tharguen.

'If you ask me,' Lóim muttered as the Dûnelorians approached, 'they don't look very happy.'

'They seem preoccupied,' whispered Mittah.

'You think they think we've intruded on their territory?' asked Ihal.

'I really don't know,' Tharguen replied.

'They are coming far too quickly, and they are too armed to be in a mood to greet us,' said Lóim.

'We're right by you, Tharguen,' whispered Celor as he floated nearby in his fairy form.

The rest of the team watched as a large group of Dûnelorians drew closer. They were clad in thin beige clothes, camouflaging with the sand, but were heavily armed. The sun reflected brightly on their weapons.

'At last, we meet you,' said Tharguen once the tall polcs reached them. 'We hope we are not disturbing you in any way. We are from Teloria and—'

'Save your stories for the Emperor's son,' said the Dûnelorian who stood in front of the rest.

'Pardon me?' Tharguen was taken aback by the man's abrupt tone.

'We are not interested in what you have to say, but our Prince is interested in who you are. We have been watching you all from the moment you stepped foot onto our terrain. Come with us.'

He turned around and started off. Many Dûnelorians came around, checking the Telorians as they walked.

'Captain,' whispered a young wizard, 'why do I somehow get the feeling these people are not interested in befriending us?'

'Don't worry,' Lóim muttered from his friend's side, 'you're not the only one with that impression.'

'Best keep quiet, Tommash,' whispered Tharguen.

He obeyed his Captain, and the Telorians followed the Dûnenlorians across the sand.

After a while, they arrived at a massive golden palace standing high and square with immense pillars. They stopped in front of the majestic gates as a guard approached the Captain of the Dûnelorian team.

'What is this?' asked the guard.

'Tell His Majesty the Prince, Rhal Majim, that we have visitors.'

The guard made a sign for everyone to follow.

When they entered the palace, they walked down a long corridor and into a large chamber where the Prince of the Dûnelorians sat atop a throne. The Telorians bowed as he stood. He was clad in a long golden cape that draped over his intricate, uniquely designed yellow-gold armour. His dark sepia skin had a golden lustre to it, and his umber hair stopped beneath the ears. Around his neck, a pendant hung housing a round yellow gem. He had a square jaw and a regal posture, and a magical quintessence that could be felt by all.

'Tell me,' began the Prince, 'what brings travellers like you here?'

'We are Telorians,' said Tharguen. 'We come with a message and a request.'

'A request!' said one of the two guards who stood on either side of the Prince.

'Yes,' said Tharguen. 'First, let me introduce myself.' He placed a hand on his chest, bowing politely as he spoke. 'My name is Captain Tharguen Sumperale, and this is my team.' He gestured towards the others. 'We are honoured to finally meet you.'

'You may skip the pleasantries, Captain,' the Prince replied, gesturing with his hand.

Tharguen nodded in acknowledgement. 'We come to tell you that Teloria is planning a grand attack against Mork for the sake of the world.'

'Let me guess,' said Rhal Majim, 'you wish for us to become your allies.'

'That is correct,' said Tharguen.

'Against Morok?' said the Prince. 'Have you gone mad?! Morok is larger in population than our realm and your kingdom combined, and that by far. No one can defeat Morok if no one can defeat Mirauk.'

'But you see, someone can,' said Tharguen, trying to inspire hope. 'Six years ago, the Dragon Prophecies came true when five Telorians set out to retrieve the *Book of Enchantment,* and the Wizardess Niome Fairhaven has already proven herself more powerful than Mirauk.'

'Has she glanced at him?' asked the first guard.

'Yes, and she thrives. The Firlanians and the Dalvarans are already with us. With your help, we can destroy Mork.'

'Your Majesty,' said the second guard, trying his best to whisper in the echoing room, 'if this is true that the prophecy has come true, then that changes everything. Are we to—?'

'Silence. Know your place,' the Prince quipped back. He turned back to Tharguen, eyeing his team as he spoke. 'I see there are those with Dûnelorian descent in your team.'

'Yes.' Tharguen felt a tinge of hope as the Prince met his eyes once more.

'But they are *not* Dûnelorian. They are Telorians, and loyal to *you*.' The Prince narrowed his eyes, glaring at Tharguen.

Tharguen's heart dropped. He was beginning to think *he* was the cause of the mistrust.

'Captain Sumperale, we would love to destroy Morok and everything related to it,' said a knight, stepping out of the shadows. His armour was less intricate than the Prince's though more elaborate than that of the guards. 'What a shame Teloria was not there to help many of us years ago.'

'If you would've asked for our help, we would've gladly given it.'

'Let me glance at you now to see if what you say is true,' said that same knight, walking closer to Tharguen.

'Oh, it is!' said Tharguen, thinking there was something familiar about this particular Dûnelorian.

'I want to believe you, but my job is to protect my Prince, especially from imposters.'

Tharguen looked at him more carefully. He recognised him. He had definitely seen him before, but he could not put his finger on it.

'Have we met before?' Tharguen asked straight-forwardly.

'Have we?' replied the knight. 'I am glad you remember. I recognise your voice, your face, the way you stand. I do not easily forget a person, although last time you were not Captain, and clad in much darker clothes. Why did you let us escape?'

'That's where I saw you,' Tharguen realised, his stomach tightening in knots. He swallowed hard. Tharguen knew exactly the moment the Dûnelorian was referring to: when Beshrig had had a group of Dûnelorians captured and decided to kill the group's leader to make an example of her.

Tharguen had stared at her lifeless body in shock. He had already devised how to free the Dûnelorians but was forced to wait till sundown. Beshrig had invited him for the interrogation; that was when Tharguen had recently been promoted as Beshrig's Second. However, the interrogation had never happened. Instead, Beshrig stabbed the leader of the Dûnelorian group through the heart. Tharguen had stared in horror, quickly thinking to pass it off as though he had expected the chance to interrogate the group's leader, for his true intentions could never be discovered.

Tharguen had freed the Dûnelorians that night and covered their escape, but he would never forget Beshrig's duplicity and the feeling that perhaps he could have done more – saved her, predicted Beshrig's plan or insisted he'd been alone to interrogate them.

The sick feeling from watching a potential ally die before he could save her overwhelmed him once more. He looked back at the Prince, his heart filled with sorrow.

'I was a Telorian spy in—'

'No! You are a spy *now!*' the knight shouted sharply as he drew a dagger. Tharguen threw his hands up in surrender. 'I do not trust you! This polc is a Morkan, Your Highness, and I do not believe a single word he has uttered here today.'

'What?' exclaimed Tharguen. 'No! You don't understand. I was a Telorian spy in Mork. I was pretending to be Morkan, but I let you all go without anyone else knowing it. That had been my plan the moment I'd learnt of your capture.'

'A Telorian spy in Morok? Hmph. Then how did you leave?'

'I left when Niome was captured; I freed her. She is the Great Wizardess of Teloria now.'

'There is no Great Wizardess!' The knight turned to the Prince. 'These are all lies, Your Majesty!'

Guards came and grabbed hold of Tharguen.

'What he says is true!' cried Gahli, a sun blonde-haired female polc, close friend to Ihal and the others. 'People admire him for it! He was part of a team of twelve knights and one of the only two survivors—'

'Take him away,' interrupted the Prince.

'Let me explain my story!' cried Tharguen. 'You must believe me! I thought we were going to interrogate your group's leader; I had no idea Beshrig was going to kill her, I swear. I am so sorry that I could not save her. Had I an inkling – had I known, I would have done everything in my power to free your people sooner. I promise you' – Tharguen's nose wrinkled with disdain towards his Morkan Captain – 'Beshrig paid the ultimate price in the end, for I killed him before escaping Mork with Niome and the others.' He took a breath. 'Please, if you cannot trust me, at least speak with my King.'

'What King? Teloria has had no King for ages,' spat the second guard. 'You have failed in your gathering of information, Morkan, and now you are paying the price you deserve.'

'No! He was the second survivor . . . it's a long story,' protested Lóim.

'Take them all away,' the Prince commanded.

Many guards grabbed several of the Telorians while others were already on the verge of escaping.

'Run all the way home!' shouted Tharguen. 'Tell Bahvley and Niome what has happened. Please hurry!'

Many Telorians ran out of the chamber as fast as they could, while others were intercepted or grabbed or tripped.

'Jeremy!' cried Lóim. He saw a few of his friends fall to the ground.

'Run, Lóim!' yelled Pete. 'Save yourself!' Pete kicked the air as a knight lifted him from behind.

The others were dragged away as Lóim ran on.

'I don't want to have to kill any of these people,' said Ihal as she ran through the long corridor, 'considering that I've never killed anyone before.'

It was true. Many of them had never been to war before or even out of the country. Only a handful had fought when the Morkans had attacked Teloria in the South, and even then, they had mostly fought with bows from the wall.

'Not to mention I'm still hoping we can rekindle the alliance that once existed between the Dûnelorians and . . .' Ihal turned her head to look at Gahli, who was supposed to be beside her, but she wasn't there anymore. Ihal looked back, running backwards, to see Gahli had been grabbed by one of the guards. Ihal fell when she bumped into Lóim. He helped her up and they ran on, though he practically was dragging her by the hand.

'Gahli,' Ihal said softly to herself.

When the group of young Telorians reached the giant doors, they couldn't pry them open.

'Tom! Do something!' cried Mittah.

'What am I supposed to do?!' Tom shouted.

'Didn't you learn a spell or something from your grandfather?' said Huck.

'My grandfather was a druid, not a wizard! It's not the same thing. He made potions,' Tom spoke as he scanned the double doors. 'See, wizards execute spells; druids are the passers-on of tradition and prayer. They often teach magic as a meditative component of life. Although many druids create potions, they do not exercise magic the way wizards do. Drúgan, however, is a druid *and* a wizard.'

'A little less lecturing, a little more spelling!' cried Lóim.

'Right – Niome taught me something.'

'What, then?' Lóim implored.

'I forget the words!' Tom said, panicked.

The guards were closing in on them. Tom wasn't used to this kind of pressure. They were only nine now, down from their original band of thirty, and he knew they had to reach home and relay the message. He supposed that that was part of training, learning to perform under pressure. Just then, Tom remembered, and he shouted in a joyful tone:

'Kelcenu! Neppo! Dan ispa!'

The doors flew open, and the Telorians ran out. Suddenly, the Kikies reappeared before them and prepared for fast-flying.

'Take it away!' shouted Lóim.

The Kikies took a good grip on each of the Telorians, and within moments they were all far from the view of the Dûnelorians.

Chapter Two:
Far From Worries

In Teloria, Telorians across the kingdom were celebrating the First Day of Summer. The Five of the Star and their friends enjoyed the festivities as well for the most part, save for the fact that they all wanted to go on another mission – though hopefully one less dangerous this time. It had been several years now since their last journey, and some of them were beginning to feel restless.

Jimmy craved the adventure. Exploration missions would be pleasant, he thought. However, he was not looking forward to the next battle they would have against Mork.

After roaming the town square for festival activities and viewing the acrobats' performance, Jimmy began to feel bored and felt like having some fun. He closed his eyes and whispered to himself, and shortly after, Meysah popped up.

'You called?' he said.

'I love this spell,' said Jimmy, grinning.

'It's practical. Tells someone where you are, tells someone to come over. And we can choose to tell one person, two persons, three persons, or every one of the others of the Star! It's great. It's ingenious. It's—'

'I'm bored,' Jimmy interrupted. 'I need some action.'

'Festival activities not up to your *adventurous* standards?' laughed Meysah. Jimmy shrugged. 'Too bad Lóim isn't here. I'm sure you would've loved to play a trick on him.'

A wide grin spread across Jimmy's face.

'You thinking what I'm thinking?' asked Meysah, and Jimmy nodded enthusiastically.

'I have a plan.'

Niome entered the Magic Lab whistling. She was very pleased with herself, for she had just returned the other day from Mistoff, where she had had an interesting conversation with the Pleessies. They had agreed to let her in on the most well-kept secret regarding the magical shield. Originally they were going to teach her the spells and help her create such a shield and assist her in Teloria, but as she was to become more powerful – enough to be able to defeat Mirauk – and needed to exercise complicated magic to grow stronger, they decided to teach her the deep secrets. Soon, she had learnt a unique spell that would allow her to cast a powerful shield around Teloria all on her own.

Niome laid her bag on the desk, then placed her book of personal notes on the desk at her seat. She then walked to the cupboard and looked through some boxes.

Suddenly, there was a loud bang and Niome yelped, startled. She quickly looked around. The window had closed; she went and opened it again. As soon as she got back to the cupboard, however, it closed again. She scowled, puzzled.

When she walked back to the window, she noticed that her book was gone. That's when she grew suspicious. She chewed her lip, pondering, then decided to play along and continue as though she didn't know her brother was somewhere in the room.

Turning, she saw her bag had been moved. *Now, Meysah could not do all this on his own.* Niome opened up her magical senses and felt two mischievous presences.

She forced herself to keep a neutral face, though she was rather amused. She wasn't going to ruin her brother's fun. Not just yet, anyway; she knew Meysah and Jimmy were fidgety for action these days. She, too, needed a bit of a change of air. In such dangerous times, however, it was not ideal to plan a vacation. It had been a while since they had travelled to visit their friends from the other kingdoms.

'Who's here?' she asked. No answer came. 'I said, who's here?'

'It is I,' said a deep and mysterious whisper. She could not tell if this was Meysah or Jimmy and had to suppress a smile.

'And who are you?'

'I who speaks wisdom.' This almost made her laugh.

'Why have you come to me, spirit?'

'To guide you.'

'Guide me to where? The drapes?!' she said as she pushed aside the navy curtains, where she found Jimmy and Meysah. 'Yes, very wise.'

'Oh, you're no fun!' groaned Meysah. Jimmy was rubbing his throat.

'Next time *you* do the harsh voice,' he said to Meysah. 'I think it damaged my throat.'

Meysah rolled his eyes, and Jimmy rolled his in response. Niome laughed. 'So now that Tharguen and his army have gone, you've found me as your new target to play tricks on?'

'To tell you the truth,' said Jimmy, 'I miss voyaging. Before, when I'd never left Teloria, I always craved adventure. When I left, I was scared. Now, I miss travelling and exploring. So to keep busy, I play tricks on people. The last time anything exciting happened was six years ago. I know we went to visit Dalvar and Firlan, but it wasn't the same.'

'We need a little more action,' said Meysah. 'Not Morkans or dragons, just . . .' He paused, moving his hands in a somewhat circular fashion, trying to illustrate his thoughts.

'I know what you mean,' said Niome. 'I crave it myself, though not in the same way.'

'We have nothing to do these days,' Jimmy sighed.

'Well, sit,' said Niome. 'We'll chat. Maybe we can go see the play they're staging this week.'

'Oh, I've always wanted to be a player and perform in front of an audience!' said Jimmy.

'You've always wanted to be everything,' said Meysah incredulously. 'What happened to wanting to be the Chief of Knights?! Speaking of which . . .'

Vigh rode his horse towards the training ground. He was on his way to meet Boreth, who was practising his archery. He had good news to tell him; he had just spoken to Bahvley, who had returned from Lani.

Boreth lowered his bow as soon as his friend approached. 'Why the broad smile, my friend?'

'Boreth, the time has come to leave again on yet another journey.'

'Do tell!'

'I just spoke to Bahvley,' said Vigh.

'Back from Lani already?'

'Yes, and he's finished double-checking the security of the completed wall. It looks like the people of Teloria feel safe again and won't be afraid if we leave for a while.'

'I admit, as much as I love this place, I do miss venturing off to the unknown. I know we went to Dalvar and Firlan, but . . . visiting and exploring are two completely different things.'

'I agree. Meysah and Jimmy are sure going to be happy to hear about it, and I think Bahvley might just come along.'

'I wouldn't be surprised. It'll be just like old times when you and I'd go on those small missions that kept us . . . what's the word?'

'Alive?'

'Yes, that's it,' said Boreth.

'Back in the days before we started teaching.' They both smiled.

'So tell me, Vigh, where will we be going?' Boreth finished gathering his arrows and placed them in his quiver.

'The Twisted Forest.'

'Excellent. When will we be leaving?'

'Soon.'

'Not too soon! I still have to pay a visit to Clahria before we go.'

'Ah, yes,' said Vigh. 'Then perhaps you should go this week.'

'Yes, that *is* what I had in mind.'

'You go there quite a lot.' Vigh quirked his brows.

Boreth blushed. 'Well, every few weeks, yes.'

Vigh smiled. 'I'm glad you're happy.'

Boreth untied his horse. 'Finally, we'll be making progress outside of home,' he said, pointedly changing the subject.

'Shall we call on the others?'

'Maybe we can go about things the old-fashioned way,' said Boreth. 'Let's go find them ourselves.'

Boreth swung his bow over his shoulder, jumped onto his horse, and they both rode off.

It was close to evening when Niome, Meysah and Jimmy left the Magic Lab. They were on their way home when they met their masters.

'Master Boreth!' called Jimmy as they approached each other. 'You want to go see the play with us tomorrow?'

Both lords had a serious look on their faces. They slowed their horses to match the walking speed of the others.

'Hello, Jimmy,' Boreth said flatly, ignoring the question. 'Meysah. Niome.'

'How are you two?' Meysah asked hesitantly.

'I don't know,' said Vigh. Both lords spoke in low, almost monotone voices.

'What's wrong?' asked Niome, concerned.

'What's *not* wrong?' said Boreth. A mistake, because he almost slipped and laughed.

'We need to talk to you three,' Vigh said gravely.

'What is it?' asked Meysah.

'Not something that can be discussed here,' Boreth muttered, regaining seriousness very smoothly. They turned their horses around, and the others followed.

'Are you upset?' asked Jimmy. The innocence in his voice was endearing. 'Did we do something wrong? If we did, we're sorry – we weren't aware.'

'It's nothing you did,' said Boreth. There was a pause.

'Who died?' asked Niome.

'No one died!' said Vigh.

'Then what is it?!' exclaimed Meysah. 'Tell us. We are agonising to know!'

'It's Bahvley,' said Vigh.

'What happened?' gasped Niome.

'He says . . .' said Vigh, 'he says . . . he . . .' He couldn't bring himself to say it, still trying to maintain his seriousness. *Good thing I have my back to them,* he thought.

'He says . . .' Boreth tried in his place, 'he says . . .' but he also kept stopping in order not to laugh. 'He says . . .'

It was no use. They both burst into laughter, saying at the same time, 'He says we can finally go travelling again!'

They laughed a while as the others stared at them bug-eyed, which made the lords laugh even harder.

'We wanted to play a trick on you!' said Boreth, wiping a tear from his eye. 'Oh, I'm sorry.' He laughed some more. 'Your faces are priceless.'

'It worked!' said Vigh. Eventually, their laugh died down to a mere giggle. 'Ah, that was fun,' Vigh sighed. 'We miss exploring, and we thought of getting some excitement by playing a trick on you.'

Then, as a delayed reaction, the other three smiled and laughed in turn, mostly out of relief.

'We tried to play a trick on Niome,' said Jimmy.

'But it didn't work,' added Meysah.

'And now you two came along, and . . .' Niome giggled, unable to continue.

'Eeyaaah,' said Jimmy, 'you two were a lot more successful than we were.'

All five laughed again. When their laughter died down, the three younger Telorians asked what this travelling news was about.

'Come,' said Boreth, 'let's all go to my house and discuss it over supper.'

At Boreth's, they lounged and ate while Vigh and Boreth told them the plan to go explore the Twisted Forest in hopes of making new allies.

'Finally, a trip!' Jimmy and Meysah were thrilled.

The next day, the Five went to see Bahvley to hear more details. Bahvley hadn't decided yet if he would go with them or not. Part of him wanted to, but he also wanted to be home when Tharguen returned to hear news from his travels. For now, he still had time to think about it.

The Five took the next few days to prepare their things so that everyone would be ready for when Boreth returned from the Old Grey House. They decided on what to bring, what they would really need, and which weapons would be most useful. They got their swords sharpened and polished, made sure they had enough arrows, and decided who would take care of their horses while they were gone, because the Twisted Forest was no place for a horse. Lastly, they made sure to have some warm clothing in case of unexpected delays before they returned home; somehow, they all had the feeling they wouldn't be home again before Winter.

On the sixth day of Summer they were ready, and Boreth prepared to leave for his visit to Clahria's.

Bahvley was at his new home in the Royal Halls. He had moved there shortly after becoming King but still wasn't used to it, for it felt so enormous and empty. In truth, he still spent most of his time in his old home with Niome, Meysah and their parents or invited them to the Royal Wing, which had a corridor that led right into the main area of the Royal Halls. The Royal Wing was the more residential area with many rooms and quarters, many of which were equivalent to a large two-in-one roomed home for a family in the village.

At present, Bahvley was busy trying to figure out how to make the place look less imposing, or how to make it seem smaller somehow. It was well decorated, but perhaps more furniture or banners would do the trick.

Interrupting his thoughts, Dex, the door ward of the Royal Halls and Royal Wing, approached him.

'Your Highness,' he began. 'You have visitors here to see you.'

'Visitors?' said Bahvley. 'Who?'

'They say it's a surprise. And they came to pay a promised visit to you and your friends.'

'Well, then, do tell them to come in. This place is too big without guests.'

'Yes, Your Majesty.'

Dex nodded and walked to the entrance, followed by Bahvley. He opened the two large wooden doors and there stood a smiling Kchalami, accompanied by Elmezni and Krystal, with many Firlanians standing behind them.

'What a nice surprise!' exclaimed Bahvley. 'It's been too long.'

'Several years,' Kchalami said. 'We've been quite busy at home, and I assume you, too, have been busy.'

'Quite,' he agreed.

'Congratulations,' added Elmezni. 'We saw the wall. It looks more than just repaired from what you had described of it before. Looks like you've done well as King.'

'Thank you. Please, come in.' Bahvley turned to Dex. 'Please tell Niome and the others that our Firlanian friends have come to pay us a visit.'

'Yes, Your Majesty. Right away, Your Majesty.'

'Thank you, Dex.'

Dex gave Bahvley a curt bow and left.

There were a dozen Firlanians, all of them friends of the Telorians: Kchalami, Akchmassiel, Elmezni, Krystal, Batel, Mishcal, Laurelmi, Petruni, Dinankch, Saviel, Falmozni and Aterel. Bahvley invited his friends and their entourage to the dining hall, where they all sat down to chat.

'Tell us what's been going on,' prompted Kchalami.

Bahvley told them everything that had happened since the Firlanians had last seen them. Afterwards, the Firlanians in turn informed them of the happenings in Firlan.

'We have seen, or heard of, no Morkans,' said Elmezni.

'But that means nothing,' Krystal interjected, her blonde curly hair waving as she spoke. 'Perhaps we have not encountered any, but they are preparing as much as we are, and we should not let ourselves be caught off guard. Anything can happen at any moment.'

'And that's precisely what they'll be expecting and waiting for,' Akchmassiel added. 'The Morkans are waiting for us to be completely off guard.'

'Then they'll be waiting a long time,' declared Bahvley, 'for Teloria is ready for anything.'

At that moment, in walked the Five, who were quite happy to see the Firlanians. They greeted them warmly, and again the Firlanians told their story, followed by the Five's anecdotes.

'Not that there have been any, really,' said Jimmy. 'There hasn't been much action around here for quite some time.'

Meysah continued, 'And that's why we're going to the Twisted Forest.'

'It's a part of Teloria that has not been visited or explored in centuries,' explained Vigh, 'and we're finally off to meet the people who live there – the people who left Teloria when the Firlanians left, if they still exist or dwell there. There have been no absolute signs that there *are* people there, but we're hopeful we'll find something.'

'With everything that's been going on since Mirauk's rise to power,' Niome said, 'many people or former allies were cut off from each other, much as Firlan and Teloria were. *I'm* hoping the people who dwell there, if any dwell there at all, have merely been in hiding and keeping safe.'

'When were you planning on leaving?' asked Elmezni.

'As soon as Boreth gets back from visiting his *beloved* Clahria,' teased Vigh as he nudged Boreth with his elbow. Boreth shook his head, suppressing a smile.

'You're welcome to join us, if you like,' said Niome.

'Sure!' said Kchalami. 'After all, we are the closest cousins of the people who live there – assuming they still live there.'

'Not to mention we know what life in the woods is like,' added Akchmassiel.

'Great!' Vigh clapped his hands together.

'I'm leaving tomorrow,' said Boreth. 'I should be back in a few weeks.'

As they all chatted, Niome went and sat next to Kchalami.

'I sense there is something you wish to share with me,' she said, her voice low. 'You seem preoccupied.'

'Well, it can wait. It is of no extreme urgency . . . yet. A matter we will have to discuss sometime soon, though.'

'Very well. I shall be all ears.'

'Thank you. It's very nice to see you, Niome.' The Firlanian Prince smiled.

'As it is nice to see you,' replied Niome. 'True friends are always welcome in Teloria.'

The pair smiled again and returned their attention to the others. They all spent the rest of the day laughing and feasting together.

The next day, Boreth left with his horse and was set to arrive at the Old Grey House eight days later. The other Telorians spent time with the Firlanians, enjoying their time of merrymaking. Bahvley was still hesitant about going with the Five, and as the days went by, he came to the decision that he would wait for Tharguen's return. Once he was back, they both would join the others afterwards. He felt a strange longing for his friend – something he hadn't felt since their days in Mork when they each believed the other was dead. A strange sensation, he thought, and he wanted to be there to make sure Tharguen got home safe and sound.

As for the Firlanians, they were quite excited about the exploration, for they had never travelled beyond the borders of Firlan except for Akchmassiel and a few others. They visited Teloria before the journey, and Bahvley and the other four made sure to show them all the greatest sights the land had to offer.

CHAPTER THREE:
A Change Of Plans

*D*ex strode towards Bahvley at an urgent pace. The Telorian King was in his study in the Royal Halls.

'Your Highness, there's an emergency!'

'What kind of emergency? Where?' Bahvley rose from his seat.

'Several of the young soldiers and the Kikies from Captain Sumperale's team have returned,' replied Dex. 'They say they need your assistance right this very moment.'

Bahvley dashed to the door. 'Then let them in!'

When he arrived at the door, he saw the Kikies along with nine Telorians from Tharguen's team.

'Where are Tharguen and the others?' he asked.

'They've been captured!' said Lóim.

'The Dûnelorians thought that Captain Tharguen was a Morkan, and they captured him!' cried Mittah.

'They recognised him from long ago in Mork,' Ihal added.

'We got away, and we need you to go back with us to prove the truth to the Dûnelorians!' said Malcolm.

'I *will* go with you, and so will my sister and the others. If they need proof, they need it from the Five as much as from me,' said Bahvley. He turned to his door ward. 'Dex, go get the others, and the Firlanians, and Selemil and Henker. Gather everyone finally.'

'I'll be back as quickly as I possibly can!' With that, Dex ran out the door.

So this is what I have been feeling – the strange sensation that I needed to be home for Tharguen's return. Tharguen needed him now, and he was going to aid him. Though something seemed untold about this event, something deeper that magic might reveal later on. For now, all he knew was that his friend was in trouble, and his stomach tightened at the thought.

Bahvley gave the tired travellers something to eat and tried to think of something else for a bit.

'There's only a week left before we leave for the Twisted Forest!' said Jimmy.

'It's funny how we're looking so forward to this trip,' said Vigh, 'yet when we think of any trip too far west, we shiver.'

'Well, I mean, it's only natural,' said Meysah. 'We're all scared of Mork, and even a step towards it scares me. But a step towards a land where friendly people dwell or might dwell, and . . .' He paused, looking out the window of Vigh's house. 'Isn't that Bahvley's door ward? He looks awfully troubled.'

There was an anxious, hurried knock on the door. Vigh answered.

'The King calls for you all! There's been some trouble in Dûnelor. The Captain and many others have been captured; he was recognised as a Morkan. The Kikies and some others escaped and came home to get help. I need to go find the Firlanians now!'

'They're with Selemil at Henker's house,' said Vigh.

'I will go and get them right away, then. Thank you,' Dex panted as he left.

'We must find out more about what happened,' said Niome, her stomach in knots. She and Meysah began to open the door.

'Oh my goodness, Boreth's not even here!' Vigh closed his eyes and muttered to himself, going into a brief trance. After a moment, he walked out the door last. 'I called upon Boreth. I hope he doesn't worry that *we're* the ones in trouble.'

It was the fifth day since Boreth had been at the Old Grey House when he felt the magical call from Vigh. He paused as though to listen to something, closing his eyes, and a few moments later he opened them in startlement. His face went white.

'What's wrong?' asked Clahria.

'They're in trouble!' said Boreth.

'What? Who?'

'I don't know what happened, but I just received a message from Vigh. He called upon me. There's been some trouble; they're in a panic. I have to go back.'

Boreth quickly gathered his things.

'I'm sorry that I have to leave now,' he said to Clahria as he gently put his hand on her face.

'I know,' she replied. 'Go. They need you.'

Boreth embraced her a long while before stepping out the door. He turned to her again and kissed her longingly, knowing he would miss her while he was away, as he always did, before he ran to the stables and got his horse. He looked back one final time to wave at Clahria before hurrying off home.

When Niome, Meysah, Jimmy and Vigh got to Bahvley's, the escapees from Tharguen's team told them what had happened. The Firlanians soon arrived to hear the news too.

Everyone's travel plans had now changed.

'I was looking forward to going to the Twisted Forest,' Meysah sighed, 'but if Tharguen needs our help, we'll prove to those Dûnelorians he really is Telorian.'

'Something about it just doesn't make sense, though,' said Niome. 'I'm sure there's more to it than that. No, there *is* more to it. I don't know what, but there is.'

'I feel it too,' said Bahvley. 'That's why I have to go with you. I just don't understand why they didn't believe Teloria has a King.'

'Because Teloria has not had a ruler in ages,' said Ihal.

'Still, Bahvley's right,' said Tithil. '*They* have rulers, Emperors, and they have not been in contact with Telorians for a long time. Long has it been since the Mittèlor banishment and exile. For all they know, Teloria could have chosen a new ruler hundreds of years ago shortly after Mirauk's rise to power. So how would they know exactly how long there has been no ruler here, or if there still is none, for that matter?'

Celor let out a low tone. 'Hnthn. Something tells me that the Dûnelorians have been receiving false information.'

'Either that, or their sources reveal strange things,' said Vigh. 'They seem too quick to judge.'

'I'm afraid', began Mië, 'that no matter how much I try to find a brighter side to all this, there is none.'

'Then we know what we have to do,' concluded Bahvley. 'The only thing is, our time is getting short before Mork decides to attack, and who knows when that will be. We need to get more allies. I know that Phynd returned to your land, but we don't know when he will return to Teloria with his ships; he and the other Kikies haven't been gone that long. We can't fight this war alone. So, who is going to the Twisted Forest?'

'We will go,' said Kchalami. 'You can go to Dûnelor, and we will go to the Twisted Forest.'

'And you have nought to worry about', said Krystal, 'since we are the closest cousins of the people who dwell there. If they are in hiding, we know where they could be and how to find them. If there are evil creatures there, we know how to fight and destroy them.'

'We will go in Teloria's name,' said Kchalami.

'And tell them all about you,' Elmezni added.

'Are you certain?' asked Bahvley. 'I wouldn't want them to think this alliance was trivial to me.'

'Don't worry about it,' answered Akchmassiel. 'We'll take care of everything.'

'Thank you,' said Bahvley, relieved. 'I really appreciate this.'

'Well, it's our pleasure,' said Elmezni. 'After all, we serve you.'

'No,' said Bahvley, 'you don't serve me. Friends don't serve each other; they help each other. Or if you serve me, I serve you when I'm in Firlan. We are all part of the same team -- a team where suggestions are given and solutions are found instead of orders demanded. I will go resolve this misunderstanding with the Dûnelorians while you go meet the people of the Twisted Forest. And then we should meet somewhere, instead of all coming back all the way here, to decide what to do next. Besides, you might want to return home after this, or I might want to meet our new allies.'

'How about we meet by the Ortim River?' suggested Kchalmai. 'On the Telorian side of the river, where you can see the path to Firlan on the other side.'

'You mean near where the Gord Plains begin?' asked Vigh.

'Yes.'

'All right, but when?' asked Niome.

'It took us nineteen days to get here,' Lóim said, exasperated. 'Shouldn't we concentrate on leaving?'

Bahvely and Kchalami looked at each other and whispered calculations to each other. Then they nodded, having agreed on a meeting time.

'We shall meet there in sixty days' time,' said Bahvley, 'on the third day of the twelfth week of this season.'

'Tomorrow being day one,' added Kchalami.

'If either team is late, the other waits,' said Bahvley. 'Same if they're early.'

'But what about Master Boreth?' asked Jimmy.

'I sent him a message, remember?' said Vigh. 'He has no doubt left for home by now. He's travelling by horse; we'll be walking. We'll meet him along the way.'

'I'll be sure to bring anything he might need that he didn't take with him to Clahria's,' said Jimmy. 'Even though he has most of his things, he left some at home purposely; he didn't think he'd encounter any trouble.'

The others nodded.

'Okay then,' said Bahvley, 'go home and rest. We have an early start tomorrow.'

Everyone stood and left the room except for Selemil and Henker, who had not yet uttered a word. They had merely sat still, listening.

'While I am away,' Bahvley said to them, 'I'm going to need the two of you to take care of Teloria, which you do, and always have done, very well.'

'You can depend on us, Bahvley,' said Selemil.

'Some may be confused, but I know how to settle these sorts of matters,' Henker said.

'After you meet up with the Firlanians at your rendezvous, will you be coming straight home?' asked Selemil.

'I will most likely go to the Twisted Forest. Out of courtesy. After all, I don't want to be rude.'

'People might worry at seeing you leave,' said Selemil. 'You've been back too short a time after so long an absence. They don't want their King to disappear for too long again.'

'You can reassure them that I will return safely. If I was gone fifty years and came home safe and well – a year is nothing. I don't worry about such things, nor should they.' Bahvley stood and took a step towards the window, looking out. 'It is Tharguen for whom I worry. I hope he's okay.'

'Oh, I'm sure he is,' said Henker.

Bahvley looked at him. 'It just isn't right. It's not fair; after all the sacrifices he's done and the risks he's taken, the least the Dûnelorians could do is thank him, if they can't *show* gratitude. But no! He's being punished for his bravery.' Bahvley began to pace to and fro. 'He saved Niome's life six years ago. He contributed to the retrieval of the *Book of Enchantment*. It just doesn't make any sense.' He stopped pacing. 'Something's not right here, and I'm going to find out what it is. Just don't tell the people of Teloria why we've gone. If this is but a grave misunderstanding, I don't want the people of Teloria to worry.'

Selemil nodded.

'Don't strain your mind with such worries,' soothed Henker.

Bahvley sat down and leaned his chin on his clasped hands.

'If only Gorthan were here,' said Bahvley. 'He could solve this case in an instant. He always had some interesting sort of magic about him when it came to such things. He was the first person people went to. Now he's gone – gone before I could see him again, before he could know I was alive, and I miss him and his advice. I really thought I'd see him again after those fifty years. At least there are the two of you.'

'Listen,' said Henker, 'if ever you need a word of advice or guidance from Gorthan, just look up at the stars at night and ask him for his help, and his spirit will give you a sign.'

'I suppose so,' said Bahvley. 'Things just were so much simpler way back when. And I keep asking myself: *Why did Gorthan have to die?*'

'Because he felt his time was up,' answered Henker. 'He knew, deep in his heart, that the fate of Teloria lay in great hands. He didn't want to be around to live what he lived long ago. He was prepared to die if he had to, and so he did, in order to protect you and the others. It was his wish. He preferred to die and be powerful still by becoming a star rather than to be killed. I, on the other hand, refuse to go anywhere until all of this has ended.' The old polc placed a hand on Bahvley's shoulder and gently squeezed, smiling wanly.

Then, Selemil and Henker left Bahvley to prepare for his trip.

The next day, everyone met up at the main gate of Teloria. Niome, Meysah, Jimmy and Vigh had met up earlier; Bahvley had joined them shortly after. Together they marched to the gate along with the Kikies and the others from Tharguen's team. The Firlanians had gotten there earlier and were waiting patiently so that they could all leave together. Selemil had also gone to wish them farewell.

'Farewell,' said Bahvley as the Firlanians began heading out through the gate. 'Kchalami, I will see you in eight weeks.'

'Good luck to all of you,' replied Kchalami as the group departed. 'May the stars shine upon you.' Kchalami stole a glance towards Niome; the discussion he had hoped to have with her would have to wait until later.

The Firlanians turned right and walked along the wall, planning to enter the forest from that side. The others went straight ahead, following the main path. After three and a half days, they met up with Boreth at the intersection. Boreth had travelled day and night non-stop so he could meet up with them quickly, though they would have waited for him anyway. They explained to him what had happened in Dûnelor. Boreth's horse was sent home with an enchantment that Niome cast, and the host of polcs and Kikies continued over the Stream of Fluidity.

As they walked, Niome started to sing, for it livened the silent mood. Some of Tharguen's team members quietly hummed along.

On we go once again,
Following the path leading forth.
We may meet fear or pain,
But never will we stop marching on.

Ahead lies the unknown,
And still, we walk to it;
For if you can guess what fate has in store,
You can choose the better path.

Distant are the troubles we know not of,
And unimportant seem the pleasures to come.
But stubborn as we are,
We will undoubtedly succeed.

She began to whistle, hoping the merry tune would alleviate her worry, for she knew that whatever had gone wrong would be cleared up – hopefully.

Chapter Four:
Growing Anxiety

In the Palace of Rhal Majim, the prison cells resembled rooms of an inn, except that they were locked from the outside and scarcely furnished. The Telorians had been put in one sizable room and held there, yet the new prisoners were at least adequately treated by the guards. Their weapons had been taken from them, but they had been allowed to keep some of their more personal items. Many days passed where the Telorians did not know what was going to happen next.

After fifteen days, many were beginning to feel antsy and expressed they thought they were going to go mad. The lot of them sat on the ground or leaned against the wall as everyone began arguing about why the Dûnelorians didn't want to listen to their story or any explanations.

'Quiet!' shouted Tharguen. He had not spoken since the beginning of this argument and could not stand letting it grow. 'Wondering and arguing about possibilities won't get us anywhere. What-ifs won't tell us the whys.' He was angered and worried.

Everyone piped down and a long silence ensued. Then Tharguen thought he heard voices. He stood up and leaned his ear on the door, and soon the other Telorians heard the voices as well. They could just barely make out the words.

'We can either believe them or not, as long as we do not break our deal.'

'Captain, what is better: ignoring them and maybe staying safe, or believing and befriending them and being attacked? If we decide to break the deal, at least we will have allies to help if we get attacked.'

'No,' said the Captain. 'And they warned us of this. We made a deal. We cannot go back on our word. It is too late.'

'We only agreed to the deal because of their threat. First, let us make sure it really is him, Captain.'

The Telorians heard footsteps nearing the room, and the door opened. Both Dûnelorians walked into the room, closing the door behind them.

'After great debate, our Prince has made his decision. However, first, we need to ask you a few questions,' said the Captain. Everyone fidgeted uneasily.

'Fifteen days, you keep us locked up in here,' said Tharguen, miffed, 'and *now* you're ready to talk?'

The Captain looked at Tharguen. 'You, what is your name?'

'Captain Tharguen Sumperale.'

'How many years did you spend in Morok?' he asked.

'About fifty polken years.'

'And you did everything everyone told you to do?' Tharguen nodded. 'As in obeying all the rules and fighting and killing if you needed to?'

'I had no other choice. It was the only way to survive. It's difficult enough as it is!'

'And I am guessing you know the language?' continued the Captain, not acknowledging Tharguen's claims. Tharguen nodded. 'You are quite clever!'

'So much that it is hard to believe,' said the Officer.

'Tell me, what was your identity in Morok?' the Captain asked.

'Why is his identity in Mork so important?' exclaimed Pete, one of the younger lads. 'He told you the truth! We are all Telorians. Why are you keeping us here?'

'I am not talking to you, soldier!' the Captain said bluntly. 'Besides, you will not stay here much longer.'

'So what! Are you going to—'

'Pete! Stop it, it's no use!' said Tharguen, a warning in his voice. He turned to the Captain. 'My name was Gowtch; my Captain was Beshrig. I was his Second-in-Command.'

'Thank you,' said the Captain. He turned to his Officer and whispered to him. They looked at each other as though processing something. Then, they both left.

'Why did you tell them?!' exclaimed Pete.

'They're going to ship us to Mork now,' said Gahli.

'Maybe not,' said Eerzin, one of the Telorians closer to Tharguen's age.

'We still don't know anything,' said Tharguen. He sat down on the floor.

'It feels like we've been here forever,' sighed Gahli.

'We've been here two weeks, and this is the first time the Dûnelorians actually come and talk to us,' said Tharguen. He paused, pondering.

'You mean more than just to bring us food and water,' said Gahli.

'And the Prince came a few times,' noted Pete.

'"After great debate." What great debate?' Tharguen muttered.

'I guess the Prince hasn't decided yet what to do with us,' said Pete. 'Maybe with Tharguen, but not us, I'm sure. Maybe that's the debate?' He shrugged.

'At least we are still fairly treated,' said Jeremy.

'No, not considering there's a particular reason for that. Apparently, we're more important than regular prisoners,' said Tharguen. 'And why is that.'

His question came out more like a conclusive statement, to which he assumed no one knew what to respond.

'What do you think will happen now?' asked Jeremy.

'I don't know,' said Tharguen. 'Try to get some sleep now. We may understand better tomorrow.'

Tharguen would not miss his chance to know more next time.

The next day they did not learn more, for they received no news. The guards outside the room knew nothing; they simply performed their duties. A few days later, the Captain and his Officer returned to ask more questions, this time about the others, and particularly Gahli, who thought it was because she was the only girl amongst them. Quite a few questions were personal, but the Telorains answered nonetheless, hoping it would prove they were not Morkans.

'You look like strong polcs,' said the Captain to many of them. 'Yes, and some of you say you can cook. And you', he said to Gahli, 'are quite the peculiar one. Normally Morkans do not send female polcs out to fight, unless they are adept in magic.'

'That's because we're not Morkan!' said Gahli, annoyed, almost rolling her eyes. 'And as you've seen' – she spread out her arms – 'I know barely anything about magic!'

'All right,' said the Captain. 'I am done with my questions. We will come back again later on.'

As he and his officer walked to the door, Tharguen gave some of his team members a look. Several of them slowly walked in their path, blocking the way. Then, as quickly as possible, Pete and Gahli grabbed hold of the Officer, and Tharguen grabbed the Captain by the collar. Eerzin held the Captain's arms so he couldn't fight back while others held down the two men to further immobilise them.

'Not so fast,' said Tharguen. 'Why are you asking us all these questions? Why wait so long, never coming to check up on us, and then interrogate us? Huh?! We want to know what you plan to do with us!'

'I am not in a position to tell you at this time.'

'Oh, I think you are. I will not release you until you tell us.' There was a pause. 'I may not be Morkan, but I sure was trained in unarmed combat, and I assure you, if you do not tell us, I will snap you in two.'

Tharguen moved one hand and closed it around the Captain's throat, gently squeezing to amplify his threat. To Tharguen's relief, the Captain called his bluff.

'You will be sent to Morok. Your people will probably stay here. Some may go with you.'

'Why?' cried Tharguen. 'What is this deal?'

'We have a deal with Mirauk so that Morok does not bother us.'

'But what's the *deal?!*' Tharguen compressed his throat a little more.

'That we do not meddle in the affairs of others.'

'There's more to it, I'm sure!' said Tharguen. 'You are meddling in *Mirauk's* affairs.'

'Rhal Majim will not change his mind.'

'I still want to know!'

'Let me go, and I will tell you.'

Tharguen released him, nodding to the others, and they released the Officer as well. The Captain steadied himself, looking at Tharguen suspiciously. Everyone in the room glowered at each other.

'It is an agreement that will leave Morkans out of Dûnelor forever,' the Captain said steadily and calmly.

'Rhal Majim wants peace and quiet from them,' said the Officer. 'And there is only one way we can get that.'

'Please, tell us more specifically,' said Tharguen in a sarcastically polite tone. 'What way is that?'

'There is a polc who betrayed Mirauk among the Telorians. Mirauk is after him.' The Captain paused but continued when his eyes met Tharguen's glare. 'He says he will not attack us or bother us if we do not help the Telorians and if we deliver his polc, or else he will destroy our dominion.' There was another pause.

'And?' prompted Tharguen, his arms crossed.

'And we promised him we would deliver the one whom he is after. You are him, are you not?' The Captain regained his composure, and his tone was challenging.

'I *am* him,' said Tharguen, knowing in his heart what he had always suspected: that Mirauk was fulfilling the promise that had been voiced by Kàtchah. Tharguen bowed his head. 'I confess it.'

'Then you know where lies your fate,' said the Captain.

'Let it be known in the records that I did not betray Mork, for I was merely a Telorian spy. Now that you have shed some light on our confusion, you may go.'

With one last glare, the Captain and his Officer walked out of the room. As they were shutting the door, the Officer complained, 'Rhal will not be too pleased to hear this. Yet, he might be satisfied with our work and the accuracy of this confirmation . . .' Then they were out of earshot.

'Well, he sure had the look of fear in his eyes,' said Tharguen. 'He must definitely think we're dangerous.' He paused shortly. 'Maybe I did press a little too hard on his throat.' He took a deep breath.

'Damn it!' said Gahli. 'Pardon me, Captain, but why did you confirm that you were the Morkan Mirauk's after? Until now, they had no real proof!'

'I gave them my name, did I not?'

'Now we're all going to die in Mork before Mirauk,' complained Pete.

'The Morkans have been after me for many years, and I already knew from the beginning, before ever coming home from Darakön. Captain Kàtchah assured me himself they'd hunt me down. I wouldn't be surprised if he came here to get me himself.' He sighed. 'What's the difference whether they try to capture me here and now or elsewhere later? Besides, there might still be a chance for us to escape or change the Dûnelorians' minds.'

'I don't understand why they would agree to such a deal,' said Gahli. 'There must be some deeper emotion behind it. I suppose Mork it is, then.'

'Anyway, why are *you* so worried?' said Tharguen. 'If anything, the Dûnelorians will keep you here to serve their Prince. You'll have a chance to earn their trust, in time. If anyone is to be shipped to Mork, it's me.'

'Then why did you tell them all that?' wondered Eerzin. 'It's suicide.'

'Honesty shows strength,' said Tharguen. 'I'm prepared for anything.' He lowered his voice. 'Except death.'

He started pacing to and fro. Then his anger swelled and he yelled, punching the wall with his fist. He took a deep breath.

'If anything should happen to me,' said Tharguen, 'I need you all to stick together. All we have is each other now, and . . . I don't know *what* will happen.'

'Captain,' said Pete, 'we'll do everything we possibly can to save you.' He paused. 'Even though we're scared.'

'Thank you,' said Tharguen. 'It means a lot to me, because I'm scared too.'

Many more days passed. Again, the Telorians were left to their confusion and impatience until finally, a week later, the Captain and his Officer returned, accompanied by many guards.

The Telorians stood, alert. *Is this it?* Tharguen asked himself. *Are we going to Mork?*

'His Majesty wishes to bring you to his father, the Emperor Billahmyé Veij Majim, to determine what to do with the rest of you. All of you are to go,' said the Captain. He followed Tharguen's gaze to the large bags several guards carried. 'His Majesty has asked that all your personal belongings and weapons be brought to his father's palace.'

Tharguen nodded carefully, but at that moment he got an idea – though he kept it to himself, for he did not know if it would work or if there was any point to trying it at all.

'Some of you might remain there or return here,' the Captain went on, 'depending on where you will be more useful.' He paused. 'Well, come on.'

Guards walked to each Telorian and bound their hands in front of them.

'Grayt,' said the Captain to his Officer. 'Take the lead. I will be at the tail today.'

Officer Grayt nodded and started off.

The Telorians were escorted out of the large room and through the hall. They were led out through a back door where what appeared to be large carriages awaited them. However, upon closer inspection, the Telorians saw that these carriages had no wheels. They were fairly roomy, and roofed with straw on cloth. There was space enough for ten inside plus the driver who steered the horses. All of these wheelless carriages were lined up one behind the other.

Rhal Majim stood ready to board his, watching as the Telorians were escorted into several of these wheelless carriages.

'Captain Loyfeij,' Rhal said to the Captain, 'keep an eye on the sand-sled containing the Telorian Captain.'

'I will watch from my sled very closely,' replied Captain Loyfeij.

Tharguen, Pete and Gahli were escorted into the same sand-sled before getting separated from their other team members.

Tharguen quickly whispered to his knights as he passed by them, 'Don't try anything unless I signal it.'

Then he, Pete and Gahli entered quietly, both followed and led by guards. They sat down on cushions as the guards surrounded them, and Tharguen noticed a large bag in front of him as he leaned back. The sand-sleds then started moving.

Tharguen observed the bag further and soon realised it was the bag that held their weapons – some of them, at least – but even if he tried, it wouldn't help him retrieve his sword. He did have a knife well hidden in his boot still, but he did nothing. Well-concealed weapons were perhaps one of the rare things he was grateful for about Mork; he could still pull off a few stunts. However, Tharguen also wondered why the Dûnelorians had put him in the same sand-sled as the weapons and realised they could be testing him. Perhaps they were waiting for him to present them the opportunity for violence, in which case he would not touch the bag nor give them any reason to accuse him of wrongdoing.

One of the guards noticed Tharguen's interest in the bag and looked at him with disdain.

'Do not even think about it, filthy Morkan!'

Tharguen seethed, clenching his jaw and balling his hands into fists. Being called a filthy Telorian by Morkans was one thing; to be called a filthy Morkan for the plain reason that he had spent fifty polken years as a spy in Mork hit him too close to home. He twitched, reflexively wanting to defend himself, but did not engage with the guard. Another guard stood and moved quickly in response before the other stopped him.

'No,' he said, 'it is not worth it.'

The Dûnelorian guard removed his hand from his weapon and sat back down, eyeing Tharguen warily. Tharguen glared at the two guards in return. He let out a slow breath, releasing some tension. No one was bothering trying to explain anything around here, and all of his conclusions thus far had been guesswork.

Tharguen closed his eyes as everyone fell silent.

CHAPTER FIVE:
Foreboding News

The host of Telorian prisoners along with their Dûnelorian escorts travelled silently and slowly for four days. It would have been quicker to walk, perhaps, but in the sand, especially on windy nights, it helped to have these sand-sleds. Besides, the sleds were built to withstand the desertean terrain and weather.

The Telorians kept quiet, keeping their thoughts concealed, only sometimes daring to whisper to each other for a short time. Tharguen had noticed they were travelling southwestwards. On the fourth day, he could see a tall palace far away and knew they would be arriving in the evening.

'Captain,' said Pete nonchalantly. Tharguen looked at him. 'Tell me, what made you stay in Mork? I mean, why didn't you just come home?'

Tharguen realised what Pete was trying to do and went along with the polc's scheme, although it *was* true he had never revealed too many details from that time to anyone but Bahvley and Niome. He took a breath.

'I had just killed a Morkan and taken his garments. I figured I wouldn't be attacked and killed so easily that way. I was sneaking up the Command Tower when I bumped into a Captain. He didn't recognise me, so I introduced myself as a recruit and explained that this was my first battle but that I had no captain. I tried to sound assertive and hoped he wouldn't notice my shaking hands. I didn't think he would buy every word of it, to be honest, but he did. In Mork, it turns out, until a soldier has proven himself skill-worthy, he is not given a Captain. Beshrig told me he wanted a stout polc like me on his team. He said, "*My name is Beshrig, and I have decided that you have just joined my army.*" I said, "*My name is Gowtch.*" I had to think of a name quickly; it was the first thing that popped into my head. Had I known I'd have it for nearly fifty years, I would have chosen a more suitable name for myself.'

'Tharguen suits you fine,' said Gahli. Tharguen smiled.

'Beshrig gave me his set of keys and told me to go get . . . medicine for the fighters,' Tharguen went on, furrowing his brow as he strove to remember some of the more specific details. 'Instead, I tried to return to Elina so she could enter Mirauk's study, where he stacks all his books at the top of the Sorcery Tower. But I saw . . .' – Tharguen winced at the memory – 'so many friends die. Elina distracted

Mirauk and looked upon his evil gaze. Mirauk let her go – you know, so she could tell Teloria of our failure. I saw her fleeing, and a look of terror was upon her. She didn't see me trying to catch up to her. Had she, she probably would've waited for me.'

The Dûnelorian guards began to listen to the story more intently, as opposed to trying to ignore Tharguen's words.

'I remember hearing a yell coming from Bahvley. Mirauk was stabbing one of our friends who had taken the hit for him.' Tharguen shook his head slowly. 'I'd never heard Bahlvey scream like that before.' He bowed his head. 'Then Mirauk went for Bahvley's decoy, Queevsil. He had killed our First Captain, too.' Tharguen passed a hand over his face, closing his eyes momentarily.

'Elina knew that the Fairhaven blood was powerful and that if Bahvley entered Mork, he needed to be protected. I don't know how much of the prophecies she knew, but she had told us one word from them: King. We knew Bahvley was meant to be the King of Teloria, and Elina sacrificed herself for us, for Bahvley. Everyone . . .' He paused, his jaw tight. 'The Team of Twelve, we called ourselves. Captain Ackerley brought an army to accompany us, three hundred polcs strong, but it was Bahvley who led us to Mork, and . . .' Tharguen let out a shaking breath.

'You, Bahvley and Elina were the only survivors,' Pete said solemnly.

Tharguen nodded. 'You can imagine how hard it was to hold back tears at that point, and many times I wept. You see, I never saw Bahvley escape, and in that moment I thought he was dead. He's like a brother to me, and I hated that I could not save him.' Tharguen blinked back tears, then smiled wanly. 'My relief upon discovering his survival and escape from Mork was immense.'

'What about Mirauk?' asked Gahli. 'Did he never suspect you?'

Tharguen shook his head. 'I never looked at Mirauk, and that battle when Elina was cursed by Mirauk was the only time I was in his presence. Except for when he ran down those stairs after Niome, the Five, Bahvley and me when we retrieved the *Book of Enchantment.*'

'Why didn't you escape with Elina?' asked Pete.

'When Elina fled, I tried to catch up, like I said. When I saw it was no use, I tried to find the rest of our scattered team, but they were either gone or dead. I stood there, in a Morkan disguise, with nowhere to go. Had I tried to flee at that point, I might have been discovered.

'I continued my charade to find out who had truly died from my team. When Mirauk left the premises, Beshrig and I checked the bodies. Bahvley and Liffwai, along with a few others, were missing. I thought they were dead, though. But I had to stay, just in case someone else was still alive and needed me. So, I turned to the only person I *could* turn to:

Beshrig. And I pretended to be a Morkan for a while more. Turned out to be a very long time.'

'How did you learn the *language?*' Pete marvelled, raising his brows.

'Quickly, cleverly.' Tharguen smiled smugly. 'I was quick at picking up the Morkan language, and I grabbed books to read what I could, used my knowledge of Ancient Telorian learnings, even if it was little, and I listened. I listened when the other Morkans spoke, replied only when directly spoken to – usually with a nod after being given an order – and observed the reactions and replies in the common tongue when Morkans spoke in the Morkan tongue to each other. It earned me the reputation of an obedient soldier, and Beshrig loved that I never quipped back like some of the others did.'

Tharguen smiled sideways. 'If I didn't do right away what I had been told to, I was either asked why I wasn't doing said thing, which told me what the order had been, or I was perceived as the lost, unsure one, and then shown how to earn my rank. As I learnt certain words and expressions, I was able to decipher more and more until finally, I knew the language as well as any high-ranking Morkan.'

'At the battle, though, if you were pretending, could you not have left and caught up with those who escaped?' asked one of the Dûnelorian guards. Some of the other guards eyed him sternly, as though reminding him of his duty. He shifted uneasily.

'I didn't know where they were,' Tharguen replied, 'and a few days later I found out that they were at the Islands. I had tried to find a way to leave without being pursued, but Mork is very well guarded, and no one goes anywhere without someone of higher rank approving it first. I was trapped there, but I also chose to cease all attempts to find a way out, and I decided to remain indefinitely and help any whom I could. At the time, I had hoped I could somehow help my friends. Bahvley was alive, and every Morkan knew it.'

Tharguen looked straight at the Dûnelorian guards in front of him, his head held high. 'I'm not the only Telorian Mirauk is after. And I'm glad I decided to stay, for I saved Niome. It was a long rise to being Second-in-Command, but it gave me access to a lot of secrets that will continue to help us defeat Mork.

'As for Bahvley, last I had heard, he and Liffwai had gotten away by boat and there was no means of pursuing them. It's a shame Liffwai died. It chagrins me that we lost everyone.' He paused. 'Still, I prayed and believed Bahvley was still alive. And that gave me hope.' He smiled fondly, thinking of the Kikies of his team. 'Those Kikies took good care of him. The lucky fool.'

'The Kikies?' said the most suspicious guard.

Tharguen told them who they were. Some guards wondered how a Morkan could come up with such a compelling story as that, voicing how they thought that maybe he was not truly Morkan after all.

Then the sand-sled halted. Captain Loyfeij came to see them.

'Okay, time to come out now.' He looked at the guards and scowled. 'Why the strange looks?'

The guards only shrugged their shoulders and looked at Tharguen.

'I see,' said Loyfeij. 'He has been trying to persuade you with his stories. Well, they are false – all lies. Now come.'

'They did not sound false to me,' Tharguen heard one of the guards mutter to another, and he was pleased. There was hope yet.

Tharguen, Gahli and Pete were escorted to the Prince's sled where all the other Telorians were gathered. The Prince walked up to them.

'This is my father's palace. You can try to tell him your story, but he already knows mine.'

The Palace was immense and rose high into the sky above them, adorned with arches and golden pillars at the front. Large steps led to the palace's double doors, which were even greater than those at the Prince's palace. It was magnificent. Silver engravings laced the tall pillars and the double doors, giving the entrance an incredibly regal allure. Drawings of former Emperors and Empresses had been painted on the walls in rich, vibrant colours.

The Telorians looked at the Emperor's palace in awe.

'Move along, I said!' said Loyfeij. 'Can you not hear me, stupid brute!'

Tharguen turned to him. He finally dared to put him in his place, yet at the same time he knew this was not an evil polc, else Loyfeij would resort to violent actions and violent words as a Morkan would. Still, Tharguen was not going to let himself be pushed around by an equal.

'I demand more respect,' he said. 'You may be Captain here, but I have learnt from your guards that you have only recently been named Captain. If we were on the same team, as we should be, I'd be your superior. But that's not what matters. I deserve more appreciation from you.'

He added a little boastfulness in his voice, though very subtly. 'If it weren't for me, Niome could have been killed, or none of the Five could've passed the guarding armies of Mork and therefore never retrieved the *Book of Enchantment*, and therefore, the world would not have been saved, and Mirauk would be in power now! And if we are to be allies eventually—'

'Allies,' sneered a guard nearby. Tharguen ignored him and continued his speech.

'You should learn to respect those who risked their lives for the sake of all the lands, including yours. You know very well I was that Morkan, but you also know I was a Telorian spy. Don't deny the fact that you know we're all innocent. At least spare my team!'

'You cannot talk back to me,' said Captain Loyfeij.

'Actually, he can,' said Rhal Majim, 'for, as he said, he would be your superior were you on the same team. But you are not, and he certainly cannot talk back to me.' He gave Tharguen a prideful smirk. 'Save your breath, Morkan . . . or Telorian.'

'My name is Tharguen, Your Highness. Captain Tharguen Sumperale.'

'And you *do* dare talk back to me.' The Prince seemed amused. 'Telorians are reputed to take risks. At least you live up to your reputation, but I warn you, *Captain* Sumperale, to hold your tongue.'

Tharguen swallowed his rebuke. He thought there was a little too much emphasis on the 'Captain' there, but he knew it was best to choose your battles, and this was not one he wished to have quite yet.

The Telorians were led into the Palace as the great doors opened with a rumble. They were led through several corridors and several rooms before finally coming to the Emperor's throne room, where an older polc sat.

The Emperor wore an elaborate robe of golden lace and ivory embroidery upon a yellow gown with long, wide sleeves. A golden crown with silver engravings sat upon his head of silver-streaked black hair; the pendant that hung around his neck bore a round orange gem. His skin was tawnier than his son's, and his face bore the lines of age and wisdom. He sat on his throne with the same regal demeanour and magical essence as the Prince.

The Emperor rose at the sight of the Telorians.

'These are them,' said the Prince, waving a hand towards the Telorians.

Tharguen could not read much from his face, but the Emperor did not seem too pleased.

'I am Emperor Billahmyé Veij Majim. I have heard your story.'

'You haven't heard the truth,' said Tharguen. 'I was a Telorian spy in Mork, yes, but we're here in peace. We Telorians want to ally ourselves with you. You mustn't trust Mirauk; he's a monster. He's going to attack you anyway. Yes, I know about your deal, but—'

'I cannot talk to anyone in that state,' said the Emperor, his voice baritone. 'You are the ones whom we are to deliver. Case closed. I cannot go back on my word. Although, I must first make no mistake that you are he who Mirauk seeks, for what if you are deceiving us in order to gain . . .' He paused.

'Gain what? Win what? We are innocent! What lies has Mirauk told you?!' Tharguen shouted loudly, desperately.

'Take them away!' said the Emperor, waving his hand, annoyed. 'Bring them to the prison cells. And then, send for the Dukes of Morok.'

'Mirauk's nephews!' exclaimed Tharguen.

'Yes,' said Rhal Majim. 'They are the ones who came on Mirauk's behalf and with whom we have been dealing since.'

'The Dukes,' said Tharguen under his breath. 'I might have known.' He clenched his teeth.

Guards came and dragged the Telorians away, ultimately tossing them into the cells. It was dark and gloomy in the basement where they were now prisoners, and it certainly lacked the cosiness to which they had grown accustomed at the Prince's palace. They were fairly large cells, all linked together, with only metal bars to separate them. They stood along each wall with a corridor between the sides. Many Telorians stood in each cell.

Tharguen held the bars tightly with both hands, yelling at the guards. Captain Loyfeij came down and told him to shut his mouth. Tharguen grabbed him by the collar in response and pulled him in; Loyfeij's head banged on the bars.

'I will yell and talk back as long as there isn't any justice made here!'

'Then you will yell for a long time. Let me go!'

Captain Loyfeij took out a knife and pointed it at Tharguen's throat. Tharguen let him go.

'Aye, *sir*,' he said.

Tharguen was beginning to hate the treatment he was getting, but there had to be some way of breaking the curse that had seemingly been laid on the Dûnelorians. The Dukes had smooth-talked the Dûnelorians into this; he knew it. There had to be some way to wake them up to the terrifying yet essential truth that they must help the Telorians against Mork.

Captain Loyfeij steadied himself and walked away.

'Who is possibly going to be brave enough to go to Mork?' asked Pete, mostly rhetorically. The others looked at him. 'To send word.'

'No one,' said one of the guards. 'We send our messenger bird. The Emperor writes his letters, and the bird takes flight with them in its beak. He is a great big brown bird. A nice sight, if ever you saw him.'

'An eagle?' asked Gahli.

'No, he is a rare kind, although very much like an eagle. But he is more of a hawk.'

'Is there only one of these birds?' asked Pete.

'The Emperor has one, the Prince has one, and the Princess has one.'

'So there's a daughter also?' Pete said.

'Who lives the most south of our land,' said the guard.

'Why is she not here, then?' asked Gahli.

'Because she does not agree with her brother or her father on this matter.'

Tharguen looked at the others. So there *was* hope after all. Then his stomach almost immediately dropped, remembering about the Dukes.

'When will the bird take flight?' asked Tharguen.

'Tonight,' said a second guard, 'if he has not already taken flight.'

'And when will he reach Mork?'

'With a fast-flying bird like that,' said a third guard, 'here to Morok, about a week.'

'And how long from Mork to here for Merlik and Garkhktak to arrive?'

'Who are they?' asked the first guard.

'They . . . are the Dukes. There are two because they're twins, and Mirauk likes things evenly split.'

'Oh,' said the first guard.

'A few weeks, more or less,' said the third. 'A dozen days by horse.'

Tharguen looked at some of the others and whispered, 'At least that gives Bahvley time to reach us.'

'Can we ask you something?' Pete asked the guards. They nodded. 'Do *you* believe us? I mean, you seem amenable to answering our questions.'

'We do,' said the second guard. 'But we follow orders, and even if we tried, nothing would persuade the Emperor or the Prince to change their minds about the deal, even though we doubt Mirauk will keep his word. Perhaps the Princess will have better luck with that.'

'What if we were to attempt to get more answers or try to escape?' proposed Tharguen. 'Would you help us?'

The three guards took a moment to confer with each other.

'Perhaps,' said the first guard. 'But only because we fear Mirauk, and only as long as it did not include harming our people.'

Tharguen nodded, then sat down to doze off into a sleep slightly less troubled than his reality.

CHAPTER SIX:
Across the Dunes

The Telorians and Kikies travelled for a long time. Many days and nights had passed since they crossed the bridge over the Stream of Fluidity. The road built by the Telorians was coming to an end, and a vast field lay before them.

One night, as they tried to get some sleep, a strange hooded figure emerged in the dark. Vigh was the first to see it. It was clad in black and walked slowly, as though it seemed to be floating by. As Vigh lay motionless, he heard a strange sound like the deep breathing of some nocturnal beast. He sat up quickly and stared at it. The others stirred.

Soon they saw that there were more of them, all coming closer and closer to where they had taken up camp. The Telorians took out their weapons.

'These somehow don't look like Morkans,' Vigh said softly.

'But they sure look like something out of Mork,' replied Boreth, his voice low and filled with disdain.

'They definitely have the aura of beasts borne from evil magic,' said Celor.

Jimmy shot his bow at one of the creatures, but it appeared as though the arrow flew right through it, for as soon as it touched the creature, it disappeared. The creature looked at Jimmy but did not attack him before resuming its course eastwards. He lowered his bow, holding it with trembling hands.

'That's not normal,' he muttered.

'Why are they heeding us without really heeding us?' asked Niome.

'It's as though these creatures are on a direct course to some destination,' said Vigh.

'If they were sent from Mork, perhaps they must obey a precise command before attacking,' said Boreth, 'else they would have retaliated already.'

'Is this a haunted place?' asked Meysah.

'Maybe,' said Ihal, 'but I don't understand. We didn't encounter these roaming apparitions before.'

There was a flicker of light in the distance as dawn arrived, and as the sky brightened, the creatures disappeared.

'Where did they go?' exclaimed Lóim.

'Ghosts?' suggested Bahvley. 'Or . . .' There was a look of dread upon his face, and he let out a shaking breath. 'I have seen these creatures before. I can't remember when or where, but somehow, I know I have. They are . . . familiar to me. We must get out of here at once.'

They gathered their things with haste and continued on their long journey for many more days to come. On the thirty-sixth day of Summer, they arrived at last at the Desert of Dûnelor. They knew they were approaching when the land became drier and the grass grew in patches; there was more brown than green, and the earth started to look lighter in colour. At this point in their journey, the Kikies shrunk to their fairy size, continuing unnoticed at the Telorians' sides. The travellers came to giant rocks that formed a gateway with a great wall made of many boulders. Once past it, they were in the magical desert, and there was sand as far as the eye could see.

The days were quite hot, the nights cold. That first day and night were enough to annoy Jimmy, who didn't appreciate the radical temperature changes. All of the next day, he kept complaining.

'I can't take this anymore! What kind of weather *is* this! It's not real Summer! How do these people live here?'

'They're used to it,' said Lóim, 'for their ancestors came from a tropical land, and if I were you, I'd stop complaining.'

'You can't possibly be saying *I'm* annoying, because I'm not *half* as annoying as you,' retorted Jimmy.

'Come on, get along,' said Ihal. 'We have to endure each other for quite some time.'

'We *are* getting along,' Jimmy replied as he eyed Lóim, a bit unsure.

'They might be able to hear us,' said Lóim. 'Last time, they told us they had been observing us for days. They're strong with magic, you know. They *are* capable of tormenting us if we insult them.'

'Naah! They won't do such a thing,' said Meysah with confidence. 'How are they supposed to torment us?'

'Do you feel that?' said Tom. 'It was still before. Now there's a breeze.'

The group stopped walking, and soon enough there were gusts of wind blowing in their faces, carrying sand along with them.

'A sandstorm!' cried Lóim.

'I applaud you,' said Meysah. 'You've got timing for coincidences. Or, you know, we're being tormented.'

'They're not *tormenting* us,' said Niome. 'They're trying to *prevent* us from continuing. That's why we must continue on stubbornly, without thinking of turning back.'

'Don't worry,' said Meysah, 'the thought wouldn't even cross our minds.'

Meysah felt very optimistic about the situation at first. But as the storm grew, everyone became more and more tired, having more and more trouble keeping up, and Meysah was the first to complain.

'I don't know', he said, quite out of breath, 'how . . .' He took another step. 'Long . . . I can . . . go . . .' He took another slow step with much effort. 'On . . . like this . . .'

'I know . . . what . . . you mean,' said Ihal, who trudged along beside him.

'Master Vigh,' said Meysah, 'you didn't happen to bring your light-cube with you, did you?'

'I'm afraid not. I didn't think we'd need it.'

'Lord Nimrod,' said Huck, 'may I ask you what a light-cube is?'

'It's a weapon that clears up fog and darkness to the eyes of travellers. It was a gift from the Pleessies. It may have helped see the way better. Perhaps not.'

'You don't suppose that the Dragon's Wind could come in handy?' asked Jimmy.

'I brought it,' said Niome, 'but I don't think it'll work.'

'It won't,' agreed Vigh. 'Besides, the last thing we need right now is more wind.'

'Lord Nimrod,' said Huck.

'You can call me Vigh.'

'Lord Vigh, then. What's the Dragon's Wind?'

'A weapon used to blow the enemy away,' Vigh answered. 'A gift from the Firlanians.'

Meysah stopped walking and plopped his bag onto the sandy hill. Many others did the same; they just could not go on anymore. Even Boreth and Vigh eventually followed suit and collapsed down onto the ground.

'I have become . . . rather fatigued,' said Boreth, sighing deeply and closing his eyes.

'We must go on. We're almost there!' Bahvley encouraged the group. 'We have to sprint. There's only a day and a half left of travelling.'

'It's too windy!' cried Niome. 'If it's to be like this, we have to turn back.'

'What are you talking about?' Bahvley scowled in confusion. 'Niome!' Desperation began to make his heart race. 'Fight it!'

'What's the point?' she replied with a sigh.

Indeed, everyone had been enchanted, and they started walking back, away from their destination, with conviction. Bahvley could not understand why he himself was not affected, and then the Kikies appeared. They had been circling above him.

'I believe I have an explanation,' said Tithil, lifting a finger. 'I spilled my brew on you before, remember? It has special powers against this sandstorm, I believe. Even a Kiki learns something new every day.'

'Well, is there any left?!' asked Bahvley.

'I spilled it all on you.'

'My cloak! It also got on my cloak. I can put it on Niome, and she maybe can cast a spell to break this curse.'

He took off his cloak and put it over Niome's back.

'Niome!' he said. 'We're talking about Tharguen here. Tharguen's in trouble!'

'I know! Let's get on with it!' said Niome.

'Everyone's been hypnotised,' said Celor, 'except for us Kikies, for we are not so influenced by foreign magic. And Bahvley,' he added quickly, 'thanks to Tithil's clumsiness.' Tithil smiled gingerly.

'How are we to unhypnotise them?' Niome said with clarity, looking at her brother's cloak.

'Is there no spell that can help?' asked Mië.

'I'm afraid not for this sort of thing,' she replied. 'For I don't know what kind of magic it is, so I don't know what kind to counter it with.'

'Then I'll have to be authoritatative and threatening to get them to come with us,' said Bahvley, unsheathing his sword. He hurried to the others and pointed his sword at them. 'You will continue on! It's an order. Anyone who defies me will regret it.'

His tone was frighteningly intimidating though his words were simple. The other Telorians all grumbled in disapproval, but soon they turned around mechanically and followed Niome. Bahvley returned to her side.

'What an older brother won't do for his younger sister,' he said. She smiled.

The others whined all the way till night overtook the sky. Then they rested a short while, and Bahvley stayed awake to make sure that no one snuck away. By early afternoon of the next day, they had arrived at the Prince's Palace, the storm had stopped and everyone was back to their usual selves.

Bahvley knocked on the great door of the beaming palace. A guard came to answer, looking at them in puzzlement.

'What is this? I thought it was the old merchant again.'

'I am Bahvley Fairhaven, King of Teloria—'

'So there *is* a King?'

'I am here to speak with Prince Rhal Majim about a misunderstanding.'

'No misunderstanding at all. So he did speak true.'

'My friend, Captain Tharguen Sumperale, spoke the truth. He is Telorian, as am I, and whoever else you see here—'

'Then all the more reason not to help you!' interrupted the guard.

'Why? I must speak with—'

'It is too late; he is gone. They have all left. They have gone to the Emperor's Palace.' Then he added curtly, 'Good day.'

And with that, the Dûnelorian guard shut the massive double doors, leaving Bahvley to shout and bang on them uselessly.

'Where is the Emperor's Palace?' Bahvley called out. No answer followed. 'Well, that went well,' he said sarcastically.

'What are we supposed to do now?' sighed Jimmy. 'We don't even know where the other Palace is.'

'We have to put our minds together to find it,' said Ihal. 'Else all we'll do is panic, and that will lead us nowhere.'

'*You* sure are serious,' said Lóim.

'And you never are,' she replied, jutting her neck out.

'You could be a little nicer about it,' said Meysah.

'I've learnt a lot on this trip, and I am simply sharing wisdom.' Lóim laughed at Ihal's statement.

'I do have some wisdom!' she insisted. 'More than you, probably. Or else you hide it well.'

'Well, we have wisdom, too,' started Meysah, 'and—'

'Just because you went to Mork, you think you know so much more than us. Let me tell you, we fought and defended our country without running away.' Ihal started walking off.

'Running away?!' exclaimed Meysah, miffed. He motioned to Ihal. 'She says while walking away.'

'Lóim, I need your help with something,' said Ihal, looking back. Lóim walked over to join her a little away from the main group.

'Hu-ho!' exclaimed Jimmy, nudging Meysah's arm.

'Don't worry,' said Mittah. 'She does this all the time. Whenever she's jealous, that is.'

'Jealous!' said Jimmy.

'Well, you got to go to Mork. She didn't.' Mittah walked to Huck, Tom and Malcolm, leaving the two friends to contemplate.

'I think *I'm* jealous,' said Meysah, looking in Ihal and Lóim's direction.

'Do I sense some love?' teased Jimmy.

'No! I don't know her that well, and I don't think I want to, either. I mean, I feel awful and I . . . think I . . .'

'You like her, you like her!' Jimmy teased some more, grinning from ear to ear.

'One day, you'll feel like I feel, and you'll see what I mean,' spat Meysah, offended. He stalked off.

'What'd I say?' Jimmy shrugged it off, chuckling to himself.

Meanwhile, the Lords, the Kikies and Niome were discussing their predicament.

'Which way should we go?' Bahvley asked, trying his best to sound diplomatic despite feeling tormented with worry for his best friend.

'If we are most north of the desert,' mused Boreth, 'the only way to go is south.'

'Yes, well, "south" is a little too general,' Vigh commented.

'You must go south*west*,' said a voice.

Everyone turned around. An old crooked Dûne-lorian with a wide-brimmed straw hat, strings hanging down from it, stood before them, turning the corner of the immense wall. He carried a walking stick, yet his walk was solid. His skin was a rich sepia, and his voice had the gruffiness of old age paired with a soothing gentleness that reminded them of Bob Tweedle. He walked right up to them, his mouth curled into a permanent smile.

'Hello . . . uh . . . who are you?' asked Bahvley.

'I am a merchant.' The Dûnelorian smiled more widely. 'I can trade you a map for, let us say, a good few pounds of gold?'

'Do you know where the Emperor's Palace is?' asked Celor.

'Yes. I also know a bit of information I could tell you for a bit more.'

'I'll make you a bargain,' said Bahvley. 'You bring us there and tell us what you know, and we'll trade you safety, gold *and* a potion.'

'But I don't . . .' started Niome, suddenly pausing. She quickly caught on to her brother's plan. 'Yes, I have just the perfect potion for a merchant.'

'Really?' said the merchant. 'Let me see it.'

Niome looked through her bag and took out the little bottle of herb tea. She knew she wouldn't need it.

'It is more of a medicinal tincture, actually,' she said. 'It's a brew.'

'Excellent!' The merchant took the green transparent tincture, his smile beaming, and put it in his large sack. Almost instantly, he started walking again. 'Come on, we must hurry. We have several long days ahead of us now.'

They all started off, and Bahvley explained the agreement to the rest.

'Do you have a name, merchant?' he asked the polc.

'Yémillahr, but my friends call me Yém – or they did when they were still alive.' He chuckled. 'Yes, that is how old I am.'

'How old?' asked Boreth.

'I do not reveal such things,' Yém replied. 'So, tell me, you are Teloria's King?' he asked Bahvley. 'Who are the others?'

They made their introductions, and Yém listened carefully. He acknowledged each one, admitting he wanted to know with whom he was travelling.

'Simpler were the times before Mirauk's reign, when Dûnelorians and Telorians could more easily be in concord. You do realise that the mighty Billahmyé Veij Majim will have my head on a platter for this – served with rich foods and delicacies,' said the old polc with a chuckle. 'Of course, I jest.'

'Of course,' said Malcolm, looking at some of the others and exchanging frowns.

'Sounds like Mirauk's type of thing,' quipped Jimmy.

'A lot of things seem rather Morkan around here these days,' said Yém under his breath, but Niome caught it. Yém looked at her. 'I hear that the reason every one of your friends was brought before the Emperor is for further judgement of what should become of them. I think some of them are to be shipped to Morok!'

'Mork!' exclaimed Niome in a high-pitched tone.

'I believe the Emperor has had some secret dealings, but I do not know of what. The Prince and his father, and even the Princess, have exchanged many letters of late, and the Prince has become strict and acted unjustly towards visitors when usually he is friendlier, even if we are a reserved people. I believe the Princess does not wish to take part in her brother's recent decisions. But in truth, I am not sure. Dûnelorians are not friends of Morkans, you know, but there is more to this story than any one of us knows, and I believe it concerns Morkans.'

'Well, I'll be damned!' said Bahvley.

'Is there a chance that they're still alive?' asked Niome with a touch of sadness.

'Oh, they are alive,' said Yém. 'Dûnelorians are not Morkans.' He gently patted Niome on the shoulder. 'Rest assured, young Niome, that your friends are all still alive.'

For the rest of the day, they all walked in silence. That night they tried to sleep, but the worry was too great, and none could shut their eyes except for good old Yém.

Chapter Seven:
The Treacherous Trek

The travellers continued their journey through the desert, led by their Dûnelorian guide. The lords were busy discussing with Bahvley and the others except for Meysah, who was preoccupied. The young knight waited for a time when Ihal was walking alone, with no Lóim or Mittah beside her. He walked up to her, though she pretended not to see him.

'Have I offended you?' asked Meysah. 'Because if I did, I'm really sorry. Sometimes I say things, unaware of how it affects others. One of my faults, I know, but I don't mean to offend.'

'You didn't offend me,' said Ihal, slightly annoyed. 'You just bug me.'

'I bug you? Wuh – why? How?'

'You get so much praise from everyone.' She shook her head. 'The rest of us . . . get cast aside. Have I ever done anything as brave as walking into Mork or fighting a dragon?'

'Well, you just never got the chance,' said Meysah. He gave her an encouraging smile. 'Coming to Dûnelor was your first trip, was it not?'

'Yes, but I feel I missed out on a lot. I did fight in Teloria, shooting arrows from the wall, but—'

'Then there you go! Trust me, you do *not* want to go to Mork.'

'But I mean, you got to go to Dalvar again – with my Captain, might I add,' Ihal continued complaintively, 'but I had to stay home.'

'Well, that's not *my* fault, Ihal. Look, I'm trying to comfort you here and you're making it so difficult! Just because someone has more travelling experience than you is no reason to be jealous. You think I enjoyed Mork or fighting that dragon? You have not come face-to-face with a Morkan yet, and until you do, you won't understand how frightening it is.'

'It's *you* who doesn't understand, Meysah. You get to go on all the fun trips. The Twisted Forest! Had *this* not happened, you'd be there right now. I want to go there, too.'

'You always need to get the last word in, don't you? Well, if your pride is all you can think of, Ihal, then too bad for you.' Meysah could think of nothing else to say.

Ihal walked away. Jimmy, who had heard every word, came to Meysah's side.

'I told you so!'

'Told me *what*, Jimmy!' he shot back, emphasising the *T*. Meysah's patience was short even for his friend.

'You like her, and now I know that *she* likes *you*.'

'Did you not hear a word that was said?'

'Every bit of it,' replied Jimmy proudly. 'Read between the lines, my dear friend. She just told you she would've liked to be *where you were*; she wants to be *where you are*. It was the same when you were in school together those few years. *And* she called you brave. It's obvious to me. Think about it.'

Jimmy winked at Meysah, which annoyed him so much that he shouted in frustration while kicking the sand.

The next day, Niome took to teaching Tom a few extra spells and tricks.

'So, if I want to get the spell's full effect, I have to speak quite loudly,' said Tom to Niome.

'It's not so loud as much as it is clear,' replied Niome. 'You'll find that a spell is most effective if you direct it to do what you need it to do. Don't fall into the trap of letting it direct you. Plus, a whispered spell can be just as powerful as a shouted spell.'

'Maybe that's why not all the spells work when I say them,' said Tom.

'Cast the spell again,' instructed Niome. 'And enunciate.'

'Still on your brother?'

Niome nodded, adding, 'He needs cheering up.'

'Okay. Here I go.'

Tom had borrowed Niome's new wand, which she had designed to work for any sort of spell, even the Tweedle Spells. The wand took the command of Niome and those close to her if ever she were unable to cast a spell herself. Tom had become her new trusted wizard friend rather than just an acquaintance, so it worked with him now, too – or was supposed to.

He pronounced the magic words.

Trip the left foot,
Lift the right,
Caper the feet,
Jump and bump!

Tom waited for a reaction. Nothing.

'No, it's "*caper* **both** *feet*",' said Niome, chuckling goodnaturedly. 'You need to get every word right.'

'Oh, I see.' He tried again, waving the wand.

Trip the left foot,
Lift the right,
Caper both feet,
Jump and bump!

Suddenly Bahvley found himself running along and jumping up into the air to perform a beautiful caper. Then he awkwardly stood still, everyone turning to stare at him. Niome and Tom laughed so hard, their faces turned purple. Bahvley then laughed too.

'One day, I'll cast a spell on you!' he said, pointing a finger at his sister.

Bahvley came up to Niome and slung an arm around her shoulders. 'Something tells me I'm not the only one you're trying to cheer up.'

Niome sobered. 'You know your sister well.'

'He's still alive, Niome,' said Bahvley, conviction in his voice. 'If Yém says Tharguen still lives, then he still lives.'

Niome nodded. Bahvley gave her a small kiss on her forehead.

Shortly after, they came to a rocky path and then a bridge. The bridge was quite a few feet off the ground, perhaps eight, but did not look it.

'Now, we must go over the bridge,' said Yém.

'But it's so low!' exclaimed Huck. 'And looks unstable. Can't we just walk on the sand beside it?'

'Not unless you want to sink into the quicksand,' Yém replied.

Everyone took a closer look. Indeed, the sand was muddy and moving ever so slightly.

'Is the bridge safe?' asked Classû, a Telorian slightly older than Niome.

'Sure,' said Yém. 'I pass by here all the time. The Emperor's guards never come by here. They do not guard it. It is also a shortcut to my shop.'

The bridge was made of wood, slanted, and very old-looking. The Telorians were quite reluctant to go by, while Yém confidently started across.

'Just be sure to walk lightly,' he told his charges.

Celor bent and observed the moving sand. 'Normally, I'd suggest a fast-run, but the sand is creating some sort of movement in the air directly above it. Fast-run is best done either on solid ground or above a hole; I do not think we should risk it above this kind of sand.'

Bahvley nodded. 'Just be alert, just in case.' The Kikies nodded.

'We'll go last,' said Tithil to Bahvely.

'And we'll go fast,' said Forthil.

Bahvley started slowly but surely. Niome followed, and Jimmy and Meysah were behind her. Vigh and Boreth started across when Yém had gotten safely to the other side. Behind the Lords, Tom and Huck walked side by side, Classû and Malcolm behind them. Then the others followed, and last came Mittah, Lóim and Ihal.

There was a cracking sound, and everyone stood still, frozen where they stood. Suddenly the plank of wood that supported Ihal collapsed, and she fell through. Lóim grabbed hold of her by the waist, but she slipped out of his clasp until only her hand held onto his. In a flash the Kikies hurried to help, but they were not quick enough to grab hold of her; Ihal fell into the quicksand below, and almost instantly her legs were buried up to her knees. It was now a race against time.

Reflexively, without giving it any thought and before anyone could realise what he was doing, Meysah ran back across the bridge and jumped down. His legs were knee-deep in the sand; Ihal's were covered to the upper thighs now.

Ihal was speechless upon seeing him jump down. She could only stare at him in stupor and blink. Meysah grabbed hold of her with both hands by her underarms and hurled her up with all his strength. Slowly, she glided up out of the sand and

Meysah grasped her at the waist, pushing her up some more as the others pulled her up completely.

Ihal was speechless and safe, but Meysah was sinking. Now, realising what he had done, what he had risked, he began to panic internally.

'*Kurssus!*' he whispered to himself.

Everything had happened so fast. He wanted to stay brave on the outside, and so he smiled sheepishly as Ihal stared at him with a worried expression.

Instantly the Kikies shrank, as they had planned on doing for Ihal, and flew down to help him with their magic. Almost as quickly as he had jumped in, he was out.

A few moments later, everyone was safe and sound on the other side.

'What were you thinking, Meysah?!' shouted his sister in disbelief. She railed at him, 'You could have gotten yourself killed!'

'Because fighting Morkans can't get me killed,' Meysah said sarcastically.

'Of all the stupid . . .' Niome stopped herself. Her shoulders slumped.

'I love you too, Niome.'

Niome hugged Meysah. 'Don't ever do that again, or I'll have our brother the King order you to never do it again.'

'Okay,' Meysah agreed, chuckling.

'What did you do that for?' grumbled Lóim, giving Meysah a stern look. 'It would've saved us a lot of trouble.'

'I don't know,' answered Meysah, turning to his friends. 'It seemed like the right thing to do.'

'Foolish, yet courageous,' Bahvley laughed in relief. 'I'd've done the same.' He let out a long sigh, smiling. 'Now that we have recovered, let's continue.'

Yém smiled at Meysah in appreciative admiration and started off again as everyone else did. Ihal said nothing but smiled shyly to herself. Mittah laughed as the two girls walked past Meysah and Jimmy.

Jimmy picked at some of the bits of sandy mud beginning to dry up on Meysah's back. Meysah soon realised he was as muddied up as Ihal was.

'They say people do radical things when they fall in love,' started Jimmy. 'I am very impressed. And did you notice the reaction?' He then broke into a chant, like a drunk polc trying to serenade someone.

There is something strange in the air,
A young maiden so fair,
Has stolen the heart of a young,
Young soldier when she walked as he had sung.

'Stop it, Jimmy! Now is not the time!' said Meysah as he rushed to join his siblings, leaving Jimmy to laugh alone.

The group of travellers walked a while before coming upon an oasis.

'It is time to rest,' said the old merchant. 'I am weary.'

He sat down and leaned against a tree. The Telorians filled their bottles up with water and followed suit. Meysah sat by the edge of the pond and cleaned his boots and trousers of the muddy sand, removing his socks and rolling up his trousers to wring them out. Ihal came and sat next to him and started to rinse out her trousers as well, dipping her bare feet into the pond.

'That was quite the random reflex,' she said.

'You need not mention it,' said Meysah, as though he were expecting her to tell him it was foolish.

'I thought it very brave of you.' Meysah froze up as a blush emerged on his face. He had not prepared what to say to that. 'To risk your life for mine. I thank you.'

'Oh, don't mention it – it was nothing,' he replied shyly but briskly. He scratched his head nervously.

'I meant to apologise to you, for my attitude earlier,' said Ihal. 'You were right. I wanted the glory that I have not yet earned. I suppose that's why Lóim and I get along like brother and sister. We are alike that way.'

'Like brother and sister?' Meysah whispered to himself.

'You have more experience than me,' Ihal went on, 'and I understand that I, too, will gain that much wisdom in time. I owe you one.'

'You owe me nothing but the trust that I respect you, and I mean not to demean your deeds.' Meysah scowled internally at how much he was fumbling even with simple replies.

'All right,' said Ihal. 'I didn't mean to quarrel with you.'

'I didn't mean to, either.'

They both smiled at each other. Meysah jumped up.

'Come,' he said, holding out his hand, 'let's join the others.'

He helped Ihal up, and together they walked back to the group.

The next day, late in the evening, Yém stopped and looked at the others.

'This is where we part,' he said. 'Continue straight over the dune and you should arrive.'

'Where are you going to go now?' asked Bahvley.

'Home.'

At that, Yém walked away in the opposite direction.

The Telorians and Kikies went on without their guide, and once night had fallen, they arrived at the Emperor's palace. Bahvley, Niome, Meysah, Jimmy, Boreth and Vigh walked up the steps to the large door of the majestic palace as the Kikies disappeared. Bahvley's knock echoed loudly through the air. There was a long moment of silence before someone came to the door.

'Well, what a surprise,' said Captain Loyfeij. 'If it is not more Telorians.'

'I need to speak with your Emperor,' said Bahvley.

'Who are you?'

'King Bahvely Fairhaven, from Teloria.'

'The Emperor will not discuss anything with you,' said Loyfeij. He turned around.

'You are holding my friends captive,' said Bahvley in a slightly raised voice, maintaining his calm demeanour. 'Why? Teloria has done nothing against Dûnelor. I assure you he's not a Morkan; Captain Tharguen Sumperale is Telorian. If you want proof that the Five did go to Mork and then to Darakön, well, here they are.'

The Five stepped forth in their star formation.

'Which one of you is the Wizardess?' asked Loyfeij.

'I am.' Niome stood to her fullest height with her head held high, letting her magical aura exude.

Captain Loyfeij observed her for a moment. 'Fine. Follow me.'

He led them to the chamber where the Emperor and the Prince sat. A stern expression occupied the Prince's otherwise handsome face.

'What is this?' asked the Emperor.

'Teloria's King and his team have come to claim their friends to resolve—' started Captain Loyfeij.

'There is nothing that needs resolving,' Rhal Majim interrupted.

'I *must* have a word with you,' insisted Bahvley.

The Prince took a breath to speak.

'Let him speak,' said the Emperor, cutting off his son.

'Long ago, I, Bahvley Fairhaven, travelled to Mork, but we failed our attempt to recover the *Book of Enchantment*. I escaped, and my friend Tharguen disguised himself. We are the only two survivors. Six years ago, my sister, the Great Wizardess Niome, and four others followed in my footsteps, and indeed the trip was a success, in part thanks to Tharguen.'

'You speak of the Great Wizardess,' said Rhal, 'but she is so young. What happened to the other Great Wizardess?'

'She passed away from Mirauk's curse,' said Niome with downcast eyes.

'I am sorry to hear that,' said Rhal, sincere woe in his voice, 'but my father and I cannot help you.'

'I don't understand why you are still holding them captive, my friend and his team,' said Bahvely. 'All we wanted was to become your allies. If you want us to leave you alone, we will; just free my people, please. Listen, Teloria is at war with Mork.'

'So is Dûnelor,' said Billahmyé Veij.

'Then why not help us in our battle against Mork?' Bahvley asked assertively.

'Because we prefer not to mingle in other people's affairs,' the Mighty Veij replied.

'You are mingling in it now, whether you like it or not,' said Niome, 'for you are holding our friends.'

'We would rather not be bothered by Morok and stay out of your business than help you and be attacked by Morok,' said the Emperor.

The Prince leaned towards his father and whispered something.

'There's more to it than that!' cried Niome, scowling. 'I know there is. Why else would you still be holding my – our friend captive. Don't you know he's innocent?'

'Oh, we know it very well,' said Rhal, standing up and walking towards her. 'If you must know, there *is* more. Indeed, we have made a deal with Mirauk.' Niome's heart sank. 'We promised we would not help you and promised to deliver the one he is after, whom the Morkans call Gowtch, in exchange for freedom, and if we do that, they will not attack us but leave us in peace. Mirauk will never bother us after this.'

'So what, are you going to just ship them all to Mork?!' cried Bahvley.

'Yes. As planned, yes,' said Rhal.

'This is so unfair!' shouted Niome. She turned to the Emperor. 'Don't you know this is a scheme? You can't possibly believe that Mirauk'll keep his word!'

'We will not be persuaded to change our minds,' Rhal replied.

'Lead them out,' said the Emperor. 'Make sure they never return.'

Guards stepped forward and began escorting them out. Niome kicked and screamed as one of the guards carried her to the entrance. After leading the travellers far away from the palace, the guards left them.

The Telorians did not know what course of action remained. Niome began to weep.

'What are we to do?' whined Ihal. 'Gahli is trapped in there, and Pete, and—'

'Tharguen,' said Niome. 'They didn't even let Bahvley finish his story.'

Lóim walked to Ihal, who stood by Niome's side, and put his hand on her shoulder. Meysah felt too riled up about the Dûnelorians to get upset about his jealousy towards Lóim, though it would have comforted him to comfort Ihal.

'Why did the Prince tell us what their deal with Mork was?' wondered Vigh.

'Because there's a reason he wanted us to know of it,' Boreth said.

'He doubts it,' guessed Jimmy. 'He is perhaps having second thoughts. Perhaps his father feels more strongly, and he is now regretting his decision.' He shrugged. 'He didn't sound or look like he was gloating.'

At that moment, the Kikies appeared.

'Telorians!' said Celor. 'We have good news. We flew to the basement to investigate and found Tharguen and the others in prison cells, but they are alive and healthy.'

'We know what was said upstairs,' said Tithil. 'No need to mention it.'

'We discovered how to sneak into their basement to save the others,' Mië added.

'The Dûnelorians don't want to wage war against you,' said Celor, 'but there is more we could not discover. They are very guarded.'

'Well, it's unavoidable now,' sighed Bahvley. 'We will get our people back, by whichever tactic we need to use. However, if we can sneak in and get them out without fighting anyone, that is what I would prefer.'

Bahvley fastened his belt tighter and fixed up his sword for a better fit.

'Come,' he said, 'we're going to claim our people back. No one is going to Mork if it's not to fight Mirauk altogether.'

'You will need to rest first,' said the voice of an old polc. Everyone turned around. It was Yém, standing nearby. 'I thought I would wait to see if your plans worked out. I can help you. Come, rest, and I will tell you how.'

Chapter Eight:
The Break-In

The time that passed was long and boring as the Telorians strove to figure out a way to persuade the Emperor and the Prince to change their views. However, some felt it was too late, for the Emperor's messenger bird had already left four days prior to bring his message to Mork. The twin Dukes would soon leave for the desert.

The Telorians sat in thought. Tharguen began to sing softly, a sad tune.

I may be far from home,
But I am not alone;
For I carry you in my heart,
Hoping that never again we may part.

I miss you greatly, my dear,
But I'll be home soon, have no fear,
For whatever may happen where I am,
Know that I love you and—

The song was interrupted by the sound of the Emperor's voice.

'I am here to inspect all of you and decide which of you are to serve me or my son, and which of you are to accompany your Captain to Morok.' His guards opened the cells and stood vigil outside them. The Emperor walked into one of the cells, guards by his side. He walked to Tharguen. 'Understand that even if I had the choice, I would still deliver you to Mirauk.'

'You *do* have a choice!' protested Tharguen.

'Would you not make such sacrifices to save your own life?' asked the Emperor. Tharguen would've liked to answer '*Never*', but he couldn't, for it was not so. Instead, he looked down. 'Indeed, you would. Indeed, you did when you let one of my people die when pretending to be a Morkan.'

Revelation came to Tharguen, and he suddenly understood a part of where the Dûnelorian Emperor stood in this matter. He wished Bahvley were here to negotiate these matters diplomatically. Then again, would it make any difference?

'Please do comply,' continued the Emperor without a pause. 'It is in your best interest.'

'I did not *let her die*,' Tharguen said through clenched teeth. 'I swear, if I could have saved her, I would have.' He stared the Emperor in the eyes. He did his best to control his emotions. 'And I freed all your people who'd been captured. I risked my life for your people, because it was the right thing to do.'

'And yet you failed to help another, *if* what you say is true,' the Emperor replied.

'If? *If!*' Anger swept over Tharguen. 'If you were not the Emperor, I would grab you by the throat and clobber you until you set my team free.' Tharguen turned his head to the side, shutting his eyes. 'I'm sorry.' He hadn't meant what he'd said. It hurt him that his team was doomed to suffer for his mistakes. It hurt him that he would pay for Beshrig's actions years after he'd left the evils of Mork.

'You are violent,' said the Emperor.

'And you are vile!' said Tharguen, looking up again. 'For you are allying yourself with Mirauk, whether you want to admit it or not.'

'Guards, restrain him. I do not wish to take the risk of keeping him loose.'

Guards took hold of Tharguen and bound his hands to chains, then tied those chains to the bars of the cell. Tharguen tried to fight them off, but it only gave them more reason to restrain him. Then the Emperor walked to each of the Telorians, making his judgements and telling them where they would serve best. At last he walked to Gahli.

'Ah, yes, definitely. I understand my foreteller's point of view. You would make a good wife to my son.'

'What? No! I don't desire to wed—' objected Gahli.

'That does not matter,' answered Mighty Veij. 'Either that, or you join your Captain in Morok.'

'I'd much rather die in Mork than live miserably here!' cried Gahli.

'I pity you.' The Emperor walked out of the cell and to the next. He approached Jeremy; while his Dûnelorian descent was far diluted, he still retained mild traits. 'You will serve my son, the Prince.' The Emperor looked at Eerzin. 'You are going to Morok.'

And thus he proceeded, judging them all and deciding their fates one by one. Then he left, leaving Tharguen and his friends more desperate and melancholy than ever.

A couple of days later, guards came and opened up the cell in which Tharguen, Pete and Gahli resided. They freed Tharguen's hands but made no attempt to move him; they took Gahli with them.

'Where are you taking me?' she shouted as they dragged her through the halls. They led her up some stairs and into a chamber where the Prince awaited her. The sun shone from the window on his face. The guards released her and exited the room, leaving them alone.

'Have a seat. I wish to chat with you.'

'I prefer to stand.'

'Very well, then, stand. Gahli, is it?'

'Okay, what do you want from me? Get it over with; just ask me. I have a schedule, you know.'

'A schedule?' asked Rhal, amused.

'Well, when I get back home, I have to go see my teachers and—'

'I am so sorry, I am afraid you cannot go home,' said Rhal. 'Now, my father has this idea that . . . you know. I have no intention of forcing you, but you have to stay here. Anyway, you would not survive a fight with a Morkan.'

'Did you just insult me?' said Gahli. 'You dare when you are alone with me?'

'What would you do to me?'

'Maybe . . . this!'

Gahli grabbed Rhal by the arm, twisted it back and threw him to the ground, crouching down over him. Rhal took her by the ankle and pulled but Gahli maintained her position firmly, tucking her knees into the sides of his armour.

'And if I had my sword,' continued Gahli, 'I might've killed you. My Captain was trained by Morkans, remember. And I trained with the best Telorians before learning from him.'

She let him go and stood up. Then, Rhal slowly stood, eyeing her warily. He crossed his arms.

'Next time, I assure you, you will not catch me by surprise. I give you a comfortable room to stay in—'

'Alone! To worry and miss my friends!'

Rhal walked to the door. He glanced at her boot, where she kept a hidden knife – at the same ankle he had grabbed – then waved a dismissive hand. He opened the door.

'I will return.'

* * *

The next day, a few other Telorians were taken from their cells and brought to serve the Prince and Emperor and '*help*' prepare the palace for the Dukes of Mork. Many served in the kitchens and assisted with cleaning the halls.

Rhal again visited Gahli. She stared at him a long time, trying to figure out why the Dûnelorians would have agreed to such an absurd bargain with Mirauk.

'May I join you?' he asked. His eyes darted to her boot.

'I won't surprise-attack you,' Gahli said softly. 'Sorry about that.'

Rhal nodded. He entered the room and shut the door. Then, after a long silence: 'I trust your needs have been accommodated?' Rhal inquired.

'Oh, I have potions, but yes.'

Rhal nodded. 'I understand. Still, I would rather you be . . . comfortable than kept downstairs.'

'And here I thought I was brought to this room because we were to be matched together,' muttered Gahli. There was an awkward silence. 'Why *is* your father so insistent to find you a wife? Has he not suggested other—'

'I have refused them,' responded Rhal.

'And so he suggested me. Why? His approach is . . . different than what I'm used to.' If she could get him to open up, perhaps they could find common ground from which to form an alliance – or at least she may learn the reason the Dûnelorians chose to side with the Morkans.

'I apologise,' replied Rhal.

Gahli sat down on the bed. 'You said you refused others. Why did you refuse them?'

Rhal opened his mouth to speak but hesitated. 'I am not certain I should speak of this.'

Gahli nodded. 'I only ask because . . . well, if I'm to stay here, I'd like to know more about you.'

'I suppose that is reasonable,' replied Rhal, taking a few steps further into the room. 'If you should know, they were not . . .'

He softened, and suddenly his demeanour seemed like that of a simple polc – grieved, his stern face becoming tender. Rhal sat down on the bed beside Gahli.

'I once loved a woman but lost her. I suppose my father merely wants to see me find love and happiness again.'

'I'm sorry to know you lost the woman you loved,' said Gahli. 'Was there no other?'

'There was, and never will be, any other,' replied Rhal.

'I can understand that.'

Rhal continued to look straight ahead. 'My father has tried before to help me find love anew, but I always said they reminded me too much of her. It was not always the truth; there simply is no other for me.' Gahli nodded. 'I suppose that is why he thought perhaps I would want a polc who was not of Dûnelorian descent. But like I've said, there is and never will be any other for me.'

Gahli placed her hand on his and squeezed gently. 'I understand.'

Rhal nodded. 'I am sorry that you and your team have been roped into this mess along with your Captain. He is the only one we wished to apprehend.' His face hardened.

'And why is that?'

The Prince shook his head, standing from the bed. 'I have shared too much. Forgive me.'

Gahli stood, wanting to reach out, feeling sorrow. She extended her hand but hesitated before letting her hand drop to her side. Rhal's eyes softened again.

'I have not spoken of her in a very long time,' he said, 'but she is ever in my heart. She was to be my wife. She was strong and brave, like you.'

'What happened?' asked Gahli, taking a step towards him.

'Morkans!' His face turned to an expression of disdain. 'And your Captain. Polcs under his command took her away from me! She was only gone on an exploration mission.'

'I'm sorry. Did you see—'

'No, I was here.'

'Then how do you know it was Captain Tharguen?'

'Because my guards were there some twenty years ago and escaped, and they recognise him today.'

'But he didn't kill her, did he?' said Gahli, her eyes pleading. 'And they weren't under his command, were they? Because it was his Captain, Beshrig, who killed her.'

Rhal bowed his head. 'The polc who did it is dead. I suppose it is easier to deal with if I blame your Captain for it.' He shut his eyes tightly and clenched his jaw. 'I need someone to pay.' A tear ran down Rhal's face. He turned away from Gahli. 'That is why when the Morkans came on their dark horses, we accepted their deal.'

'Can you not see that the Morkan responsible has already paid the price for it? Tharguen did everything he could,' insisted Gahli. 'He wanted to free all your people, everyone. He didn't know what Beshrig had planned.'

There was a long pause. Rhal had opened up to her; perhaps he himself was searching for that forgiveness within himself. She would pry it out of him if she had to, but there had to be a way for him to forgive Tharguen.

'He was present, and posing as a Morkan. That is enough for blame to be bestowed upon him.' Rhal turned abruptly to face Gahli again. 'I do not know where this conversation is going. I have already said too much.'

Rhal left swiftly and didn't come back the next day. But he did come back eventually, and Gahli was able to get him to open up some more, and she opened up in return about friends she had lost to Morkans. Rhal was hurting, and she wished she could make his sorrow go away. Changing his mind about the deal with the Morkans, however, would be more of a challenge, but she was determined to get there.

On one of the days of their imprisonment – the Telorians had lost count by this time – the Emperor came down, his eyes full of anger, or perhaps was it worry. He walked to Tharguen's cell and looked straight at him.

'What can you tell me of King Bahvley Fairhaven?'

'What do you mean?' asked Tharguen.

'Is he known to make any surprise attacks?' said Billahmyé.

Tharguen then saw in the Emperor's eyes a new threat, and he was filled with hope. If his friends had come to Dûnelor, he would not give away their tactics to the Emperor, so he simply said, 'No. But he will never give up.'

The Emperor took a moment more to stare at Tharguen, then, without a word, briskly turned around and walked away. When the Telorians were alone with the guards again, Tharguen looked at Pete.

'Praise be the Spirit of Elina that lives in all of us! For this means that Bahvely came here and attempted to change the Emperor's mind!'

'So he's going to save us!' said Pete.

'I think. I hope,' replied Tharguen, smiling fondly.

'It was today,' said a guard, 'that they came and were thrown out.'

Tharguen laughed from relief; he was so happy to hear this. The other Telorians who remained in the cells smiled with hope. From that moment on they all waited for something to happen, but nothing did – not until a few nights later, when they kept hearing strange noises.

Thump, clatter, pitwee! One of the old statues in the storage chamber, not far from the cells, had been knocked down and gradually rolled to the first guard, who had sat down to rest. He stood, walking quietly to the storage chamber. An arm grabbed him, and a pommel knocked him unconscious. He fell to the ground.

'It's okay,' whispered Tharguen loudly. 'They're on our side!'

'Oh,' said a voice, and out popped Bahvley's head from the room. The third guard sat his friend up.

'We agree with your friends but have not yet figured out a way to help. We are but guards in a basement.'

'Exactly, but you know secrets, right?' Bahvley smiled at him. The guard nodded. 'Great.'

'It warms my heart to see you, my friend,' said Tharguen.

'Believe me, it warms mine,' replied Bahvley.

Bahvley made a sign to the others and they quickly came into the room. As soon as Niome saw Tharguen, she ran to him. He took her hand from between the bars, interlacing their fingers, and reached out to her face with the other. She kissed him through the bars, and they embraced as closely as they could.

'You can't imagine how relieved I am to see you!' said Thagruen. 'They've held us in here for weeks.'

'Where are the others?' asked Mittah.

'They've been taken to different parts of the palace,' said Pete.

'We have to get them out of wherever they are,' replied Malcolm.

'The young girl is probably in the north wing,' said the third guard, 'but the others, I do not know.'

'Gahli!' exclaimed Ihal.

'They want to marry her with the Prince,' said Jeremy.

'What?' shrilled Ihal. 'We have to stop it!'

'We should split up into teams,' Bahvley proposed. 'Four teams. One to find Gahli, two to go find out where the others are, and one for around here. We should find out all about the secret passages, the patrol schedule of the guards . . . and quietly, therefore slowly.'

'Why are you looking at me?' said Meysah. 'When did *I* make a ruckus?' he continued, pointing at the fallen statue his brother had knocked over. Bahvley gave him a look. Meysah shrugged.

'There is a secret passage to the rooftop nearby. This way,' said the second guard, pointing down the hall. 'It will be easy to find . . . Gahli that way, but for the others, you may need to sneak through the halls.'

'It sure is a good thing these guards are on our side!' said Meysah.

'Okay, there should be team leaders,' instructed Bahvley.

'I'll be one!' volunteered Meysah. 'And I'll go exploring through the halls. Who's with me?'

'I'll accompany you,' said Neyith, one of the Kikies.

'I'll go with you,' said Lóim.

'Me too,' Ihal chimed in.

Another Telorian and Dessimë joined Meysah.

Meysah grinned, proud to be in charge.

'Okay,' laughed Bahvley.

'I'll be the second team, then,' said Jimmy.

Huck and Tom joined him, as did one of their friends and two Kikies, Mimulus and Zend. They decided to go find Gahli. Vigh and Boreth formed the third team, along with Mittah and Malcolm, and Miё, Tithil and Forthil of the Kikies. They would go through the halls too. Then there was the fourth team, who would take care of the basement and protect Tharguen. This team was comprised of Niome, Bahvley, Classû, another Telorian, Celor and two other Kikies, Hёya and Nana.

'The secret tunnel up to the roof is through this old door,' said the third guard. 'No one has gone through there in ages, so it should be quite safe and isolated.'

'A way to the halls,' said the second guard, 'is by under the floor. Between the basement and the first floor, there is a large enough space, so you can crawl around and hear all.'

'We're not claustrophobic, right?' said Meysah. The others nodded.

'Right!'

'Or sneaking through is more tricky,' said the second guard. Vigh nodded.

'Good luck, everyone,' said Tharguen, 'and thank you, and be careful. This is truly a miracle; let's not curse it.'

Jimmy opened the old rusted door and started up the metal ladder hooked on to the wall of the small tunnel. Meysah popped open a hatch in the ceiling, and each of his team members passed through. Bahvley closed the hatch behind them. Then Vigh and Boreth and their team went through one of the many stairwells. Bahvley had given them all the explicit instruction of figuring out where their friends were and how to get them out, and to come to report it before doing anything. The last thing he wanted was to alert the Emperor of their presence just yet. Everything had to be meticulously calculated.

'So, how did you get in?' asked Tharguen.

'Oh, by the window of the storage room,' said Bahvley matter-of-factly.

'Clever.'

'We met an old merchant who helped us and, after we've rescued you all and run away, he will distract the Emperor and the Prince. Let's hope we can get you out before nightfall tomorrow.'

'You mean today?' said Tharguen. 'It's almost morning.'

'Technicalities,' replied Bahvley, smiling.

The first guard woke up and looked about. The others explained what had happened, and Bahvley apologised for knocking him out. The guard chuckled as he agreed to aid them too.

CHAPTER NINE:
Putting the Puzzle Pieces Together

The sun was rising when Jimmy's team reached the roof. Already were they exhausted, for they had climbed nonstop at a steady pace for what seemed to be a dozen levels, so high was the palace.

Jimmy looked about. The air was warming up quickly, even if dawn had not yet become morning.

'Let's have breakfast!' said Jimmy. His stomach gurgled.

'Your stomach sure does gurgle a lot, Jimmesh,' said Huck.

'It does, Huck. And you can call me Jimmy, simply.'

'It's a good thing you didn't volunteer to crawl under the floor,' said Zend. He laughed in his Kiki voice. 'You'd blow our cover! Or should I say, your stomach would.'

They installed themselves and started to eat.

'How are we going to figure out where Gahli is?' asked Peyvil, a light-haired Telorian.

'We'll fly about to find where she is,' said Mimulus.

'Someone should go talk to her,' Peyvil suggested.

'You can go, Tommash.'

'Or maybe you can go, Hûcklo,' Tom replied teasingly.

'How?' asked Peyvil.

'By the window,' replied Jimmy as though it were obvious.

'Yes,' said Peyvil, 'but how?'

'Rope?' suggested Jimmy. He shrugged.

'I'm not hanging from a rope!' exclaimed Tom and Huck at the same time. Everyone looked at Jimmy.

'Who, me? Oh, I . . . it's so high, it's scary. I don't even know Gahli. You all know her; I never had the chance to meet her. We never studied together. I don't even know what she looks like! How will I know it's really her?' The others merely stared at him. 'Fine, I confess. I'm afraid of heights.'

'That explains a lot,' said the Kikies simultaneously.

'Not that we didn't already know,' added Zend.

'Mind reading?' Jimmy rolled his eyes.

'Sorry, we're still training our minds to not reflexively read everyone's minds as we do in our land,' said Mimulus.

'You're also very easy to read,' said Tom, 'even for non-mind readers.'

'Okay, but I mean, I don't want to fall.' Jimmy motioned behind him with his arms.

'Well, if you die, you'll come right back to life again,' said Tom. 'You're the Telorian with a thousand lives.'

'How do these stories get so exaggerated!' said Jimmy, pinching the bridge of his nose. He looked at the others and sighed, resigned. 'All right, I'll go.'

They finished up their snack, and the two Kikies went to find the window in question. Indeed, at the north wing window, the most north centre window, they found Gahli alone in a small but cosy-looking room. Then, after reporting their findings to the team, Jimmy tied a rope to his belt. The others held the rope to bring him down, while the Kikies floated by him in case he needed assistance.

Jimmy started down, then grabbed hold of the roof, leaning over it, his legs dangling down in emptiness.

'Now wait here,' he said. 'Why can't you Kikies go, hm? With your fast-flying and floating in fairy size?'

'You're a point of the Star. It will be more comforting,' replied Mimulus.

'More comforting? You're her teammates!' He paused, scowling. 'You're scheming something.'

The Kikies just stared at him, blinking. The others smiled innocently.

'Tom? Huck?' No reply. 'Peyvil?' Another pause. Jimmy narrowed his eyes. 'Fine, bring me down.'

The window was closed. Jimmy's first goal was to try to open it, by pushing himself off the wall to give himself a swing, but instead he crashed into it, breaking the glass and colliding with the floor.

Gahli had been sitting ponderously on the bed, and at Jimmy's grand entrance she bounced up, startled out of her wits, and let out a little yelp.

Jimmy stood and shook the glass parcels off him, then looked at Gahli. For a moment, he forgot what he was there for. Then, sudden embarrassment invaded him.

'Uh, hi.'

'Who are you?'

'Oh, I'm Jimmy, and I came to tell you that the others and I have come to save you, and Tharguen and everyone else, so don't lose hope. *We* are here.'

'Who's "we"?'

'Well, Bahvley and the rest of your team, and Niome, Meysah, Master Vigh, Master Boreth and me! And I know that you are Gahli.'

'Jimmy, as in the Jimmy who's part of the Five, who died and came back to life?'

'Well, yes, that's me,' said Jimmy, blushing. Then he grinned proudly.

'It's nice to meet you,' said Gahli.

'Same here,' Jimmy replied as if in a daydream.

'Do you always break in through the window when rescuing someone?'

Jimmy shyly shook his head at a loss for words.

'Oh!' He snapped out of his trance. 'We divided into teams, and my little team came to save *you*, so we should know of any, uh, secrets you'd know about the guards' schedule, corridors or passages . . .' He trailed off.

'I think there are guards outside my door,' said Gahli. Jimmy looked at the door, making an *Uh-oh* with his mouth, then looking at the shattered glass on the floor. 'I think they're asleep,' continued Gahli quickly. 'If they were awake right now, they would've heard you.'

'Won't the Prince get new guards when he sees these are sleeping?' Gahli shrugged. 'Well then,' said Jimmy, 'we'll just have to carry you out the window.'

'Now?'

'Later,' said Jimmy. 'We have to report back before so that the rescue is well coordinated once we know where everyone can be found.' Gahli nodded. 'I think I've seen you around.'

'It's possible. Originally I'm from Dulma, but since I joined Captain Tharguen, I've been staying with Ihal in Teloria City.'

'That's far,' said Jimmy, referring to her hometown.

'I was lucky to be visiting my relatives in Teloria City when the Morkans attacked from the South, and that's how—'

They heard the Prince's voice from out in the corridor.

'It's Rhal Majim!' whispered Gahli with a hint of panic.

'Oh, then, I'll go back to the roof, but' — Jimmy took her hand — 'I'll be back later today. I promise.' He ran to the window. 'What will you say about the window?'

Gahli glanced at the shattered glass before looking back at Jimmy. 'That I broke it. Don't worry. The Prince has been opening up, and . . . I'll tell you later. Quick, hurry! You mustn't be found!'

'Bye!' said Jimmy. Gahli smiled.

Jimmy tugged on the rope and was pulled up. Gahli giggled to herself, looking up out the window.

The Prince entered. Gahli looked at the floor.

'What happened?'

'I tried to open the window, but it was jammed. I guess I was too rough, 'cause I broke it accidentally.'

'And why would you be trying to open the window?' asked Rhal, sticking his head out the window, looking up and down and all around.

'To get fresh air in here. Why else? The air is stagnant enough, thank you very much.'

Rhal turned to a guard who was standing by him.

'Be sure to remind me to get it fixed. And you,' he shouted at the guards outside, 'stay awake!' He turned to Gahli. 'What good are guards if they cannot even do their jobs properly?'

'Should I chat with them from my side of the door to keep them awake?' asked Gahli.

Rhal chuckled and muttered something in the Dûnelorian tongue.

* * *

Jimmy was flung onto the roof, helped by the Kikies.

'And so?' asked the others.

'She's fine, yup, all right,' said Jimmy. He stood, dusting himself off.

'She's *fine*,' teased Huck. Jimmy blushed.

'The Prince was coming, so that's why I tugged. Uhm, he goes to see her every day, and she mentioned him opening up to her.'

'Opening up about what?' asked Tom.

'She didn't have time to even start explaining. She said she'd tell me later, so I have to go back, later. Uhm, guards guard the door, though. I thought we could bring her up with the rope once it's time for the rescue.' They all nodded.

Eating while slithering was most inconvenient, but at least they ate. Meysah discovered a few hatches in the floor for whenever they'd want to get out.

The team paused to listen when they heard someone stomping above them. Indeed, there were two voices, but through the floor it was difficult to tell if they were voices either of them recognised. They were so muffled they couldn't make out any words. However, the manner in which the two spoke sounded very Telorian.

'We have to find a hatch,' said Meysah, 'and get to the very room we're under.'

'But what if it's not them?' objected Lóim. 'It's too risky.'

'We're never going to know anything if we don't risk anything,' said Meysah.

'But it's dangerous,' argued Lóim. 'I don't want to come face-to-face with a Dûnelorian.'

'Neither do I,' said Meysah, 'but if we do, it's no big deal.'

'No big deal!'

'What, are you scared, Lóim?' Meysah turned his head enough to have Lóim in view. 'Because there's nothing to be scared about here. I mean, it's not like they're Morkans. Coming face-to-face with a Morkan is much more terrifying than this.'

'I wouldn't know.'

'I thought you fought—'

'From very far,' admitted Lóim. 'I was an archer only.'

'So much for all that boasting,' Meysah muttered, turning his head back to face front. 'Well, I hope someday you come face-to-face with a Morkan. It'll do you good.'

'Hey,' said Ihal, 'he has a point, you know. I, for one, agree.'

'Great,' Meysah said sarcastically. 'Take his side.'

'Why don't we take a vote, yah?' said Fimrel calmly. He was a slightly older Telorian, quieter, and one of the only Telorians in the kingdom with a Firlanian name.

'Okay,' said Meysah. 'Who wants to get out of here? I do.' There were three other '*I do*s' before he announced, 'Four to two.'

They all slithered some more, bags squashing them down at the tighter spots, to find a hatch nearby. Once this was done, they waited for the guards to leave and for the Kikies to double-check that there was no one else coming. The coast was clear.

Vigh wished he had no shadow, for sneaking along the side of the walls was the biggest strategic challenge he had met yet. It was tougher than sneaking into Mork, for then he had been in disguise among many, while here he and the others had to be so quiet, so careful and practically invisible. It was a good thing that the two Kiki brothers were floating about and could whisper in Vigh's or Boreth's ears if anyone was coming or describe what the corridors ahead looked like. They were on the third floor, for there was less activity, and therefore it would be easier to hear and guess the activity downstairs and upstairs. Guards walked to and fro near a specific hallway, and two more stood by one door.

'They must be in there,' said Boreth, his voice just above a whisper, 'otherwise, there wouldn't be so many guards in that area.'

'Then I thank our instincts for having come to the third floor,' said Vigh.

'Notice how they pace back and forth there, but some sort of corridor leads right beside the door, yet no one is checking that,' said Mittah.

'If there was a way to get to that hall and pass those guards, then we could get to the room,' said Malcolm.

'Can't the Kikies simply go instead of complicating it for us?' asked Mittah.

'Perhaps for now, but eventually, they will need us,' said Vigh.

'We'll have to distract them,' said Boreth. 'Eventually.'

'If I could get my hands on some Dûnelorian armour, I might be able to pass as a guard,' said Malcolm, 'but it would have to be from a spare lying around somewhere. If we take any armour from a guard we knock out, it will alert them to our presence.'

'Then we'll leave such a possibility out as an option for now unless an opportunity presents itself,' said Vigh. Malcolm nodded.

Tithil quickly appeared.

'Forthil and I will pass under the door and alert our friends of our plans.'

Then he disappeared again. A few moments later he reappeared, as did Forthil.

'There are more upstairs,' said Forthil. 'But guards guard the stairs now. I think they might've heard us, without heeding us.'

'Then how are we to get upstairs?' asked Boreth.

'Nth . . . I have an idea,' said Tithil.

After explaining his vision, everyone hid in a closet. Then Mië appeared down the hall.

'Could I get some assistance?!' she hollered.

One guard went to see in an adjacent room that led to other adjoining rooms. Mië kept calling out from more distant rooms, luring the guard further and further away from the corridor.

Forthil appeared before one of the two remaining guards and smiled, then he disappeared again. The guard blinked. He tapped the other's shoulder.

'There was a strange polc here,' said the guard.

'But there is no one,' said the second.

'But I saw him.'

'You *saw* does not mean there *was*.'

'I am not going mad! He was here and disappeared!'

'Come, you must lie down. You have not slept in days.'

'Maybe it was a Morkan spy.'

'Come, come.'

And the guards walked away. The three Kikies reappeared and the little band slipped through the door and up the stairs, giggling silently before going through the double doors of the fourth floor. No guards were around that door, luckily for them.

'Okay, it sounds like the Prince is long gone. Time for me to go back down.'

'Why are you so eager, Jimmy?' mocked Huck.

'Oh, I'm not eager – only to hear about what the Prince shared . . . what?' Everyone looked at him, smiling awfully suspiciously, he thought.

'Nthnn-nthnn-nthnn!' Mimulus hummed, wiggling his shoulders.

'Mimulus! What!' There was a pause. Jimmy took the rope and tied it to his belt. 'I don't care what anyone thinks.'

They helped him down.

'Knock knock,' said Jimmy, peering in.

'Come in!'

Jimmy jumped in. 'So, uh, how did it go with the Prince?'

'Fine. Yah, I, uh, think I managed to convince him to let us go.'

'Really? That's great!'

'He seems sympathetic enough. The problem is the Emperor, who wants to marry us, but I don't want to, and he—'

'I won't let him marry you.' said Jimmy a little too quickly. 'Against your will . . . uh . . .'

'The Prince doesn't want it, either.' Gahli smiled at him. 'He told me that ever since his wife-to-be died in Mork, his father has been trying to match him up with others and—'

'Wait,' said Jimmy. 'If the woman he loved died in Mork, then why do the Dûnelorians have a deal with the Morkans?'

'It was Beshrig who killed her, and Tharguen, as Gowtch, was present when it happened.'

Jimmy nodded, taking that in. 'Tharguen is haunted by his past in Mork, but I can't see him harming innocent polcs.'

'Beshrig's actions surprised even Tharguen,' said Gahli. 'They were supposed to question the captives. Tharguen had already devised how to free all of them that very same night. And he freed all the others.' Gahli bowed her head. 'Rhal has been hurting ever since then and looking for someone to blame.'

'Beshrig is dead,' said Jimmy, 'Tharguen killed him in front of us, and if the polc to which the blame falls is not alive to suffer punishment, then I can see how someone would direct the blame to another who was present and seemingly on the Morkans' side.'

'Yes, and because of that, when Mirauk offered the Dûnelorians the deal, they accepted,' said Gahli.

'What exactly does the deal consist of? I know a bit, but . . .'

'Shipping Gowtch to Mork. He's wanted. And with him traded in, the Morkans will never bother the Dûnelorians again.'

'And they think that by giving Tharguen to Mirauk, they won't be attacked?' exclaimed Jimmy.

'Lower your voice,' Ghali warned.

'Don't they know Mirauk's a liar?' Jimmy whispered. 'What I know of him is he's cunning.' Jimmy looked from the door and back at Gahli. 'A liar he is, and all he wants is to get rid of Tharguen since he poses a threat to him, like when he was looking for Bahvley all those years because he, too, was a threat to him. And then he'll try to get rid of us Five!' Jimmy's whispers became louder. 'But *never* will he leave the Dûnelorians alone. It starts with one favour, and then another and another and one too many and *bang!*'

'Quiet, Jimmy! You'll alert the guards!'

'Sorry.' Jimmy smiled sheepishly.

'I can persuade the Prince, I think, of the truth. When do you have to report back?'

'Tonight!'

'How will *they* not suspect that Telorians are sneaking in and out of their palace when they hear odd sounds and odd things start to happen?'

'Ah, we got an old merchant to help us. He's at the door, bugging them.' Jimmy laughed.

They spoke for a little while longer before Jimmy gave Gahli a little hug and left.

Meysah slowly opened the hatch, peering his head out to take a look around. Then he nodded and slunk out from under the floor. The others followed as he crept to a corridor. It was a long corridor, but it seemed empty.

'What if it's not really deserted?'

'What, do you want to crawl back under the floor, Lóim?' said Meysah. 'Be my guest, but I'm going to find your friends.'

He started off, and everyone else followed.

'It's not normal for it to be so quiet,' whispered Ihal.

'All I ask is that you trust my judgement.'

'We do,' said Lóim, 'it's just that sometimes you're a little arrogant about it all.'

Meysah gave Lóim one of those looks and said, 'Well, I think I have the right to be.' Then: 'May I remind you of how you used to be, and still are, a little?'

'Scht!' said Fimrel. 'Seriously, it's a good thing a more mature polc is here with you. You're behaving just like children.' There was a pause. 'Do you hear that?'

Voices could be heard.

'It's Yém,' said Meysah. 'Hurry, this way.'

As they headed around the corner, they saw, standing by a large table, a few Telorians setting plates. Shocked to see their friends, they almost dropped a few plates, but there were no inadvertent accidents. Meysah and the others explained to them what was going on, and the three captured Telorians told them where they stayed at night. Lucky for them, there was a hatch on the floor just outside their prison room, but unfortunately there were guards around all the time. At least now the team knew how to get to them.

Then, the team snuck back to the hatch and slunk back in.

'I hear voices!'

'Where, Malcolm?' said Mittah.

'Here!'

Two distinct voices could be heard behind the wall, but there was no door.

'How is it possible for them to be in there if there's no door?!' wondered Vigh.

'Maybe there is one,' Boreth mused, 'but we just can't see it. Remember the secret passageways in the Prison Tower of Mork?' Vigh nodded. 'I think this door is a secret door, to a secret room.'

Boreth gave a big kick at the wall, and indeed a crack was heard, but no door opened.

'It must open up the other way.' Boreth tried to pull on it.

'I think it's locked,' said Vigh with a grin.

Boreth knocked. 'Hello there, I'm looking for two Telorians. Is this their room?'

'Indeed, for we are they. Who are you?'

'It's us, Jackley,' said Mittah, 'Mittah and Malcolm and Tithil, Forthil and Mië, and two of the legendary Five Telorians. We're one team out of four. We're here to save you all.'

'Well, good luck! They locked us up in here after we broke out of the other room.'

'Don't worry,' said Vigh, 'when we come back, we'll bring Niome with us. She knows a spell to unlock doors. Or we can perform it; only I forget the first part.'

'Okay, then.'

'We'll be back,' said Malcolm. 'Promise.'

They went back to the stairs and down to the basement quietly.

In the basement, the prisoners had been chatting with the others.

'Please tell me,' Niome implored Tharguen, 'what's bothering you so much?'

'I don't want to worry you more than you have been,' said Tharguen.

'We all know they're trying to get you to Mork,' said Bahvely.

'Yes, but . . . *they* won't dare bring me there.'

'What are you saying?' asked Niome, already guessing at his reply.

'The Morkans are coming here to get me. And the Duke brothers on top of that, so even if we convince the Emperor to change his mind, Morkans are on their way.'

'So, we'll just have to run as fast as we can,' said Bahvley. 'Eh.'

'This is no joke! Mirauk's nephews are almost as bad as *he* is. The last time I saw them . . . they never liked the looks of me, anyway. They may try to kill me. No, they *will* try to kill me.'

'So we'll fight them,' said Niome. 'I don't fear them. I'll make them fear me.'

The door from the passageway to the roof opened. Soon after, the other teams returned and they all discussed their plan for a while. They concluded that the only way to free everyone was to take over the palace, and they had to do it now.

They all hid in the passageways, ceiling, and storage room. The guards called for Billahmyé Veij, Rhal Majim, Captain Loyfeij and Officer Grayt, telling them that Tharguen had a very important announcement to make. And indeed they all came late that night, along with two guards each.

'What do you wish to tell me, Captain?' asked the Emperor.

'Watch out for my friends!'

'What?'

At that, the Telorians popped out of their hiding places and surrounded the Dûnelorians. Some succeeded in disarming a few guards.

Perfect so far, Tharguen thought to himself.

However, Dûnelorian guards rushed in from the stairwell, ready to fight.

'It would appear I was correct to have had my suspicions,' said Emperor Veij Majim.

Jimmy's team remained hidden in the passageway and decided that they should climb up. Suddenly, guards opened the door and were after them. They all hurried to the roof.

'The guards are close to the top! What are we to do?' panicked Huck.

'We'll all go join Gahli,' said Jimmy.

'And escape through there?' cried Tom.

'I have an idea, Tommash,' said Huck.

With the help of the Kikies and the rope, they each took turns going down. Peyvil went first and explained the situation to Gahli. Jimmy was last, for he did not use the rope but the fast-fly technique of the Kikies, which he was getting used to by now. They were all gone by the time the guards popped the hatch open and spilled onto the roof.

'I'll cast a spell on the guards outside the door so we can flee as they fall into a deep sleep with a nice dream,' said Tom.

Nodding, Gahli knocked on the door.

'What do you want?' said one of the guards.

'There are people in my room,' said Gahli. 'Come in, quick!'

The guards opened the door, and Tom pronounced a few words that knocked the guards out.

The Telorians passed through the threshold and out into the hall.

Luckily for Meysah's insight, he and his team had stayed in the basement ceiling passage, unnoticed by anyone.

'I must say, you do have good judgement,' said Lóim. 'Sometimes,' he added quickly.

'And you, good ideas, I have to admit,' replied Meysah. 'Come, we'll go find those Vigh and Boreth spoke of.'

In the basement, many guards had been seized by Telorians and Kikies while others were still wrestling. The Telorian captives had been freed and stood ready to defend themselves, though they were weaponless. The other Telorians and Kikies had not used a single weapon thus far, hoping that it would prove their honesty and nobility to the Dûnelorians.

Bahvley walked up to Billahmyé Veij Majim.

'Order your people to stop this nonsense at once!' cried the Emperor, his baritone voice reverberating in the large room.

'Will you back down on your deal with Mork?' asked Bahvley.

'No!'

'Then I'm afraid, Emperor Veij Majim, we'll have to settle this otherwise. Ruler against ruler!'

Bahvley took several steps back and unsheathed his sword. 'We fight to disarm and overpower.'

The Emperor followed suit. 'Very well then!'

The two began to duel, and they both fought with honourable skill; everyone else stopped to look. A parry here, a parry there, a cut and thrust, a lunge. They fought faster and faster and more and more aggressively as they duelled on. They seemed to tire a little but kept on as though running a marathon.

'I know they agreed to disarm and overpower,' said Tharguen in a low voice, 'but if they continue like this, one of them is going to get hurt, and I don't want that.'

The Emperor cut close to Bahvley's cheek, almost grazing him, but the Telorian King leaned back, swinging his sword about, forcing the Emperor to take several steps back. The Dûnelorian ruler came at Bahvley once more, harder this time, and Bahvley blocked him, their swords' clang echoing in the room as they pushed against the other.

'Stop!' cried Rhal. 'Stop! This is ridiculous. No more fighting.'

Bahvley and the Emperor stopped to look at Rhal, who had a stern expression upon his face. Bahvley nodded to the Emperor and took a step back, sheathing his sword. The Emperor held his sword aloft but retreated as well.

Rhal walked to Tharguen. 'I know I should not blame you, for I understand that you were merely a bystander, but I did, for all these years . . . *hate* you. It was some twenty and a few odd years ago when an army of Dûnelorians went to Morok by my command. Their mission was to investigate and explore only. My wife-to-be was the Captain of that team, and she died.' Rhal cast his eyes towards the floor and took a beat.

'My people were caught and brought to the caves of Morok,' he went on. 'Although I am grateful that a strange Morkan, which I hear is you, let the team escape, that same Morkan had watched his Captain kill her.'

Tharguen closed his eyes, momentarily pained by the memory.

'There were many witnesses among those who escaped,' said Rhal. 'I now know this Beshrig acted out of impulse, but I blamed you for it, thinking you could have foreseen his actions. Perhaps you had known, perhaps you could have cried out, fought him, stopped him, saved her.' Rhal's eyes reflected much sorrow. 'I know now you did all you could within your power, and that you were doing your best to survive and not to be discovered; I understand that now. You did not kill her with your own blade, but it felt as though you had contributed to her death all the same.

'I thought I was doing the right thing in agreeing to this deal with Mirauk, but that will never bring her back.' He let his sword fall to the ground. He stared at it blankly. 'You came here to help us and are still here, along with so many others, trying to save us . . . from the biggest mistake of our lives.' Rhal looked back at Tharguen. 'Even with everything we have done to you, you are still trying to show us the path of friendship. Mirauk will never leave us alone. We cannot possibly believe him! I was doing this for revenge, but I should also think of the future of Dûnelor. I apologise for this, Captain' – Rhal looked at the Emperor – 'and I hope you share my opinion, Father.'

There was a long pause.

'I am deeply sorry for what happened,' said Tharguen. 'I didn't know what Beshrig was planning. *I was supposed to be questioning the team, not him. I thought I would lead the escape then. I knew I had to wait till sundown, but I was hoping I could clue them in on the plan. Beshrig pierced her heart, and perhaps I could have run to her and done something, anything, but she was dead the moment Beshrig removed his blade. I truly wish I could have done something to stop him and save her, I truly do. Standing there, mouth agape, shaking and unable to say anything. I felt so ashamed. I passed it off as shock because he'd lied to me.'*

Tharguen shook his head. 'Witnessing that was one of the most difficult moments I'd had to face in Mork since seeing my friends die at the hands of Mirauk. I wanted to kill Beshrig then, believe me, but all that was going through my mind was *"Do what Beshrig says if you want to see the day you flee back home."* I remember that moment so well, for it grieved me to witness it. The look in her eyes . . . and I prayed for her soul, for her to forgive me in the afterlife for what I had failed to do.'

Tharguen took a step towards Rhal. 'What happened was wrong. And as I had set out to do, I let the others escape that night. As for Beshrig' –

Thargen crinkled his nose in disdain – 'I finally did kill him in order to save Niome. It was about time, too.' He swallowed.

'Justice has been made, then,' said Rhal. 'And you coming here to ally yourselves in order to help us is apology enough, I think. If Teloria offers aid, then we do not need a deal with Morok.' Rhal shook his head. 'Putting blame will not make her return to me, nor will it save either of our kingdoms. Teloria is powerful. The Desert of Dûnelor is far from my people's homeland and cannot stand against Morok if it is alone. I think that is also why we accepted the deal.'

'Indeed, yes,' said the Emperor, his voice soft. 'But if it is at the expense of becoming enemies with those who should be our friends, I will not do it – not anymore. We were unwilling to go to Teloria and ask for help and therefore accepted Mirauk's offer.' He sheathed his sword and walked up to Bahvley. 'You need our help, and we need yours. I think we can reach an agreement. I . . . . apologise for my rash decisions in the past weeks, the past years.' He paused. 'We have just enough days to set some traps to this palace and figure something out to trick the Morkans.'

'Then we, too, accept your apology,' said Bahvley. He bowed to the Emperor, placing his arm across his chest, and the Emperor acknowledged with a bow of his own.

Rhal held out his hand to Tharguen. 'You did all you could. There is nothing to forgive of you, but it comforts me to say that I forgive you after years of blaming you.'

Rhal smiled mildly. Tharguen took his hand and they shook hands. He returned the smile.

'Welcome to Dûnelor, Captain Tharguen Sumperale. It is a pleasure to finally . . . be civilised with you.' They both chuckled mildly. 'Welcome, saviours of the world,' Rhal said to Niome, Vigh and Boreth.

'Hmm,' said Bahvley. 'Two are missing. See, they escaped and went to save the captives.'

'We should inform the guards of this change,' said Billahmyé. 'And find your friends.'

'This ought to be awkward,' muttered Niome.

Jimmy's team had snuck to the fourth floor, thinking of those captured in the wall.

'I hear voices,' said Gahli.

'Are you sure it's this wall?' asked Huck.

Jimmy felt the wall, trying to find the secret door. He walked along the wall with both hands on it to the corner and bumped into someone. Realising they mustn't be seen, he shouted, 'Quick, take cover!' and turned around to run.

But the person grabbed him by the back of his collar, and he was left running in place.

'Take cover? What do I look like?' Jimmy turned his head and saw his best friend along with his team. 'Guess I look like a fool, then, huh?' he laughed. 'You heard the voices, too, I suppose.' Meysah let Jimmy go.

'I have just the spell to unlock the door,' said Tom. 'Niome taught me it.'

As Tom pronounced the words, Meysah and Jimmy discussed their little escape.

'I thought you were fighting downstairs,' said Jimmy.

'No, we stayed under the floor, just in case.'

'Oh.'

The wall opened up, and there stood two puzzled Telorians. They quickly explained the situation and then everyone left the premises. They got to the stairwell and came face-to-face with Captain Loyfeij and Officer Grayt.

'It's that Captain I was telling you about,' said Gahli.

'Oh, no!' exclaimed the others in synchronicity.

'You're wanted,' boomed Captain Loyfeij. 'Come, follow me.'

'Wanted?' muttered Jimmy.

They followed, though Jimmy thought it strange that there were no guards to surround them. They were led to the grand throne room, where all their companions stood.

'Oh, no!' said Huck. 'We'll all be sent to Mork!'

'Nonsense,' said the Emperor. 'We called you here, for while you were freeing the others, you missed what took place here and the decision we Dûnelorians took to stand our ground and renege on the deal we made with Morok. And for that, we need your help. We made a truce with your King.' The young Telorians were still confused.

'Don't look so surprised,' said Bahvley. 'I told you we'd get to the bottom of this. Teloria and

Dûnelor are now in alliance. And right now, we need to help them.'

'Okay, how?' asked Meysah.

'Mirauk's nephews are coming to bring me to Mork,' said Tharguen. 'Merlik and Garkhktak. So, we need to arrange an ambush.'

'Oh. Oh! Now I understand,' said Meysah. 'How much time do we have?'

'We do not know,' replied the Emperor.

'Morkans coming here?' said Lóim. 'That's a scary thought.'

'Let us start right away,' urged Rhal.

After a long discussion, they had formed a plan. The Dûnelorians welcomed Yém into the palace, for he, too, was going to play his part. While they awaited the arrival of the Morkans, they made the most of their time to arrange as many traps as they could but also made preparations for the feast they would offer the Dukes of Mork in order to maintain the semblance of their alliance with Mirauk. The Telorians and Kikies helped with all the preparations as well.

'You are of Dûnelorian descent, are you not?' the Dûnelorian cook asked Jeremy. The Telorian nodded. 'Very distant, as I can see.'

'Yes, that side of my family moved to Teloria millennia ago.'

'Have you heard of Imperial bread?'

Jeremy's eyes widened. 'The rolled sweet bread?' The cook nodded. 'My grandmother used to make it all the time.' He went into explaining the recipe and method his grandmother employed.

'Well, well,' said the cook, smiling, 'it appears *some* traditions have survived the ages. Well, then, come now, begin on the batter; we have many loaves to make.'

'Yes, sir.'

And as the Dûnelorians, Telorians and Kikies prepared the palace, they all became better acquainted with each other, thus strengthening their new alliance.

It was the sixth day of the sixth week of Summer when the Morkans arrived. The watchmen came to tell the Emperor as soon as they had spotted the black horses in the distance. The Emperor then gathered everyone up in his throne room.

'Do you all know what you have to do?' he asked. *Yes.* 'Are there any final questions or re-quests?' *No.* 'Then go now to your posts. Good luck, everyone.'

Chapter Ten:
An Unexpected Turn

The Emperor and the Prince, along with Captain Loyfeij and Officer Grayt, stood at the palace's double doors to greet the Dukes of Mork together. The dark horses approached the palace and halted. There was a large militia of Morkans with the Dukes, more than double the number of Tharguen's. Perhaps they wanted to appear more threatening, but the Emperor and Rhal were not afraid of them.

The four Dûnelorians who stood outside invited the Morkans inside the palace. Rooms had been prepared for them, and stables had been furnished for their horses. The Emperor invited the two Dukes to dine with him, and the guards kept a close watch on the Morkans as they served them. At the table were Billahmyé Veij Majim, Rhal Majim, Captain Loyfeij and Officer Grayt, Merlik and Garkhktak, a Morkan Captain called Yûrk, and a few high-ranked knights.

The two Dukes were almost identical. Merlik had longer, darker hair, was thinner, and was not nearly half as ugly as his brother. Taking away the sternness and evil in his face, he looked like a decent polc. Garkhktak, on the other hand, had a bigger build and looked more imposing; his hair was much shorter, his shoulders squarer, and his voice was an entire octave lower than his brother's. Captain Yûrk was an ugly polc with sickly hued skin and pale hair.

'I wish to see Gowtch right after supper,' said Merlik, 'as well as the others. They may yet be of use.'

'We were thinking some could stay here with us,' said Rhal. 'We could use them too. But if it is so important that you must take them all—'

'You may keep some of them,' said Garkhktak. 'In fact, keep them all. Mirauk wants Gowtch, and Gowtch only.'

After the meal, Emperor Veij Majim brought the six Morkans with whom he had dined to the room where Tharguen was being held. They all entered.

Tharguen was sitting on a chair, hands bound. Though his restraints had been very lightly tightened, it didn't show.

'Well, if it isn't Gowtch,' crowed Garkhktak. 'You're quite clever, you know.'

'You've been the subject of gossip for years,' said Merlik, sizing up the room.

'Well, he *and* his filthy Telorian friends!' said Garkhktak.

'*Fi akereth sonoykhë wokhsi fiklayeth, fisit thme toworfo kuyokh!*' said Tharguen with disdain.

'Oh, so now *we're* filthy,' said Merlik. 'Interesting, since I'm not the one who betrayed his ruler and killed his Captain.'

'Well, first of all, I'm not Morkan. Never was and never will be. I was a Telorian spy. If that ruler of yours is so great, why didn't he ever discover me, huh?' The Dukes only looked at each other. 'Secondly,' he continued, feeling smug, 'my name is Tharguen. Besides, my "*filthy*" friends are more powerful than Mirauk himself, so I'm not worried.'

'Oh, yes, that wizardess friend of yours,' said Merlik. 'She's going to die, I can assure you, before she even gets the chance to test her might on Mirauk again. And you want to know why? Because if I see her, I will eviscerate her guts and serve them to my uncle on a platter of—'

Tharguen stood, still bound to the chair. Merlik shut up.

'This is going too far! How dare you!' Tharguen spoke through his teeth.

The Dûnelorian soldiers placed their hands on the hilts of their swords, ready to defend their ally.

A smirk formed in the corner of Merlik's mouth. 'Oh, we found the weak spot.' He scowled. 'Sit!' Tharguen sat back down as Merlik looked into his eyes. 'Well, if I don't see love.'

'This is perfect!' said Garkhktak. 'We get rid of you, it saddens the Wizardess, therefore she weakens, therefore the bond between the Five weakens, which makes it that much easier to split them apart, which in all weakens them, and, in the end, it's as easy as that' – Garkhktak snapped his fingers – 'to kill them all.'

'You'll never kill me,' Tharguen growled.

'*Kuyokh reka largaëd iadekhed!* At least you are to me,' said Garkhktak.

Merlik and Garkhktak looked at each other.

'Could we have a moment with him alone?' Garkhktak requested.

Tharguen gave one subtle nod to Rhal and the Emperor.

'Of course,' said Rhal. 'Do whatever you like.' He gave Tharguen an uncertain look, imperceivable to the Dukes. Tharguen knew the Prince wouldn't be too far, and the Dûnelorians stepped out, leaving Tharguen alone with the two dukes.

'What would you possibly want from me, Duke Merlik and Duke Garkhktak, nephews of Mirauk?'

'A lot! You hold the key,' said Merlik as he and his brother circled Tharguen. 'If it hadn't been for you, those stupid Telorians wouldn't have successfully passed in and out of Mork.'

'You don't know that.'

'Don't get smart!' said Garkhktak, slapping Tharguen behind the head. 'Bahvley isn't all that powerful; I doubt he would have slipped out so easily a second time had you not been there.'

'You were almost there,' said Merlik, his tone condescending. 'Mirauk was planning on finally letting you meet him and promoting you by recommendation of Beshrig.'

'I'm glad I never got there, then. Meeting him would have cursed me. Because you very well know I was never a Morkan, same as you very well know the lies you've been telling the Dûnelorians to get them on your side.'

Merlik gave Tharguen a harsh look, his eyes reflecting the decades of bitter rivalry between them.

'You should've seen Mirauk's devastation and anger,' he continued without replying to Tharguen's comments, 'after many years of putting trust in you when he found Beshrig dead in one of his weapons chambers. *Weapons chambers!*'

Tharguen laughed. 'Jimmy and Meysah can be quite clever sometimes when they play practical jokes—'

Tharguen grunted as Merlik punched him in the stomach.

'Did you kill Beshrig?' demanded Merlik.

'I did,' Tharguen said through gritted teeth, 'to save Niome's life, and then two friends of mine disposed of the body.'

'There we go,' said Garkhktak. 'All better when you comply and answer a question directly. No?'

'No!'

Merlik gave Tharguen another punch, this time in the face. Tharguen spat out blood.

'Now, about those books . . .' began Garkhktak.

'What books?' Tharguen asked.

'*What books?*' Merlik repeated mockingly. 'Don't "*what books*" me.'

He hit him again, backhanding Tharguen and giving him a black eye, at which point Tharguen stood up suddenly, freed his hands, and took his knife from his boot. He held it to Merlik's throat as he grabbed him. Garkhktak then took out his sword and pointed its tip directly at Tharguen's throat. Tharguen let go of Merlik and gave up his knife.

'The two books you speak of were destroyed,' he said.

'Where? When?' both Dukes exclaimed.

'At Darakön.'

'You're lying!' And another hit, this time from Garkhktak. Tharguen staggered back.

'The dragons took them and threw them into the fire to burn, for the Portal was theirs and theirs alone. No one was ever meant to go through it – not Niome, not Mirauk, not anyone.'

'Do you believe he's telling the truth, Garkhktak?' asked Merlik.

'It would explain the reason no one went through it,' said Garkhktak. 'Had the Wizardess gone through, the world would be changed. It would have changed the instant she came out, and Mirauk would have felt it. Mirauk knew she didn't go through it. Although Kàtchah feared she had.'

'Yes,' said Merlik, looking at the ground. Then he looked up at Tharguen. 'You know, Gowtch, or . . . Tharguen, Captain Kàtchah was awarded for bringing home the news about you, for reporting and confirming that *Gowtch* was the traitor Mirauk had perceived when probing Niome's mind.'

'Good for him, but I don't care! All of you have been after me, Bahvley, Niome and the others, but you will never succeed.'

'Oh, really?' Garkhktak said conclusively.

Grabbing Tharguen, he opened the door and threw him at Rhal.

'I did not think you would wreck him,' said the Emperor.

'Before we see the other prisoners, we should inform you . . .' began Merlik, pausing.

'Yes?' inquired Rhal.

'*Nivakhed achnad takereth vorenwo!*' Merlik boomed. Tharguen understood, and great worry overcame him. Then Merlik turned to Rhal and announced matter-of-factly, 'We're taking over the palace.'

'You cannot do that!' objected Emperor Majim.

'Oh yeah? Watch me!'

In the blink of an eye, the Dûnelorians and Tharguen were surrounded by too many Morkans to count. The Dukes did nothing but stand and watch. Merlik's orders had been magically heard by all the Morkans, and the sounds of weapons unsheathing were heard throughout the palace.

'I cannot and will not let you do this!' warned Veij Majim.

He looked at one of his guards who stood far behind the Morkans surrounding them. The guard nodded and hurried away. Soon after, a large bell sounded off – the guard had sounded the alarm, and soon enough, there was movement all over the palace. Out the window, Emperor Veij Majim saw his great bird flying away.

And thus the battle began, many Morkans against many Dûnelorians. The fight began on the first floor, conveniently for the Dûnelorians.

A large group of Morkans chased after many of Emperor Majim's polcs, and though they had trapped the Emperor's warriors in a room, they were the trapped ones, for more Dûnelorians came behind and pushed them into the room. Then, the floor beneath them gave way and all those Morkans fell into the prison cells below.

The Dûnelorians looked down, smiling proudly at their handiwork. One small victory.

There had been so much commotion that the soldiers had forgotten about the Dukes, and now the Prince found himself alone with the twins and a few of their guards. Tharguen and the Emperor had been separated from Rhal in the tumult.

Luckily for Rhal, the hatch down the hall popped open and out ran Meysah, followed by Lóim, Ihal and Fimrel. Taking advantage of the distraction, Rhal drew his sword and struck down the Morkan who had seized him. The Morkan brothers fled, but when their guards tried to follow, the two Kikies from Meysah's team appeared before them.

Lóim came face-to-face with a Morkan and suddenly could no longer fight; he was too scared to move. The imposing figure, dark eyes glaring malice into Lóim's heart, had three times his muscle power.

'I told you this was a bad idea,' he muttered.

'Too late now,' said Meysah as he knocked the Morkan down.

Lóim took a deep breath, letting his fear pass and be replaced by composure, and he steeled himself to fight another Morkan. This was his first real fight with a Morkan, and he hoped he would one day be brave enough to boast about fighting these fearsome adversaries.

Another Morkan grabbed Ihal as she struggled to break free. Meysah and Lóim both pounced to help her, but she had already, cleverly, done the job herself. She looked at the lads.

'Told you I could take care of myself.'

'Who's showing off now!' they both said, and Meysah and Lóim both suppressed smiles at each other.

They kept fighting alongside the Prince, and soon after, no Morkans in the area remained; the Prince was safe.

'Thank you,' said Rhal.

'Don't mention it,' the others called as they hurried off.

'Come,' said Meysah, 'let's go help Master Vigh and Master Boreth up on the other floor.'

'Is that such a good idea?' asked Lóim. 'Shouldn't we go to the grand balcony and wait?'

'It's not wise to—'

'Okay, let's go,' said Ihal, changing directions.

'Fine,' said Meysah, 'but I won't be responsible if—'

An arrow flew by. They all ran to the grand balcony.

'Next time, I get a say in this,' said Fimrel as they ran.

The balcony was on the west side of the palace, accompanied by a grand dining hall and concert hall. The entire wing was beautiful, made of marble and adorned with many windows that they had to duck down against the wall outside to conceal themselves from the Morkans inside. Meysah and Lóim were below one window, Ihal and Fimrel below another at a fair distance from them.

'Remind me why we came here,' whispered Meysah.

'To hide,' said Lóim.

'You don't hide in battle; you fight!' Meysah replied.

An arrow flew out through the window and struck Lóim's thigh. Meysah quickly checked what was going on whilst putting a hand on Lóim's mouth so he wouldn't yell out or be heard.

'You're lucky no one knows we're here,' said Meysah, putting his hands to Lóim's wound. 'The arrow hasn't gone in deep. A Morkan only missed his shot. But hiding will get us all killed if we stay here. Once the coast is clear, I'm out of here to get you some help.'

'I'm sorry,' said Lóim. 'You're so brave, and look at me.' He suddenly felt like a failure as he stared at his blood.

'Lóim, courage comes with experience,' said Meysah, taking care of Lóim's wound as best he could. 'I'm scared too, but perhaps to a lesser degree. Either that, or I can control it or deny it to myself better than you can.' He ripped a piece of Lóim's shirt and tied it tightly around his thigh. 'That, too, comes with experience, hiding fears.'

'You had Mirauk running after you.'

'Don't remind me,' said Meysah, shivering.

'Can I ask you something?'

'I guess.'

'What do you think of Ihal?'

'Did Jimmy put you up to this?' Lóim looked at him blankly. 'Uhm, never mind that. Well, she fights bravely . . . she's nice. Uhmm, why?'

'I don't think she likes me very much,' confessed Lóim. Meysah slapped his forehead with his hand. 'What's wrong?'

'Nothing.'

'Do you think she likes me?'

'Can we talk about this some other time?'

'What if there *is* no other time?'

'Lóim, you're not going to die from a thigh wound. And a battleground is no time to talk about our love lives.' Meysah pointed at the wound. 'Just keep putting herbs on it and pressing on the wound.'

Lóim did so, taking the sack of herbs out from his pocket. Meysah nodded three times to him as Lóim nodded back, and he quickly plucked the arrow out of Lóim's leg; the injured polc gritted his teeth but did not scream. His eyes were teary from the pain, but the arrow had not gone in deep, and the blood that came out was thick and slow.

'Dessimë and Neyith,' said Meysah to the floating Kikies, 'stay with the others while I go get help, in case they need to fast-fly. And while I'm at it, I'll find out what's going on, why the Morkans have attacked. *We* were supposed to ambush *them*!'

'I'm going with you,' said Ihal.

They nodded to their friends and ran out into the now empty room and out of sight.

Up on the third floor, Vigh, Boreth, Mittah, and Malcolm fought with the help of the three Kikies of their team along with quite a few Dûnelorians. Soon, Captain Yûrk approached to confront them directly.

'It sure is a good thing you're with us,' Malcolm said to Boreth.

'Why? Is he of importance?' asked Captain Yûrk, cornering Malcolm and Mittah.

'Perhaps you'll recognise my name: Lord Boreth Culmik,' Boreth said, inching towards Yûrk.

'And Lord Vigh Nimrod! We are part of the invincible Five!'

'Well, let's see if you're invincible now!' yelled Yûrk.

He violently duelled them both, their swords clashing and clanging for a long time before there was any rip or scratch. Yûrk's fighting skills were beyond any other, meaning he must have been one of Mirauk's higher-ranked and most trained and trusted Morkans, as his nephews and Kàtchah were. Luckily for the four Telorians, the three Kikies and the Dûnelorians got rid of Yûrk's polcs, and he was alone now with one other Morkan. Realising their odds, they staggered away before either of them got hurt.

'Come, let's pursue them!' said Vigh. 'Before they can pull the same trick on less skilled Telorians or Dûnelorians.'

'I agree,' said Mittah, 'but that was a close one. He almost killed us all.'

'Don't exaggerate,' Malcolm scoffed. 'But it *was* a close call.'

'I actually killed my first Morkan with an arrow from high above,' said Mittah. 'But this . . .'

'I know it's awkward the first time you come face-to-face with the enemy,' said Vigh. 'But you get used to it.'

The group hurried after Yûrk into a large dark room where there was what appeared to be a giant sled, only half constructed. Metal ladders leaned against the apparatus while stone stairs and platforms climbed along the wall.

'Wow, what could this be for?' whispered Mittah.

'To defend themselves on their own terrain of sinking and flying sand,' Vigh deduced.

'Looks like they've already begun to prepare for Mirauk's attack,' said Boreth. 'Looks like they've got some magical weapons in place there, or a place for more weapons.' He pointed at various parts of the contraption. 'They probably suspected—'

They heard footsteps above somewhere. Boreth got his bow and held it taut.

Jimmy, Tom, Peyvil, Huck, Mimulus and Zend raced to the basement where, as a decoy, Gahli, Pete, Jeremy, Eerzin and the others had been put into cells. Unfortunately, they were still stuck there, and Tharguen had not yet come with the keys to get them out as they had planned.

Many Morkans stood in other cells trying to poke the Telorians with their swords. Luckily for them, their weapons had been hidden in the storage room, and Jimmy and his team quickly retrieved these weapons and passed them to their friends.

'Is there a trap above this cell?' asked Jimmy.

'I don't know,' said Pete.

They all heard the cling and clang of swords over their heads. Suddenly, the ceiling above the cell burst, and down came tumbling a good number of Morkans. Above, they saw Tharguen fighting with other Morkans. He stood precariously at the edge of the hole, where the Telorians were already defending them-selves from the Morkans.

'Jimmy!' Tharguen cried out.

Jimmy looked up just in time to catch the keys. Tharguen smiled at him. As Jimmy unlocked the door, he said loud enough for Tharguen to hear, 'No dead body to hide this time, though.'

'Memories,' said Tharguen to himself.

The cell door opened and out came the Telorians and Morkans. More Morkans from above jumped down to join the fray.

Tharguen worked to keep his balance and not fall onto any weapons down below. When the cell was clear, he jumped down.

'Talk about being outnumbered,' said Tharguen as the Telorians continued to fight.

'What happened to *you*?' asked Jimmy, discreetly handing the keys back to Tharguen.

'Merlik and Garkhktak's handiwork,' said Tharguen. 'They're trying to take over the palace. Can you imagine, *they* ambushed *us*!'

'Are you truly surprised?' asked Jimmy. He kicked a Morkan, who fell onto a Dûnelorian's sword.

'No. I fear more Morkans will be arriving shortly.' Tharguen moved away from the cluster of fighters.

'Well, in the meantime, I'll get rid of these for you so you can recover a bit,' said Jimmy, waving his hand towards Tharguen's face.

'Thanks, Jimmy, I could use a short break.'

'Come on, to the roof!' cried Jimmy.

'Jimmy!' Gahli grabbed Jimmy's arm, which made him bounce back very close to her. She then shyly moved her hand. 'Uh, be careful.'

'I will,' said Jimmy, smiling shyly back.

He took her hand and squeezed it gently. Then he ran to the passageway and yelled out to get the Morkans' attention, 'No Morkan can catch me! I'm part of the invincible Five!'

'But what happens if they do?' yelled Huck in the same way, playing along. 'They'll kill you, and then the Wizardess will weaken.'

'I'll just come back to life!' answered Jimmy, almost laughing.

'You should've been part of the players for the stage,' said Tom softly.

At that, the Morkans' attention went indeed to Jimmy and his companions, and they started after them.

'Oh, Stars!' cried Jimmy as they all climbed the passageway's ladder to the top, Morkans at their tails.

'Well, that got rid of them,' said Tharguen, leaning against the wall.

'Are you okay, Captain?' asked Jeremy.

'I'll be fine. Yeah, I'm already fine. Come, let's get ourselves upstairs and see if anyone needs our help, eh?'

They all followed him to the stairs.

Meysah and Ihal snuck through the hall and came to an intersection. Ihal started to the right.

'What are you doing?' Meysah halted her.

'I'm going this way,' replied Ihal.

'Wouldn't we have better luck going that way?'

'How would you know?'

'My instincts tell me so!' Meysah had learnt to trust them as Niome had urged him to.

'But what if my way's better?'

'Trust me, just . . . you owe me one.'

'You said the event with the bridge was—'

'Well, I changed my mind. I did say you needed to trust me. Trust me now.'

'Fine,' agreed Ihal. 'But that makes us even, then.'

They went left, and it brought them to the staircase.

'I don't think we should go upstairs,' said Meysah.

'Why not?'

'It'll bring us too far from the others. It's too risky.'

'But what if we don't find help near here?' argued Ihal.

'We will, *trust me!*' Meysah emphasised. 'We should wait here a few moments. Please, stop contradicting me.'

'Lóim would not agree with you, Meysah, and in this case, he'd be right.'

'Why bring *him* up? What difference does it make now?' He paused. 'You trust him more than you trust me.'

'Yes, I admit it, yes,' said Ihal. 'I've known him longer.'

'It bothers me that you put all your trust in him when there is more cause to trust me!'

'Why does it bother you so much that I trust him more than I trust you?'

'Because! . . . He's a coward. You wouldn't understand.'

'Is it your arrogance?' Meysah gave Ihal no reply. 'Well, we're never going to get anywhere if we just stand still and argue about it.'

'Lower your voice,' Meysah whispered urgently, glancing from side to side. 'You'll bring attention to us.'

'Why can't you just tell me why it bothers you so much? It doesn't make any sense.'

'Shshsh! Quiet!'

'I'd expect you to be more . . . I don't know, and here you are, shouting at me because I—'

Meysah grabbed Ihal's face with both hands and kissed her. Letting go of her face, he looked at her timidly. 'Uh . . . uhm . . . please be quiet.'

Ihal herself was shocked as the two stared at each other.

'And if I decide to keep on arguing?' she teased, bringing her lips close to his.

Meysah's breath hitched. 'I just might have to . . . uh . . . kiss you again,' he replied, looking into her eyes, 'because it's the only way to, uh, shut you up.'

Ihal closed the distance between them, and they kissed a long time, arms wrapped around each other. Meysah deepened the kiss even more before hearing people in the stairwell. They took a step back from each other, breathless and smiling.

The two glanced quickly into the stairwell; it was Tharguen and his team who approached. Meysah and Ihal giggled. Ihal kissed his cheek before the others went through the doors.

'What happened to *you*?' Meysah asked Tharguen, almost in the same tone Jimmy had asked him.

'Oh, I just got beaten up,' said Tharguen, a little too casually to *not* be sarcastic. 'The Morkans decided to ambush us and take over the palace.'

'That's why everything's been so weird,' gathered Ihal.

'Are you two okay?' inquired Pete.

'Oh, very much, yes,' said Meysah with a wide grin before sobering himself. 'But Lóim got hurt, and we went to get help.'

'Then we'll help you,' said Tharguen.

'I don't know where my brother and sister are, so . . .'

'Neither do I, but I'm sure they're fine.'

Meysah and Ihal led them carefully to the ballroom; there was no longer any activity near there. They ran to the grand balcony.

Lóim had a new piece of cloth on the wound. He had applied more Firlanian herbs before putting the new cloth, he explained.

'We need to get him somewhere safe,' said Tharguen. 'Can you walk?'

'I can't even stand,' replied Lóim.

'Isn't here safe enough?' Fimrel asked.

'Not anymore,' said Tharguen, looking off into the distance. A throng of Morkans upon horses was approaching at great speed. 'Quick, let's get out of here.'

Up and up Jimmy climbed, as quickly as he possibly could. Tom was last in line; the Morkans kept grabbing his feet and pulling him down, but he was swift enough, and with the help of his sword he was able to shove them off.

The Telorians reached the roof and hid behind the magical beacon, a large transparent sphere. They only needed to speak magical words to ignite it – a raging fire, hypnotising the specified enemy to a state of uncontrollable relaxation and drowsiness. Of course, this was only good for small groups of weak-minded Morkans, not anything that would help the war against Mirauk, but it would buy them some time for now.

Before running back down to lock the hatch, they looked afar and saw an army of Morkans in the distance.

'Uh-oh!' said Peyvil. 'This isn't good.'

'No, it isn't,' said Jimmy.

'What do we do about these Morkans now?' asked Huck, looking at their unconscious forms.

'This is part of the trap,' said Jimmy. 'When they awake, they'll go downstairs and find themselves locked up. That's why this hatch will be locked but open.'

'Oh, the top hatch locks from the outside! I get it now,' said Huck.

They started down.

Boreth stood with his bow ready, aimed above him. The Telorians walked slowly, looking all around. Then Vigh made a sign to the others.

The Kikies, he mouthed, no sound coming from him at all, *say he and the others are there.* He pointed right above them.

Yûrk was leaning his back against the wall, practically holding in his breath, sneaking along so slowly and quietly. Vigh listened carefully to what the floating Kikies were whispering into his ear. He then started up the wall, grabbing hold of the spaces between the bricks. The others stood along the wall.

When Vigh got to the top, right under the platform, he grabbed hold of the platform's edge and jumped onto it, leaping at Yûrk and tripping the two Morkans. Boreth shot the arrow at Yûrk but the Morkan captain was too quick; he got up and jumped to the next platform where there was a door. The others hurried up the stairs as everyone ran after him.

The Kikies appeared before Yûrk, and he bumped into them and fell. They jumped on him and disarmed him while the Telorians pinned his companion to the ground. They grabbed hold of the two polcs and dragged them along to the basement. With all of them holding on to Yûrk and his soldier, the Morkans could not break free, no matter how much they fought back.

A Dûnelorian guard opened up a cell for Yûrk and the other Morkan. They threw them into the cell and closed it up before the other Morkans inside had time to try to get out.

'That's done,' said Boreth with relief, rubbing his hands together.

* * *

'I should have known better than to trust those Morkans in the first place,' mumbled Emperor Veij Majim, pacing to and fro.

'You couldn't have guessed which decision was best then,' replied Bahvley. 'I know now that being King is not an easy task.'

'We acted more on fear,' said Rhal. 'But we are no longer afraid.'

At that moment, Yém ran in. The leaders and their companions had gathered at the entrance, waiting for Yém to bring in the weapons he had planned to steal from the Morkan supply bags. He had many tools with him now but also a look of devastation upon his face.

'Morkans!' he cried. 'An entire army! Right outside, approaching fast!'

'They're not going to reach this palace,' said Niome. 'I'll give them a piece of my mind.'

She strode outside where many Dûnelorians already stood, and more followed her.

'Niome! Wait!' cried Bahvley in protest. He ran out after her, along with the others of their team.

'I think we should stay here,' said Rhal, 'to defend the palace here, and fight and capture the Dukes.'

'Where are they, anyway?' asked the Emperor.

'Out there!' said Yém. 'Joining the front line.'

'Niome! Wait! Don't! NIOME!' shouted Bahvley as he ran out after her in the sandy field. 'It's too dangerous!'

'I'm not going to let them reach the palace. I'll stop them.'

'Are you out of your mind?'

'I don't fear them,' said Niome, almost annoyed, as she and Bahvley strode towards the Morkan army.

'But they don't *only* want to attack the palace; they want Tharguen,' he objected. 'They don't know of your presence. Don't make them go after you!'

'I won't let them go after Tharguen!' replied Niome, readying her sword. 'Let them know I'm here and let them report it to Mirauk, but no one's laying their hands on Tharguen without a fight.'

'Well, you're quite protective,' muttered Bahvley. 'Good thing the Dukes aren't women. Remind me to never get between you and Tharguen.'

'Hang on, Bahvely!' cried Celor, who had taken his full size again.

Bahvley turned around and realised that his whole team was following him and Niome in great strides to the battlefield, weapons at the ready, heading right into the midst of all the fighting.

As they drew nearer, the Telorians and Kikies could see Morkans leaping at Dûnelorians, polcs throwing attackers off them. They could hear yells of pain, shouts of anger and revenge, steel crashing against steel, and before they knew it, they had arrived at the swarm of chaos.

'I'm not too sure this was a good idea,' Bahvley said quietly.

'Well, we're here now,' replied Niome. 'No point going back.'

'When do you suppose this ends?' asked Classû as he ducked, avoiding an arrow.

'Certainly not at the end of the day,' said Jackley.

'This battle? Or this war?' asked Bahvley.

'Both,' said Classû.

'When Mirauk is overthrown!' said Jackley. 'Until then, I fear it will go on and on. When do *you* think it'll end, Your Highness?'

'This battle, when we or the Morkans retreat. This war, when Mirauk is destroyed.' Bahvley unsheathed his sword, ready to join the fight.

'There will be no retreating, Your *High*ness!'

The Telorians turned around to find one of Mirauk's nephews standing before them, his long dark hair moving with the wind.

'So, at last we meet,' he said. 'King Bahvley Fairhaven. Mirauk foresaw your royal worthiness; that's why he tried to get rid of you.'

'He can try all he wants,' remarked Bahvley. 'He won't succeed.'

'No? But I will.'

He leapt at Bahvley. Bahvley defended himself as best he could, but the Duke was too greatly skilled, using kick techniques mixed in with magic and regular sword techniques. The Morkan's skills were no match for anyone in Teloria, except perhaps Tharguen and Niome. Indeed, Niome and the others hurriedly jumped towards him and pulled him away from Bahvley.

'Back off, Merlik!' she cried.

'How is it you know my name? You, such a young and weak and worthless Telorian—'

'Don't!' cried Garkhktak, approaching. 'This must be . . .' Niome kept looking at them sternly without blinking or turning her glance away. 'Niome Fairhaven, here to stop you from winning.'

'Oh, no, brother!' said Merlik, amused. 'She may have guessed my name, but can she truly read into my mind? Tharguen must have described us to her. Yes. And Niome, you are yet our best catch of the day.'

They both grabbed her and pinned her down, and before the others could do anything, they, too, were pinned down by Morkans.

'You ease your way to the front to see better, and this is what you get,' Garkhktak sneered.

The Telorians were overpowered and bound; they could do nothing about it. They could no longer even move. Niome closed her eyes. She took a deep breath and spoke strange words, relaxing her body as though allowing herself to be bound. No matter how much noise there was around her or how many times she was told to be quiet, she went on.

As she spoke, Morkans bound her hands and feet and tied everyone else up, immobilising them even more to disarm them completely.

Ehelt reiûeh, op foëhelt raëstessë vireva,
Rofehelt norgadës thaginest lilëfes ëimi.
Assuöregoluc rethoreb dana taniliav dineref,
Assuörecig retessam dana iyerthow taginehk,
Dana derziäw, regonest natihina rehot nicagimë relo.

This verse Niome repeated and kept reciting over and over again, at first in a whisper, then louder and louder as though she were hypnotised by it. The more she said it, the deeper she fell into a trancelike state. Her hands began to shake, and her face began to twitch as she lay flat, her back on the ground. Then her legs began to quiver spasmodically as she began to shout the verse.

Many Telorians felt frightened, for they did not understand what was happening. The Morkans thought she was succumbing to her fear of Mirauk, and they began to mock her. Bahvley yelled at them to stop, believing in her magic and waiting to see what was going to occur, but the Morkans kept on mocking anyway. Niome did not react to them; she did not react to anything. She simply kept repeating her words.

Then, Niome suddenly stretched out, and the rope that bound her hands and legs broke with a snap. She then opened her eyes, still reciting the verse, and stood up. Merlik and Garkhktak poked at her with their swords just enough to threaten her, but she merely turned her head slowly, looking at them blankly. There was absolutely no expression on her face. Her eyes looked glazed over, possessed.

Merlik pushed her and struggled to get her on the ground. Guards surrounding her assisted him, but the more he pushed her, the less she staggered back. It was like punching air; her resistance was beyond understanding. Garkhktak stabbed at her, but once again it was useless. Niome reflexively grabbed the sword, and she was so strong she took it and threw it down without any sign of effort, baffling Garkhktak.

Finally, she stopped reciting and took a deep breath. She then began to glow; an aura glimmered all around her like a magical shield, giving her a majestic look. The first time she had tried magic of this kind, it had taken her energy and made her tired. This time, it *gave* her energy.

The Morkans shrieked in fear, retreating back. Niome meanwhile unbound her friends and looked at the Morkans.

The Dukes stood in terrified awe and loathing admiration; Merlik's eyes were fixed on hers.

'Go tell Mirauk he shall not wage war on any people without having to deal with me!' Niome said, gazing upon the army. Then she turned to the Dukes of Mork. 'You, come with me. I'm sure Emperor Majim has a message for you to give to Mirauk.'

Niome stopped glowing and grabbed hold of them briskly by the arms. *They* were the captives now, and the Morkans were too scared to fight her or defend their leaders. The Dukes allowed her to grab them and lead them to the palace, and other Telorians took hold of them as well to help Niome escort the two captives to the palace.

Back inside the palace, wherever Vigh, Boreth, Meysah or Jimmy were, they felt a strange strength fill them and take over them. They felt as though a huge blast of adrenaline had hit them. Wherever they were, whoever they were fighting, they defeated them exceptionally well and moved faster than usual.

Meysah, after bringing Tharguen to Lóim, carried Lóim through the battle, all while fighting Morkans. Lóim cowered over Meysah's shoulder, closing his eyes tightly as Meysah had a rush of adrenaline and ran ahead, clearing the way for the others until they got to the basement, their designated meeting spot.

Jimmy had gone around the palace, inspecting all the grounds. Suddenly he was not afraid of bumping into any Morkans and had succeeded in capturing quite a few. Along the way, he met Vigh and Boreth and told them about the army of Morkans he and the others had seen. They all stepped outside, but when they reached the front of the palace, Niome was walking back briskly with the two Dukes at her sides.

Bahvley briefly explained to them what he had witnessed. Vigh nodded, understanding what had taken over him, but Niome spoke not a word as she marched further into the palace. Vigh felt as though their strength as the Star had permanently grown – not as radically as during Niome's trance moments earlier, but similarly to their shared experience with the guardian creature in Firlan. He knew they were somehow changed.

Niome and Bahvley shoved Merlik and Garkhktak into the basement where Meysah and many Dûnelorians awaited. Several Dûnelorians grabbed hold of them.

'I think we all have something that we want to say,' said Emperor Veij Majim. 'I will let my son begin.'

Rhal walked towards the Dukes.

'You thought you could just march in here and deceive us all! I have to admit, we planned the same thing: ambush.'

Rhal walked to one of the prison cells. 'When we agreed to the deal, we were afraid, but now we know who our true allies are, trying to warn us of you. Teloria stands beside Dûnelor as Dûnelor stands beside Teloria. We are stronger than Mirauk thinks, and we fear him not.' He paused. 'At first I agreed to your deal, for I thought I could avenge myself in this way for the death of my love, but I realised that Tharguen was innocent. Now' – he opened the cell and pulled out Captain Yûrk, putting his sword to his throat – 'would it make up for her death if I killed a faithful Morkan Captain?' There was a pause. 'No!' He threw Yûrk back into the cell. 'No matter how many Morkans I kill, it will never be compensation enough.'

Rhal stared down the Dukes of Mork, who merely stood there frozen, jaws clenched.

'Merlik,' said Tharguen as he approached him, 'tell Mirauk that Gowtch is dead. He existed for a time, but now it's Tharguen, who's back and not a very happy Tharguen. If he wants to kill me, he has to come after me, addressing me as Captain Tharguen Sumperale of Teloria. Oh, and you can tell *everyone* in Mork that I did Mirauk a favour when I killed Beshrig, for he would've betrayed him sooner or later. You should've heard some of the things he'd say about the two of you!' Tharguen snickered. 'He was not a faithful Morkan. I did you all a favour.'

He got right in Merlik's face. 'This is for before.' He punched him in the stomach – Merlik doubled over, grunting – then Tharguen walked away and shook off his anger. 'Okay,' he whispered to himself.

'Tell your King that I declare war against Morok,' said Emperor Billahmyé Veij Majim. 'Is there anything else anyone wants to say?'

'Yeah, I'd like to give these two Morkans a piece of my mind,' said Meysah. 'You don't scare me! In fact—'

Vigh put his hand on Meysah's shoulder, leaning into his ear. 'Don't say anything foolish,' he whispered.

'You know what,' said Meysah, 'it can wait.'

Everyone looked at each other.

'Leave!' ordered the Emperor. 'You Morkans are no longer welcome in Dûnelor.'

The Emperor's guards dragged the Morkans out of the cells and threw them out of the palace. Some of the Morkans wanted to attack, but the large army outside convinced them not to until they received further instructions from Mirauk, for they were too scared now after witnessing Niome's magic firsthand.

As the Dukes were escorted out, Niome stared at them sternly. Garkhktak glanced at Tharguen angrily, but Merlik kept looking back at Niome, mouth agape as though in awe of her power, and he stared at her until he turned the corner. Before they departed for good, Garkhktak's rage roared up. So powerful was his shout that everyone heard his angry words.

'*Kuyokh reka gokinago gerterk sikht, Gowtch!*' he shouted. '*Mirauk iliw sohowro kuyokh akwen denkag-fitonikh fo fessurkhin thig telnex charankhec ekh khetesg!*'

Tharguen stood with an angered look, face bowed down.

'What did he say?' asked Bahvley.

'He's trying to instil fear,' Tharguen replied dryly.

'But what did he say?'

'Nothing!' snapped Tharguen. After a while: 'I'm sorry, Bahvley. In short, he said that Mirauk is going to make me suffer.'

'Well, he won't succeed,' Niome replied.

Tharguen sat down on a bench. Niome walked to him and sat down beside him.

'Don't let this trouble you,' she said softly as he leaned his head on her shoulder. 'Let it go. I know it's difficult at times, but just let go.'

'I know,' Tharguen said with a sigh. 'I guess I let it get to me more than I should.'

Some of the Kikies sighed in sympathy in their Kiki way, not so different in tone than a saddened puppy, and Tharguen smiled.

'Well, that was an interesting day,' said Bahvley. He smiled meagerly.

'Actually,' said Rhal, 'it was two days, though none of us noticed it at first. We all kept on going.'

'Yes, well, I'm ready to collapse now,' said Jimmy. 'And eat!'

'Me too,' added Meysah.

Tharguen smiled as Niome laced her fingers with his. He looked at Rhal and the two nodded, relief on both their faces.

CHAPTER TWELVE:
Another Deceivable Change Of Plans

*E*veryone rested well that night. Many who had been injured had their wounds tended to, Dûnelorian and Telorian alike. The Dûnelorians knew they would probably find themselves in battle again soon, but they also knew they had time before the Morkans regrouped and recovered. Emperor Veij Majim had already begun preparations long before any of this occurred, and he would not be taken unawares again.

The Telorians and Kikies offered their aid to the Dûnelorians for as long as they remained in Dûnelor, while Bahvley also offered to send word to Teloria for fighters to come as reinforcement in the event the Morkans attacked the Dûnelorians again. Both he and Emperor Veij Majim knew that had Niome not frightened the Morkans with her spell and trance, the enemy army may have taken over the palace, if not invaded the entire desert.

A few days after the battle, Bahvley approached Niome with an issue that troubled him greatly.

Niome was in the room she and Tharguen shared in the palace, organising some things and looking for a gift to give to Yém. She wanted to thank the old merchant for helping them; after all, he would continue to help them by being their guide through the desert until they hit the plains on their return to Teloria.

'Niome?' said Bahvley from the other side of the door, knocking. She opened the door to let him in. 'Can I talk to you?'

'Sure. What is it?'

'It's about the other day.' He paused. 'What happened to you?'

'What do you mean?'

'What were you saying? A spell? What did it do? You were neutral, and yet there was a glint of something sinister in your eyes. I know it's the Dukes, but the way you looked at them was unlike the way you've looked at anyone before. Why were you so overcome with emotion?'

'One question at a time, please,' Niome broke in. 'Why are you so worried?'

'Something happened to you when you were reciting your spell, something other than strengthening the Star,' said Bahvley. 'And since then, you've been keeping this door locked. Back home you tend to leave your door wide open. Heck, even in Firlan you left the door to your room unlocked or ajar.' He took a step towards his sister. 'I know there's something going on.'

'Nothing happened,' Niome said evasively, turning around and rummaging through some clothes.

'Come on, Niome,' pleaded Bahvley. 'I know I'm no wizard, but I do sense things, and I sense—'

'Look, nothing happened,' Niome said defensively, cutting him off. 'Case closed.'

'No! Case *not* closed. You knew something before it happened, and you know something now. You let them capture us. You could've used the Dragon's Wind; you could've fought back. But no, you let the Morkans take you and tie you up, as though you knew the spell would only work if that happened. And then, when you looked into Merlik's and Garkhktak's eyes, you saw something. What did you see?'

'Oh, Bahvley, I think you're tired. There was no abnormality. You may think—'

'I'm not stupid, Niome! I saw it in your eyes. I'm your brother; I know you! The same magic runs in our blood. Just because I cannot cast spells does not mean I cannot detect or understand magic.'

'Well even if I did see something, what's it to you?'

'You're hiding it from me, and I don't like that!'

'I'm not hiding anything,' retorted Niome incredulously, almost laughing from trying to hide it so much. Her brother did know her, and better than she thought. In most cases, it was a good thing. He was only trying to protect her. She turned around. 'Now, please leave me to my meditation.'

Bahvley walked up to her and turned her around.

'I don't understand,' he said. 'Why won't you tell me? I'm your brother. Don't you trust me?' He looked at her carefully. 'I hate to have to do this, but you leave me no other choice.' Niome scowled at Bahvley. He drew himself to his full height. 'As King of Teloria, I demand you to tell me!'

'And as Great Wizardess of Teloria, I counter that command, for if I would've seen something, I could not and would not tell you. For the protection of Teloria, as well as yours and mine.'

Bahvley looked at her angrily. He nodded his head very slowly, pursing his lips. He opened his mouth to speak, then shook his head and backed away. He looked at her one last time in hopes she would change her mind and tell him whatever it was she knew, but Niome merely turned around. Unsure what else to do, Bahvley stormed out of the room.

Niome sat down with her head bowed.

In the hallway Bahvley met Meysah, who right away saw that something was troubling him.

'What's wrong?' he asked, concerned.

'Our sister's being difficult to the point of defying the King. Maybe it's because it's me.'

He walked away. Meysah scowled, pondering, and went right away to see Niome and asked her what all that was about.

'Meysah, he mustn't know – no one can – but I did see something. I wanted to tell him, but we need to protect everyone and ourselves. No one must know.'

'Well, you shouldn't quarrel. I mean, we're finally going to be off to the Twisted Forest.'

'We're not going,' said Niome. 'Not you, not me, not Jimmy or Boreth or Vigh. Another path lies ahead for us. I'll explain later. We have to meet tonight, all five of us.'

'I don't understand. Can't you tell me now?'

'I can't repeat myself; I must protect the good magic. I'll say it when we're all here, and I'll say it once only.'

Meysah nodded in understanding and left.

Right away Meysah went to find Jimmy, who was spending time with Gahli, Pete, Jeremy and the others. There were several Dûnelorians with them as they all hovered over a platter of delectable pastries.

'You lot look thick as thieves,' noted Meysah.

Jeremy looked up at him, grinning and speaking with his mouth full, 'Only enjoying the fruits of our labour.' He swallowed and wiped his mouth with the back of his hand, holding up the piece of pastry he held. 'Well, the bread of our labour.'

One of the Dûnelorians let out a spontaneous laugh and nudged Jeremy with his elbow. He looked up at Meysah. 'Join us, if you like! We baked enough for everyone.'

'Thanks, maybe later,' replied Meysah. 'Jimmy?' He motioned the hallway with his head. Jimmy wiped his hands of crumbs on his shirt and joined Meysah, who took him by the arm and led him away from the group. A few moments later, he told him what Niome had mentioned to him and about the quarrel between Niome and Bahvley.

'Huh . . . are you sure that's what she meant?' asked Jimmy.

'Yes!' replied Meysah. 'There's a meeting tonight, late, all five of us, and she's going to explain it all.'

'Where?'

'In her room, I guess.'

Jimmy nodded and then they both joined the group again for a while longer, enjoying the Imperial bread and other pastries. If the others asked what was going on, Jimmy and Meysah answered that they were simply speculating about some sort of surprise.

While this was going on, Bahvley stormed through the hallways looking for Tharguen; the polc had been injured a bit more than he had anticipated. While he thought he'd been only bruised from the punches, Tharguen had actually been scratched in the back and hadn't noticed at first. It had reached many nerves, and as it healed, he endured back pains and needed to do exercises and steady his breathing, even if it wasn't severe. After all, he was Captain of a team that needed to be in shape soon enough to leave to meet their friends, the Firlanians.

The Dûnelorians had shown Tharguen some relaxation techniques that were very soothing to his muscles and aided in the healing of his injuries. He was in one of the rooms they used for such exercises now, a room they called the healing chambre.

When Tharguen saw Bahvley, he was ready to recommend a few breathing exercises himself, for Bahvley looked like he could've seriously used them.

'I feel like I'm going mad,' seethed Bahvley after telling him the story. 'I mean, I'm not paranoid, and I didn't imagine it. Niome's absolutely hiding something from us.'

'Maybe she doesn't know herself what she saw,' said Tharguen.

'Oh, no, she knows.' Bahvley fumed in the silence.

'Are you sure?'

'She's the Great Wizardess of Teloria!' Bahvley paused. 'That's it! She's the greatest wizardess of all time and becoming ever more powerful as she gets older. Perhaps there are powers Mirauk used on her in their first encounter that she is developing herself.' Bahvley seemed to have had a revelation. 'You remember when we were in Mork the first time, and Mirauk could see into another's mind when looking in their eyes? He did the same thing to Niome and probed her mind. Niome cast a spell, looked into the eyes of the Dukes, and I saw on her face that she saw something.'

'What are you saying?' asked Tharguen.

'Niome's no longer having coincidental predictions anymore but prophetic visions, and she won't tell me about them. Perhaps she cannot tell anyone. I realise now that maybe she needs to protect what she saw.'

Tharguen furrowed his brows. 'I'm not sure I'm following entirely, but maybe I can talk to her and see if I can get a bit of information out of her.'

'Seriously, what did you tell Jimmy?'

'I told you, Ihal, it's a surprise,' said Meysah, his voice steady.

'You are aware that I can read lips, right? So can Mittah, and you did not say anything about a surprise. You spoke of Niome and Bahvley. You said something about "*no one can know*" and other things like that.'

'My point exactly: you are not allowed to know anything! It's a surprise.' Meysah stared at Ihal. 'Besides, if I lead Jimmy *away from the group,* then you shouldn't follow behind to try to eavesdrop.'

Ihal tilted her head to the side. 'What's wrong with you telling me?'

'You know, I have a lot of things to do,' Meysah said evasively. 'I'll see you later.'

He gave Ihal a kiss on the cheek and hurried off, leaving her to talk to herself.

'Yes, go and be independent again. I wouldn't insist so much if you wouldn't be so strange about it.' Lóim came by. 'He's not acting normal for such a thing, Lóim.' She paused. 'I have to figure it out. What if it's serious? What if someone's ill?'

'I doubt it's anything like that,' said Lóim.

'Well, since this morning, he's been different with me.'

'He's been different with all of us,' Lóim responded. 'Perhaps he thinks he's too good for us.' Ihal gave him a look. Lóim rolled his eyes then sighed. 'I'm sorry.'

Ihal and Lóim kept on talking for a bit, discussing the sudden and strange shift in their friends' behaviours.

'Oh, Master Boreth, I'm so glad I found you!'

'What is it, Jimmy? You seem rather perturbed.'

'Niome wants the five of us to meet tonight in her chambre for some mysterious announcement – something about us not being able to go to the Twisted Forest. But tell no one!'

'Not being able to go to the forest?' said Boreth. 'Are we not allowed suddenly? I don't get it.'

'Something like "another path is laid before us"; I don't know. Meysah only mentioned it in passing.'

'Has he told Vigh?'

'I don't know.'

'And we have to wait till tonight to find out.' Boreth paused. 'This must be more grave than you make it sound.'

'I barely know anything, and I was looking so forward to going to the forest. Maybe we'll be going after wherever else we have to go.'

'Can't we inform the others of this change?' asked Boreth.

'Not to my knowledge,' said Jimmy. 'Niome insisted it was kept secret until after we've returned from wherever. She couldn't even tell Bahvley; that's why they got into a huge fight.'

Boreth looked away, puzzled but somehow understanding. He nodded to Jimmy and started off.

'Tonight,' he said to himself. 'Tonight, it'll all become clear.'

Boreth went to Vigh and told him what Jimmy had said and what he had understood from it. He was afraid it was extremely serious but that Jimmy, and perhaps Meysah, had not yet realised the implications. Vigh agreed and wondered how the two would react once they truly knew the whole story.

'And you say Niome specified to keep this between us and us alone?' queried Vigh. Boreth nodded. 'Then that is our biggest clue.'

As the day progressed, Jimmy, Meysah, Boreth and Vigh each strove to figure out what the mystery was, but all their speculation was useless. They waited impatiently for evening to come, avoiding speaking of the matter amongst themselves in order not to arouse suspicion.

If anyone asked what was distracting them, the Lords simply replied that the events of the previous days had troubled them, or that they feared Mirauk's anger and revenge towards the Dûnelorians. If Bahvley or Tharguen spoke to them about their concerns for Niome, they pretended not to know anything, careful not to be too evasive, and said they figured she was having trouble adjusting to her new abilities.

To Jimmy and Meysah, the day felt longer than any other. They were constantly expecting something, anticipating what was to come nervously, yet never knowing what lay ahead.

As for Niome, the day went by too fast. She did not want to have to say this aloud or know it, for that matter, but she did, and she would've done anything to suspend time if only she had the ability.

Once supper had been eaten, once the sun had set, once everyone had retired to their rooms and all was quiet, the four faithful Telorians joined Niome in her room. Tharguen and Bahvley were meeting with Rhal and his father now that they had heard back from Rhal's sister and had much to discuss. It was the most opportune time for the Five to meet inconspicuously.

As soon as the other four entered, Niome locked the door and made sure the drapes were closed, the windows were shut, and all the lights in the room were out.

'Oooooo, spooky,' said Meysah as he sat down on the bed, the others following suit.

'This is no time for jokes,' said Niome in a half whisper. 'I need you all to listen very carefully, for I'll only say it once. We will discuss this tonight and never speak of it again, ever. Not in whispers, not alone amongst ourselves – not *ever.* You can think, or maybe gesticulate subtly, but nothing more. We cannot let this reach . . . and I won't even say his name, just in case.'

'You make it sound so frightening and urgent,' said Jimmy.

'It is,' said Niome. 'Although I denied it to Bahvley – for his protection and everyone else's – I did see something when I was speaking the spell. Yes, it replenished our strength, but something more happened to me then, before, during and after. I somehow knew that at that moment, I had to recite that spell, as though a voice inside of me was saying, "*Niome, there's something you need to know, and this is how you can see it.*"

'So, I began the spell, and I experienced something similar to what I lived on our way to Darakön. I saw images: fire, people running, us causing the fall of Firlan because of our unwanted carelessness. I saw . . . Em . . . laughing in his great big room, on his great big throne, as he observed us all through his crystal. I saw Teloria's brand-new wall being torn down because we chose to go one way and the enemy followed us wherever we went. I saw spies, secretly following us by mind and by travel. That's why we must change our course – so the others can do their business without great interruption by the enemy. I saw other faces of other Great Wizards. I saw Elina's face. I saw the number five.'

'What could all that possibly mean?' Vigh asked. 'We need to figure it all out.'

'Before we get into deciphering,' said Boreth, 'what did you see after?'

'When I opened my eyes and stood, for just an instant I saw through the Dukes and into their minds, and there I saw caverns and secret tunnels where a secret army was preparing. Morkans who were living underground for the time being, preparing an ambush, digging their way to make sure what had been announced was true. They were digging towards Darakön, which makes me believe Em thinks that the books are still intact, hidden inside Darakön. I saw the Gord Plains and the Ortim River, and I saw a Morkan wizard use his magic to dry up the river and dive into it when the water was only waist-high. I saw him enter a secret door and then the river returning to normal again. Though I did not see his face, I believe it was Kàtchah.'

'Does that mean,' began Meysah, 'that when you said we weren't going to the Twisted Forest, we're going there instead?'

'Indeed. The creatures I saw people flee from were ghost-like, floating about and waiting for us at the Twisted Forest.'

'The ghosts from the field . . . those were them, weren't they?' said Vigh. Niome nodded.

'So not only will we be stopping the Morkans from reaching Darakön . . . we'll be protecting ourselves from possible death,' surmised Boreth. 'Not to mention protecting our friends from foes who follow us around.'

'The creatures were sent out after us and commanded by Em to wait there for us, since he must have picked up on our intention of going there,' Niome continued. 'Everyone was talking about it, and it was planned and shouted out loud. All of Teloria knew. That's why we mustn't go; he'll try to kill us. Indeed, you are right, Boreth. But if we go to the secret caves, the ghosts won't find us and won't hurt the others, I hope, unless they already have hurt the people who live in the Twisted Forest. Unless . . . Em sends them a message, through his thoughts, to go back to seek us at the caves under the Gord Plains. Even at that, the others will be safer.'

'But then shouldn't we inform the others?' asked Meysah.

'No one can know,' Niome reiterated. 'It's for their own protection. If we talk about it, it'll be that much easier for Em to pick up the vibes from everyone. How he got a whiff about us going to the Twisted Forest in the first place, I do not know, but he is extremely powerful, and therefore caution is required. If Em sends an army after us . . . he doesn't need to know our friends are elsewhere, otherwise he may send armies everywhere. They can handle a battalion or two, but a whole army, let alone several . . .

'We don't need to cause an attack on Teloria, for that's where this path leads. Instead, it's us helping the dragons, us protecting our kingdom and ourselves in order to save our kingdom, even if it means, in a way, running away. So that's why you can't tell anyone, Meysah.'

'Not even one person?' Meysah asked in dismay.

'I can't even tell Tharguen or Bahvley. That's why we got into that big argument, Bahvley and I. Something awaits us all there, in those tunnels, otherwise I would've seen another place, other things. We must go *there*. I'll use my magic to create a drought, and then we will "fall into the river", be "swept away" by the tide and disappear. The others are strong; they can take care of themselves. They will assume it was a trap for us only and go on to the Twisted Forest without us. Do you all understand the importance of our mission?'

The sudden gravity of this was understood. Meysah's heart felt heavy with dread.

They all nodded, looking at Niome.

'But after our mission, we can go to the forest, right?'

'Yes, Meysah.'

'And how long will we be gone?' asked Boreth. 'A few weeks?'

'A few days, a few weeks, a few seasons. I don't know,' said Niome. 'As long as it will take us.'

'No. Why?' objected Boreth, scowling. 'You're asking us to abandon our friends for who knows how long, who knows to what end—'

'A better end than if we went with them!' Niome interrupted.

'To let them worry and wonder if we're alive or dead.' Boreth shook his head in consternation.

'It's bad enough that the people at home thought we were dead when we were gone not even a year,' said Vigh. 'Plus, Bahvley and Tharguen were gone for so long, and now us.'

'They may have been gone long, but look what it did. It got us through Mork, it saved our lives, it gave us allies and the best of funny friends,' said Niome. 'It's not like we're going for fifty years. We have no other choice!'

'We understand,' they all said after a pause. Boreth nodded, finally resigned.

'Then let's get organised,' said Jimmy, 'and figure out this number five thing, because I doubt it just means us. There is more to it, I'm sure. Perhaps this vision will also help us in years to come.'

'It was seen after you saw Elina's face, right?' said Vigh as he took out a notebook and ink jar. Niome nodded. 'Perhaps it has something to do with her?'

'But what if it has something to do with Em?' said Boreth. 'It could be good or bad. I think bad.'

'If it was that, I wouldn't have seen Elina's face,' said Niome. 'She was not sad in my vision, but normal, like always. Brave.'

'So it could have to do with Elina,' said Vigh.

'What if she was telling Niome a date, or how long we'll be gone or something?' offered Jimmy. 'The fifth day.'

'Of what, you fool?' said Meysah. 'The fifth week of the fifth season? It doesn't exist. Or the 555th of the year, which doesn't exist either?'

'Maybe it's the fifth day of the fifth week only,' said Jimmy in his own defence. 'Perhaps next season.'

'But we don't know what will happen then or where we'll be,' said Niome.

'We need to leave in five days?' suggested Meysah.

'This is useless,' said Niome, letting out a discouraged laugh. 'We're just guessing here, and I think we're missing the whole point. Perhaps it's a riddle we need to figure out, or perhaps there is no riddle and it just means us. Why look too far?'

'Or,' said Vigh, looking up from his notes, 'it's a riddle from Elina giving us hope and encouragement. The answer, I think, is you.'

'Me?' Niome tucked her chin in surprise.

'Yes. You saw Em and Elina and old Great Wizards and then five. What do Em and Elina and the old Great Wizards all have in common?' Vigh asked.

'They're Great Wizards,' Niome said conclusively.

'*Exactly,*' said Vigh. 'And not just *wizards*, but *Great* Wizards. There were endless wizards and wizardesses, and powerful ones, too, but only the most powerful earned their title of Great Wizard.' He paused briefly. 'Who were the five Great Wizards of Mork?'

'The brother of King Firlan Mittèlor, Bortah Mittèlor, who founded the Land of Morok, which later became Mork as we know it today. Moritûg – he was a scary one – tried to send magical blasts of fire to Teloria; he was the first one to create his own nature-based disasters.

'Then there was Mekhtel, who attempted to kill all the dragons single-handedly and was killed by them as he was in the process of entering the Portal with magic so powerful, he needed no spell. The dragons flew his body back to Mork, along with any stragglers who had survived, so the dragons' victory could spread throughout Mork.

'Malgar was Em's grandfather, who faked his death before being declared dead for real. He organised and led many battalions and attempted to broker a truce with Teloria on many occasions, both during his reign and after conceding rule of Mork to his grandson. And now there is Em,' said Niome. 'Funny enough, they all have names beginning with *M*. Must be a Morkan tradition.'

'Maybe,' said Vigh. 'Well, not Bortah. Well, Mittèlor . . .' He shook his head. 'Okay, now who are the five Great Wizards of Teloria?'

'Lessaguen, who thwarted Bortah Mittèlor's attacks, having predicted great armies coming from a distant kingdom. He grew to be a powerful prophet and struck down Bortah Mittèlor himself. Delivah was equally powerful in nature-based magic, born a couple of centuries after Moritûg's first few magically-created disasters. He developed his abilities in hopes of stopping Moritûg. In the end, their magics collided and they destroyed each other.

'Heessamiv was a Dragon Prophet who, aided by the power of the dragons, gave the final blow that struck down Mekhtel before the Morkan wizard could completely enter the Portal. Then there was Elina, whose power was said to be equal to Malgar's and who conquered him before his death. And then . . . there's me.'

'Both you and Em are the fifth in line,' said Vigh, 'and therefore equal. You are his perfect match.'

'Also, observe how every time a most powerful Morkan comes into being, so does a most powerful Telorian,' added Meysah. 'It's as though the dragons' magic is just that powerful, they lend their magic to ensure the protection of the Portal.'

'That's profound,' said Jimmy, wide-eyed, 'and deep magical insight. I told you you were becoming wizard-like.'

'So we have a riddle,' began Boreth, 'with many possible answers to keep in mind: us, Niome and Em, the five Great Morkan Wizards versus the five Great Telorain Wizards, wherein Niome and Em fall into the same position. It is also the only time in history where the previous Great Wizardess and Great Wizard, Elina and Malgar, were the current one's masters.' He looked over at Vigh. 'I hope you've written this down, Vigh.'

'I have. I also wrote down possible dates, just in case Jimmy's on to something.'

'So, what are we supposed to do now?' asked Meysah.

'Close the subject.'

'Forever?' Meysah's brows lifted.

'For as long as we're gone,' said Niome. 'I'll let you know when it's okay to talk about it.'

Everyone looked at each other, searching for something more to say, but there was nothing. They all nodded solemnly. The case was closed, and since there was nothing else to talk about, they all left in silence for bed.

A s soon as Niome had unlocked the door and sat down to think, Tharguen walked in. He looked at Niome and saw that she was preoccupied.

'What's the matter?' he asked. 'How come you're not asleep?'

'Uah . . . nothing.' Niome looked at him. 'I see your meeting with the Emperor took longer than expected.'

'It did. There was a lot to discuss.' Tharguen pointed a thumb behind him. 'Was that Vigh I saw out in the hall walking to his room?' Niome didn't answer. 'You knew it would take that long for me and the Emperor to discuss the Morkans' attack pattern, didn't you?' Again no reply, but Niome turned her head away.

'Niome.' Tharguen's voice was soft. 'Bahvley spoke to me about your argument with him earlier. It's fine if you have a secret meeting with the other four, but it's no longer secret if I guess it. You don't have to tell me what's going on; I just want to *understand* what's going on, and I want to understand why you can't tell me or Bahvley!' No reply. 'Niome?' Tharguen was worried.

'I can't tell anybody anything,' Niome said finally. 'I wish I could tell you, believe me, I do, but . . .' She looked at Tharguen. 'Whatever information was discussed was for Meysah, Jimmy, Vigh, Boreth and me alone to discuss.'

'So you can't even tell me a hint of what it's about?'

Niome shook her head. 'Trust me, it's for the better. You should be happy you don't know.'

'Okay then,' said Tharguen, cupping Niome's cheek with his hand. 'I understand, I think.'

And that was that. As confused as he was, Tharguen did understand in a way, and he took Niome tightly in his arms and didn't bother her about it again.

When he saw Bahvley the next morning, Tharguen was somehow able to make him understand without telling him about the secret meeting he deduced had happened, though Bahvley still insisted he had the right to know what Niome had experienced. He had even asked the Kikies to find out for him by reading Niome's mind.

What Bahvley didn't know was that they already had, with Niome's permission, so that they'd know her secret and could help protect and look after the others. She knew that since the Kikies were so full of good and cuteness, Mirauk could never feel their energy; otherwise, he would have known of their existence long before they had come to the Great Ocean Valley. That's something they all had learnt over the years: that somehow, the Kikies were immune to many evils from Mirauk. They knew how to take care of the others and encourage them without revealing any hint of knowing any secret.

Thus, Niome had decided to let them know. They were all wizards in their own way. However, they told Bahvley that in such cases they don't read people's minds, for they knew they could never speak of it. They also knew that if Bahvley could read minds, Niome would have let him know her secrets a long time ago, just so she could hear his brotherly councils, but that was not the case here. And so, an unspoken secret it remained between the Five and the Kikes.

Although none of the Five were to talk about it anymore, they thought about it every day, perhaps too much; the more they tried not to, the more it haunted them. Meysah and Jimmy even tried to find a whole nickname for it and called it *TC* for 'the change' so that they could say things like, *'Don't worry, soon enough TC will be over with!'* or, *'I'm bothered by TC!'* And that was it. In the end, however, they used it seldom, because deep inside, their fear of Mirauk's ability to feel vibes and thoughts was too great.

Meysah had been so preoccupied these past few days that he became negligent of Ihal and found himself in a very tight situation. Ihal felt that Meysah was not open with her enough. In truth, he didn't know how to deal with the fact that Ihal might go to Lóim, especially after finding out he was gone once that day came. He'd miss her greatly. How was he supposed to act around her now, knowing they would be separated for a long time?

'Meysah,' Ihal said, upset, 'either you tell me what's going on, or I don't know what's going to happen.'

'What do you mean you don't know? Ihal,' Meysah pleaded. 'There's nothing for you to worry about.'

'I know you're lying, Meysah. It's written all over your face.'

Meysah swallowed hard. 'I can't tell you.'

Ihal nodded angrily. 'Right.' She stalked off.

Meysah called after her, but she ignored his calls. Sighing, he leaned against the wall and bowed his head. He got lost in thought, alone in the corridor, until his thoughts were abruptly interrupted.

'Meysah!' came Lóim's angry shout. Meysah straightened. 'I don't know what you're playing at,' the other polc said menacingly, 'but if I were you I'd start being honest with the polc you have a relationship with.'

'Ihal spoke to you about our troubles?' said Meysah.

'Of course she did. I'm not going to stand idly by while you mistreat her like that.' Lóim's voice was filled with resentment.

'I'm not mistreating her,' Meysah said, pointing a finger at Lóim. 'I care about her. But there are some things that, as one of the Five of the Star, I cannot divulge.'

'You're certainly going about it in a very strange way,' scoffed Lóim. 'If *I* were with Ihal, I wouldn't treat her this way, shut her out like that.' He paused. 'Look, the way you've behaved hurt her. I understand if you have secrets with the other four, but don't act like you're unhappy to be with Ihal, because that's what she fears is going on. She's worried you regret your new relationship with her.'

Meysah stared at Lóim, mouth agape. 'I care, and I'm happy.'

'Then tell her! And maybe she'll believe you.'

Meysah nodded and stepped away from the wall.

'Not now; she wants to be on her own.' Lóim placed a hand to stop Meysah. 'Let her cool off first.'

'Thanks.'

'I'm not doing this for you,' Lóim said dryly before he walked away.

Meysah leaned back against the wall. 'What a mess this is!' he said to himself. He leaned his head back. 'How am I supposed to explain the unexplainable? I'll sound like an idiot!'

Meysah closed his eyes. He felt he was in quicksand, trying to get out but sinking in deeper, and he distinctly recalled what quicksand felt like.

Jimmy, on the other hand, spoke of *TC* in confidence to Gahli, even if he knew he shouldn't or that it might confuse her. All he said was that he was preoccupied with something he couldn't talk about, and that no matter what happened on the trip, it would be okay.

He was proud of how he handled things with Gahli, and yet she had no idea how he truly felt about her; they were not in a relationship like Meysah and Ihal now were. He didn't understand his friend's mess, but he certainly wouldn't get into the same situation.

'You have to trust me,' he repeated. 'I can't tell you what's going on, but trust me and know that something might happen, we don't know when, and that's the reason we're all acting oddly.'

'Okay,' said Gahli. 'I think I can help Meysah with his problem.'

'Me too,' said Jimmy.

'Meysah, listen,' said Jimmy. 'Tell her about *TC*. It won't really be breaking the magical rules. And most importantly, tell her the truth about how you feel. Fears and all.'

'But Jimmy—'

'Don't "*but Jimmy*" me. I told Gahli how I feel.'

'But you didn't tell her how you feel about her!'

'Meysah! Okay, at least I'm not denying how I feel, which you did at first, and . . . I'm not even in a relationship with her and I'm handling myself better than you are! We're not children anymore. What are you afraid of?'

'Everything.' Meysah turned away, facing outside. 'I'm afraid of not returning home.'

Meysah was right, Jimmy realised. What if they'd be gone far too long in order to succeed? What if, once they returned, Teloria was changed? They all found themselves in this unavoidable problem; it was simply that Vigh, Boreth and Niome had a lot less difficulty hiding their emotions. The truth was that the two Lords and the Wizardess were as frightened as Meysah and Jimmy were, maybe even more so, for in Vigh's and Boreth's case, being more experienced, they had a better idea of what was going to happen. Niome, on the other hand, being the bearer of the news, felt burdened. Yet somehow, she also felt confident in their success.

That night, Tharguen had a nightmare. It was about Mork, or he thought it was, but he was not completely sure since his dream kept jumping from image to image. As he slept, he tossed and turned, spoke in his sleep and had hot chills and cold sweats. He could have been picking up on Niome's vibes regarding her secret, he had mused to himself afterwards.

He dreamt that he was walking in a forest, and a phantom, stained in blood, pounced at him. He fought it off and drew his sword. Suddenly, he found himself floating in a tunnel, very much like the dragon's lair but smaller and without any purple mist. He was looking down on people, a crowd. He couldn't make out any faces, but they were all arguing. In his dream, he tried to figure out whether it was the future he was seeing.

Then he saw Selemil talking to Gorthan; that was from the past, he knew. They were discussing the fate of Teloria. It sounded like an argument about who was to go talk to Niome for missing the meeting. Then he saw Jimmy and Meysah near Darakön looking on the ground, searching for something. Vigh and Boreth were up in a tree. He saw himself again fighting the phantom, shouting out, '*Go back to Mork! Return to Mork!*' Then he saw Niome, lost, not re-membering who he was, and then everyone around her not knowing who *she* was and what she meant to them, as though she had never existed.

Tharguen woke up gasping and bolted upright. His breathing was erratic as he struggled to under-stand his dream. He looked at Niome to see she was sleeping soundly. She was so beautiful to him. He kissed her cheek and lay back down, facing her, putting his arms around her, too afraid to let her go.

When the Telorians went to the dining hall for lunch, they found Emperor Veij Majim sitting with a young woman. She was very beautiful, and her armour was as intricate as Rhal's, except where his had yellow, hers had red, and the cape that hung at her shoulders was vermillion. Similarly, the gem that hung on a pendant around her neck was red. Her umber skin had hints of a russet glow, and her face was thin and proud, but a sadness lingered in her eyes.

The Emperor stood when he saw the Telorians approach, as did she.

'May I present to you my daughter, Naëj Majim. It is her army that arrived this morning.'

The Telorians bowed politely. Naëj returned the bow.

'I came as soon as I received word from the messenger bird about my father's alliance with Teloria,' she explained after introductions had been made. 'I did not agree about the deal with Morok and thus refused to take part in any such dealings.' She looked at her father. 'Somehow, I knew they would come to their senses. I am glad to be with my family and very pleased to hear about the alliance.'

'Likewise,' said Bahvley.

The Emperor bid the Telorians join them as they continued to chat and eat.

Naëj had come in her grand sled, she explained to her new allies. She lived in the south of Dûnelor, where lay the great pond dubbed the Pool of Water, near one of the few villages that housed many of their people. Naëj was a wizardess; all three Dûnelorian rulers were magical, practising their magic differently than Telorian wizards did. Everywhere she went, Naëj brought luck, courage and protection. That was part of her power. She emitted a power to her palace that made Morkans unable to penetrate it. That's why she had come to her father so quickly – so that the grand sled could be completed and no Morkan would attack before they were completely ready for them.

Billahmyé had been telling Naëj about the Telorians, and she was very pleased to meet them. Niome saw in Naëj's eyes that she carried great woe with her, but the others did not notice the sadness, for it was hidden deep.

The Telorians also learnt that Naëj was not only powerful in presence, but she was learning to expand her magical abilities and was quite prophetical. In the beginning, she only saw things concerning her own family in dreams. Then she saw the present, events happening elsewhere; most recently, she had seen Bahvley's trip with the Kikies in her dreams while it actually happened. She was glad to meet the polc of whom she had dreamt, glad to know her dream was true and that Teloria was in such good hands.

Nowadays, Naëj saw the future. Though she did not reveal this to her new allies, Naëj had seen something that concerned Niome but didn't know that Niome knew already what was going to happen, and that saddened Naëj also. Many things, many mysteries and tragedies, whether linked to her or not, made her sad, for she had empathy for all living things. She even felt sad for the blind mindless Morkans who followed Mirauk's orders to the death when they could turn away and change their fate if they only trusted in good magic instead of evil.

Niome approached Naëj after lunch.

'What is the cause of your woe?' she asked.

'What is the reason for your asking?' replied Naëj with a stoic expression.

'I see it in your eyes that you fear the Morkans, but why worry when the Dark Lord is already losing?'

'Whether you destroy Mirauk or not, the fact remains that lives will be lost, such as it was with the event long ago that caused my entire family to lose hope, and there will be more events that will cause doubt and fear in people's hearts – the hearts of all peoples. And that may change much.'

'What sort of event?' asked Niome.

'The past one or the future one?'

'You can start with the past,' said Niome.

Naëj nodded and invited Niome to sit with her. The Dûnelorian Wizardess clasped her hands together.

'My people used to have many wizards, *Great* Wizards, and my mother was one of them,' started Naëj. 'Together they formed a bond that repelled the Morkans, even Malgar. Malgar tried once to invade, failed, and never bothered us again. Even going back to the time of the other Morkan Great Wizards, they did not enter our land.'

Naëj bowed her head. 'But with Mirauk, his might was so strong and his malice so poignant, their magic faltered, and all those wizards became evil. We were forced to kill them. Some fought back the evil power within them, and they died.' She looked at Niome. 'Never has anyone practised magic since, not like that. I am taking a great risk in doing so. We remained isolated, trying to understand how Mirauk did it, for he never set foot in Dûnelor.'

'That's why Dûnelor shut its gates to outsiders,' concluded Niome.

Naëj nodded. 'It is only recently that the Morkans came, and then only his nephews have, as you already know. Mirauk wanted to bribe and threaten us before, though, and my mother's death still grieves my father greatly. He grieved a long, long time, for he had to strike her down himself. She tried to fight back the evil within her, knowing it was not her own and did not belong to her, but in the end, it consumed her. My father only threw the last blow, protecting his children from the evil that dwelt inside her.'

Niome reached a hand to Naëj's and squeezed gently. Unsure what to say, she merely looked at her. The Dûnelorian princess smiled meagerly and nodded in thanks.

'After that event, Mirauk set another curse on us – that we all forget what happened, as though those wizards and wizardesses who died, those whom we loved and had no choice to kill, had only died of illness or old age. Few of us remember, and those of us who do,' she said, pointing at herself, 'are magical. However, not all magical Dûnelorians remember.

'I am the only one in my family to remember. Even though my father still grieves my mother's death, he does not know the true cause, how she shouted her love for him before leaping to hurt Rhal and me, before he jumped between us and her, and struck her.

'There are others in my palace who remember also. It is a shame my father and brother do not know. For even if I tried to tell them, they would not completely understand, and the grief of my mother's death will be even more of a burden than it was in the beginning. That is why I do not tell them. If Mirauk ever finds out about my abilities, I may be turned into an evil polc and become a threat to Dûnelor. I would rather die if that happened than live on. That is why I am sad.'

Niome looked at Naëj, now understanding the grief and weight the woman carried with her. She admired her courage and saw her magical power; she was a force to be reckoned with.

'Is there anything I can do to help?' asked Niome.

'You have already done much,' said Naëj, her smile warm this time. 'You are one who understands such burdens, a new ally I know I can trust. I can feel it. You are a fellow wizardess and I feel, even if we've only just met, that I can already call you my friend.'

'I'm glad of it,' said Niome. 'If ever there is anything you need of me, you only need ask.'

'Thank you,' replied Naëj. 'As for the vision I had of what is to come, it is only a concern that I have about a certain event – that is all.'

'And what sort of event is that?' asked Niome after a short pause.

'Just an event. Be careful.'

'I will be. I'm very wary of a lot of things. Perhaps I already know.'

'I hope so, for your sake,' said Naëj, 'but I cannot speak of it.'

'Nor can I,' said Niome, and a feeling of mutual understanding passed between them.

Naëj reached out to Niome and took her hands. 'I believe we share a common ability. If you will allow me to look into your eyes, please look into mine.'

Niome nodded. The two focused intently, looking past each other's eyes, and it seemed to Niome as though they could perceive each other's thoughts. Niome gleaned some advice from Naëj and hoped that she could receive hers as well.

Naëj let go of Niome's hand. 'There is much hope for Teloria, Niome Fairhaven.' She smiled amiably.

'There is much hope for Dûnelor, Naëj Majim.'

The two wizardesses chuckled. Naëj stood.

'Come, enough talk of woes. Let us take a stroll and chat of other matters – lovers, brothers, and magical prowess.'

Upon waking, Tharguen spoke to Bahvley about his nightmare.

'You speak of the future as though it's the past,' said Bahvley.

'I don't know if it's the future,' said Tharguen, 'but I'm afraid, and for the first time in my life I . . .' He stopped.

'You what? Tharguen, speak to me.' Tharguen only looked down, feeling shame. 'Do you fear for Niome's life? Do you fear for your life? Tell me!'

'I regret having stayed in Mork. I think Mirauk is trying to poison my mind, and it's working. Ever since he found out about my "betrayal", he's been trying to get at me some way or another. He's all about revenge.'

'You can always take medicine from the Kikies and it'll help you, but you can't possibly think that this is his doing.'

'I'll see if I have another dream.'

And indeed he did. This time, he was drenched in blood and crawling on the ground. He kept hearing a voice saying, *'This is what you deserve!'* And then Gorthan's voice: *'I told you something like this would happen! I warned you, didn't I?'* Perhaps it was his own subconscious telling him his own thoughts. Tharguen started to scream in the dream. There was fire all around him, a ring of fire, and everything was burning except for him.

Tharguen bounced up out of bed and ran to Bahvley's room.

'I had another one!' After explaining the particulars of this dream, he sighed. 'I think I will take that Kiki medicine.'

'Why are you telling *me?* You should be telling Niome!'

'I'm telling you because you're my best friend and . . . I feel insecure, like a child.'

Bahvley sat more upright. 'Tharguen, whatever you live, I'll live with you, and my sister will too. She needs to know about this, so tell her.'

'I love her so much, I don't want to let her go.'

'Let her go where?'

'No, let her go – stop holding her.'

'Oh. Sorry, I'm still half asleep.'

'That's okay.'

'Well, go hold her then!'

Bahvley smiled as Tharguen left and put his head back on his soft pillow. Although Tharguen's dreams troubled him as well, he let the fear pass for the present moment.

Tharguen returned to his room and sat on the bed next to Niome. He shook her gently and whispered her name. She stirred and opened her eyes, then sat up.

'What is it?' she asked.

'Bad dreams. I've been dreaming of Mork and of a whole lot of awful things. I dreamt that everyone forgot who you were, that you forgot who I was, that we were separated! I don't want to lose you.'

'You won't.'

'I fear that Mirauk will throw doom upon me in revenge. For the first time in my life, I regret having stayed in Mork.' He paused. 'I was warned of things like this.'

Tharguen, for just a brief moment, drifted into a memory.

* * *

'Tharguen, you don't know what you're getting yourself into!'

'Gorthan, I won't change Bahvley's mind, because you won't change mine. We are going to Mork. We already have a whole big team ready.'

'You're too young! I can't afford to lose a good fighter like you.' The polc placed his fists on his hips.

'Trust me. Good things can come of this. You'll be happy I went.'

'Anything can happen, Tharguen. Good things *and* bad things. I fear for you; it saddens me. What if you die? What if you fail? I'm not saying you will, but what if you get trapped or discouraged? *Whatever happens there will haunt you for the rest of your life.*'

'What could possibly happen that will haunt me?'

'I don't know, Tharguen. I'm no prophet.'

'You're skilled and have been through a lot. Why don't you come with us, Gorthan?'

'I can't – you know I can't. My place is here in Teloria City. You have to be careful.'

'Hey, how many people have I saved and helped so far?' Tharguen grinned, cocky.

'Yes, I know, but you may do some things that you might live to regret. People do foolish things sometimes when unaware of the things around them. You'll be focusing strictly on your life as a priority. Survival. I know how people feel in the midst of battle. You will be helping, but you may unwittingly do something terrible and live to see the dreadful outcome.'

'I'll be careful, then.'

'Extremely careful!' This was clearly intended as an order.

'Hey, you're the Chief, but I'm the one who will survive this trip. Maybe you and Selemil and Henker are afraid for us, but I know that Bahvley and I will survive. I can feel it, and I hope and I'm sure that the others will too. We'll go and be back before you know it. I mean, we're talking about Liffwai and Queevsil, and Cahti, and all of your best apprentices, Gorthan.'

'That's why I'm afraid.'

* * *

'Tharguen?' said Niome. Tharguen was brought back to the present moment, realising now the truths behind Gorthan's words. He had been younger than Meysah was today back then, as young as Meysah and Jimmy were when they had left for Mork, perhaps too young still. Yet good *had* come of it, but so had so much bad.

'Gorthan warned me of such things, and now I have to face them. I live, yes, but to regret them.' Niome looked confused. 'Promise me you won't do anything you'll regret.'

'I promise.'

'And be careful out there.'

'Tharguen, what are you talking about?' Niome wondered if he somehow knew of or sensed her change of plans.

'I don't know.' Tharguen gently placed his hand on her cheek. 'I love you. I love you, Niome, and no matter what happens to any of us, promise me you'll never forget me.'

'How could I possibly forget you, Tharguen? I love you. You are forever in my heart and in my thoughts, even when I'm not thinking of you. It grieves me to see you like this.' Niome wanted to say, *'I'll miss you!'* but she only repeated, 'I love you.'

Tharguen took her in his arms and held her tightly for a long time. A tear trickled down his cheek. He leaned his cheek on hers.

'There's something I want you to have,' he said softly.

He reached into his pouch and pulled out a ring, a beautiful ring with emerald gems on it. Niome gaped, awestruck, as Tharguen took her left hand, holding her ring finger.

'I found it in the Tweedle Woods. Call it a fluke, but I think that old ghost put it there purposely. I wouldn't be surprised if a spell came with it.' He smiled and slipped the ring on Niome's finger. 'This is my promise to you, to love you for the rest of my life. And when we're back home in Teloria, to bind that love to you with magic.'

Niome smiled. 'I'd love nothing more. I promise it, too.'

She wished she could say more but did not think she could express it adequately, so much was there to say. They simply held each other tightly and kissed, and for a while they blissfully forgot about anything that troubled them.

* * *

When the sun came up, the Telorians set to work on their business, but as the day progressed, the more nervous Niome felt. Each heartbeat seemed like a thousand; she wondered if the others could hear it. This was the Telorians' last day in Dûnelor. They would leave tomorrow, on the fifty-sixth day of Summer.

Niome was afraid of what lay ahead and did not wish to go, even though she knew she must. Niome wanted to stay in Tharguen's arms all day, and she held onto him very tightly that morning, but the two Lords were better at controlling their emotions. However, Meysah wanted to crawl into a hole and hide. He isolated himself and sat alone the entire morning. Jimmy had to literally drag him out.

'Don't let you-know-what bother you so much!' encouraged Jimmy. 'Forget about it all, just for today.'

Jimmy dragged Meysah to the room where most of their friends had gathered.

'So what's this secret?' asked Mittah.

Meysah had to hand it to Tharguen – he had picked very sharp polcs, smart and quick.

'Yeah, we want to know,' Lóim said eagerly.

'All about this apparent surprise,' added Malcolm.

Not to mention how fast word travels between them, Meysah thought.

'And what's up with your brother and sister, Meysah?' asked Pete.

They all blurted out their questions almost simultaneously, but Meysah heard them all.

'Hey,' said Meysah, 'whatever arguments go on between them, I don't know of, and don't bombard me with questions! If Bahvley and Niome argue, it's probably about an issue for him, the King, and her, the Great Wizardess, alone. It doesn't concern me.'

'There he goes again with his arrogance,' said Lóim, rolling his eyes. 'His brother the *King* and his sister the *Great Wizardess*.'

'How is that being arrogant?' Meysah asked, exasperated.

'If you weren't so caught up with yourself,' Lóim said pointedly, 'you wouldn't have anything to hide from us, especially from Ihal.'

'What does this have to do with—'

'Okay! Let's forget about that,' said Jimmy. 'I mean, lads, tomorrow we're leaving on a new adventure!'

However, everyone continued to hassle them about the so-called surprise. Luckily, they had noticed Niome's ring that afternoon and told the others about it. However, Ihal still suspected Meysah was hiding more from her, and Meysah's situation kept getting worse as the day progressed. He and Ihal were very much alike, and both of them knew very well that each of them was, at this point, too hard-headed to consider somebody else's advice.

Meanwhile, Niome was creating more tension between her and Bahvley, and Tharguen could only think of his nightmares.

He walked about gathering his team to speak to them. He led them to a large room.

'I hope you're all ready for this trip.'

'All our things are already packed, Captain,' said Huck.

'I'm talking about your souls, your hearts, and your minds.'

'Oh.'

'Many perils lie ahead. Many secrets are being kept from us. This may be to protect us, but it also means danger is coming our way. We have to be ready for the worst.'

Suddenly, Ihal had a certain understanding about Meysah, as though all this disastrous argument was simply because he wanted to protect her. She looked at Gahli, who was whispering with Tom, and she seemed to have the same resolve on her face about Jimmy keeping secrets to protect her. Ihal sighed. How could she have been so self-centred? She felt sad now.

'You make it sound so irksome.'

'Yes, Mittah,' said Tharguen. 'The phantoms are irksome indeed. Remember them? Bahvley spoke to me of them. And lately, I have been having dreams, and what I described to Bahvley that I saw in those dreams were definitely, according to him, those creatures. We have to beware, because if they are what I think I got a glimpse of in Mork, they are very dangerous.'

'What are they?' asked Pete.

'I don't know,' replied Tharguen. 'But I believe they are somehow linked to Mirauk's mind. I don't want to lose any of you, ever. That battle with the

Dukes was just the first of many we are going to emerge victorious from together.'

'But I thought it was going to be a fun and safe trip!' voiced Jeremy.

'So did I,' said Tharguen. He lowered his voice a good notch. 'Something has been going on in Niome's mind. Maybe she foresees something, but she is strange of late and we must keep an eye on her. Remember, the Morkans aren't just after me, but after Niome, Jimmy, Meysah, Boreth, Vigh and also Bahvley. We will have to keep a close watch at night and make sure they're safe. Do you understand?' Tharguen's last question was a troubled one, and he could hear his own sadness in his tone.

The Telorians acknowledged his words, and Tharguen nodded. Some admitted they were not ready after all, never having realised the implications, but reassured each other that they would prepare for the worst but hope for the best; Bahvley had said the maxim several times. Though he knew not what the worst was, Tharguen assured himself that they would find out once it had happened, but having prepared, they would be ready – or so he hoped.

Ihal went to find Meysah, who looked up at her in mild surprise. She smiled, then walked up to him and kissed him for a long while – they wrapped their arms around each other, hands passing through each other's hair.

'What's that for?' he asked when they'd finally pulled away.

'For being stupid and stubborn!' He scowled in confusion. 'Captain Tharguen had a chat with us and he told us that there were many secrets being held from us in order to protect us, protect him, protect Bahvley and the rest of us. I need to know the truth, Meysah. I know you're keeping something from me. Is it to protect me?'

'You, Teloria, and everyone else. I truly can't talk about it; Niome had us vow on our lives.' He paused. 'I'm sorry. I've been a right fool about the whole situation.'

'Me and all,' replied Ihal.

Meysah gave Ihal a sideways grin. 'Am I forgiven, then?'

'Maybe.'

'What?' His eyes widened.

'I'll think about it.' Ihal smiled coyly.

'Well, in the meantime,' said Meysah trying not to roll his eyes, 'can I hold you in my arms?'

Ihal didn't reply but took his arms and wrapped them around her.

At the first sign of dawn, Yém, old as he was, was up and wide awake. Wasting no time, he went to every Telorian and woke them up. Niome wondered how it was that such an old polc had so much energy and was always safe. Even Henker and Drúgan were slower and less carefree.

Elina had spoken to Niome of such people when she was much younger. As she thought about it, she remembered Elina's words.

Silegena *appear to anyone in necessary times. They will seem to pop out of nowhere, and disappear into nowhere. They will never reveal an age, for they have none, because they are just there. They will be bright and smart, friendly yet wary and won't talk much of their past. They will play their part until they are no longer needed.*

Then she heard her own voice asking: *But do they only exist for that time and for those people?*

No, Niome. They are actual real polcs, but the spirit of great polcs live inside of them. They're usually simple polcs with no special life or title, and who don't possess any magic, but they're born with the wisdom, and sometimes prophetic *wisdom, of lords, kings, queens, wizards and druids who died long ago but never became stars, and that lord or wizard lives in them, in a way. But it isn't like being possessed or anything like that; it's simply a spirit residing in a host as an observer whilst lending one's wisdom.*

It had always been a myth no one had ever truly known for sure, because these folks were always so mysterious. Now Niome realised it was no myth, and she wondered which noble person, or persons, lived in Yém, or perhaps it didn't matter.

In any case, he was certainly a *Legena*. And Emperor Billahmyé Veij Majim, proud ruler of Dû-nelor, had recognised Yém as a worthy merchant after his aid during their recent battle and offered him to be part of his court. But the modest merch-ant turned down the offer. Yém explained he enjoyed his simple life as it was and needed no change to make it better, but he would not hesitate to knock on the doors of the Emperor's majestic palace if ever he needed to.

Emperor Veij Majim lent his visitors sleds for the trip out of Dûnelor; Yém had the one in the lead. A few guards went with them to bring the sleds back afterwards, though Yém was told he could keep his, a gift from the Emperor that the old merchant appreciated.

Captain Loyfeij and Officer Grayt bid the Telorians farewell.

'I am pleased to have found a distant cousin,' said Officer Grayt with a smile.

'Me too,' replied Malcolm, embracing the Dûnelorian.

'Safe travels, distant cousin,' said Grayt as Malcolm beamed at him.

Rhal gave the Telorians his best wishes at the door.

'I hope we have not inconvenienced you too much by our ignorance,' said Rhal. 'I am glad to have befriended you and am truly grateful for your help.'

'So are we,' said Tharguen. 'And no, there has been no inconvenience. Besides, it was justified, given our history, and I myself have learnt a lot, thanks to you. The Morkans would've come anyway, looking for us wherever we were at whichever time. We're glad we were here to aid you when you needed us.'

Rhal smiled and nodded. 'Have a safe trip,' he began. 'And my greatest apologies, once again, for all of you whom we kept prisoner. I feel awful about it, and I am pretty sure I have repeated that many times.'

'As I've repeated to you that I am the one who apologises,' said Tharguen.

He held his hand out to Rhal, but instead of clasping it, Rhal stepped forward and embraced Tharguen warmly. The two smiled at each other.

'You're a good polc with good intentions,' Gahli said to Rhal. 'Do me a favour: find yourself someone. *She* would have wanted it.'

'Thank you. I will consider it.'

And off the Telorians went to go join their dear Firlanian friends.

*I*t took the host of travellers a week to get back to the green fields, where the Five were reluctant to step foot, knowing their dreadful path that lay ahead. They sat in the sleds, silent, pensive, burdened and woeful. The others seemed unaware of their internal struggles save for Bahvley and Tharguen, who had their own worries to contend with.

The Kikies' hearts were heavy, for they knew all but could not tell nor comfort. As for Yém, he seemed to be in his own little blissful world. Now that Niome knew Yém was one of the rare *Silegena*, who had hearts where only good reigned and evil could never reach, she was ever more comforted by his presence. She knew that they would be safe as long as they were in Yém's company. If it hadn't been for the fact that she had to leave the others, she would have asked him to come along, but his destiny lay in Dûnelor. Billahmyé, Rhal, and Naëj needed him to stay and protect the lands, if only by the essence of his presence.

The company disembarked the sleds as Yém and the guards attached them together for an easier ride home. After a brief farewell, the Telorians started off.

Yém clutched Niome by the arm, turning her around. He inclined his head forward and gazed at her intently.

'Do what you have to do,' he said. 'Your friends know what *they* have to do. The Star will thrive.'

Niome wondered how Yém knew about the change of plans. Perhaps he didn't. Anyone could have said those words and meant anything by them, but it was the tone in his voice, cautious yet reassuring at the same time, that told Niome he knew. There was a grin on the side of Yém's mouth that quickly spread into his usual warm smile. Niome thought she saw a glint of might reflected in his eyes.

'Is everything all right?' he asked

Niome smiled. 'It is. I just thought, for a moment, I saw a different face in you.'

'Well, you know, we Dûnelorians at my age can look quite alike.' He winked. 'Besides,' continued Yém, 'I am no Melthaneij, you know. He was something, but that's a story for another time. Take care of yourself. I will see you later, however long that may be.'

Niome thought for a moment. Melthaneij was an old Dûnelorian warrior of whom Rhal had spoken. Perhaps Yém was not a *Legena* as Niome had originally thought, given his age, whatever that was, but perhaps he *was* Melthaneij – old and simple now, his days of battle long gone. She felt certain no one knew for sure, but Niome would find out, at the end of the war. This was something she would put aside for now; there were more pressing matters to deal with first.

Smiling, Yém turned around and walked away to the sleds. Niome joined the others.

The plains ahead seemed dead and empty like a cemetery of green tombs with its patches of dryer grass here and there. Several days passed, and an itch for chanting and merrymaking overcame many of the Telorians. They had no ale with them, but Tom figured the upbeat energy would be contagious and help ease the worry he observed in the Five, Tharguen and Bahvley.

Huck approached Tharguen, who was walking way ahead alongside Bahvley.

'Captain! Sing us a song, will you?'

'A song?'

'Uh-huh,' said Jackley. 'Like you always do when we're travelling.'

'Let me see,' said Tharguen, chuckling. Many of his team members quickened their steps to join him as they walked. 'Oh, I know.'

> *The Sun may be setting,*
> *The wind may be blowing–*

'No, not a sad song!' Malcolm interrupted. 'Some of us are down in the dumps enough as it is.'

'It's not a sad song!' protested Tharguen. 'The tune is far from sad. It's a love ballad.' He looked back at Niome, who was quite behind with some others, and felt a touch of sadness in his heart that he could not explain.

'Well, nothing emotional,' said Jeremy. 'Or with a saddish tune.'

'Sing something happy, something with step, to make us feel giddy,' said Huck.

'I know a jolly song!' Bahvley exclaimed. 'It's a lovely Telorian song I taught the Kikies while I was in their continent. It goes something like this . . .'

> *Tap-thump-pit go my feet,*
> *until I stop to eat;*
> *As I walk and as I run,*
> *racing with the Sun.*

'Oh, we know that one!' shouted Jackley. 'Why don't we all sing it?'

'Yes, why don't we!' said Forthil excitedly.

'We Kikies want to sing, too,' said Tithil.

They all started singing, recreating the sounds of funny instruments quite accurately with their mouths and with their feet as they bounced around and sang loudly and merrily. The happiness did indeed spread, for Meysah and Jimmy, looking up and at each other, ran up and joined in, and eventually Niome did too, as did Vigh and Boreth after a while.

Tap-thump-pit go my feet,
until I stop to eat;
As I walk and as I run,
racing with the Sun!

Clip-clop-stomp goes my horse,
galloping with wind's force;
To a marvellous land,
where I'll sing with the band!

Slump-swish-sloosh go we both,
in rain or snow go we forth;
The puddles grow as rain falls
on the walls of beautiful halls!

Tap-clop-swoosh we are here,
arrived at our friends dear;
Let us all go back out,
and do it again, as we come about!

And the chant started again, this time at a slower tempo, and the third time it was sung extremely fast. Everyone was stumbling on their words as they sang, and some were out of breath.

Gahli plopped down onto the grass. 'I need a few moments to catch my breath.'

'Let's have a bite to eat,' offered Bahvley, panting and laughing. He lifted his flask and gulped down some water.

'Mighty Spirit, that was fun!' said Jimmy.

'Why does everyone always say that? "Mighty Spirit" this or that?' Lóim mused.

'Uh, maybe because she's the Mighty Spirit,' replied Jimmy sassily, as though it should be obvious.

'Yes, but people also say "Stars" or "Magic",' replied Lóim, placing a fist on his hip.

'No one says "Magic" like that,' laughed Jimmy. 'Why would anyone exclaim to "Magic"?'

'Oh dear,' muttered Ihal.

'Because magic exists in everything and creates everything,' said Lóim, as though this should also be obvious.

'Here we go,' said Mittah as the two young knights gained an audience.

'Magic didn't create anything!' objected Jimmy. 'The Mighty Spirit did.'

'So we assume,' argued Lóim, 'but she used magic, and it obviously existed before she did.'

'What are you on about?! The Mighty Spirit existed before anything else did. *She* created magic.'

'She created *with* magic!' Lóim insisted.

Jimmy scowled. 'Are you saying the Mighty Spirit doesn't exist?'

'Not quite what he said,' warned Ihal.

Meysah and Bahvley exchanged a dubious glance before Meysah looked back at Jimmy, unsure of whether this argument was going to remain a friendly one or degenerate into something worse.

'All I'm saying is, we don't know that the Mighty Spirit created everything herself. That's all,' Lóim responded.

'But she's the Mighty Spirit!' insisted Jimmy. 'She created the world.'

'Who created the Mighty Spirit? Huh?' Lóim asked quickly.

'Okay, suppose we explore that,' said Jimmy, becoming aware that everyone's eyes were on them. 'Did magic create the Mighty Spirit, or did the Mighty Spirit create magic?'

'We don't really know, eh?' said Lóim with a satisfied smirk. 'So, you can't say it's definitely the Mighty Spirit.'

'Then you can't say it's definitely magic – ahah!' Jimmy laughed in triumph.

'You know,' said Meysah, stepping between the two of them, 'maybe there is truth to what both of you believe. It occurs to me now that maybe they both helped each other create the world.'

'Thank you,' said Lóim. 'I'm glad to see at least *someone*' – he turned from Meysah to Jimmy, emphasising every word – 'keeps an open mind.'

'Besides,' continued Meysah, his voice becoming grave, 'does it really matter who created everything we hold dear? I think what matters right now is who's trying to destroy it.'

There was a pause. 'You have a point there, Meysah,' admitted Lóim. 'A very valid one at that.' He turned to Jimmy. 'Let's agree we don't know and we're both exploring the possibilities.'

Meysah was somewhat surprised at Lóim's agreement, and he appreciated it.

'I can do that,' said Jimmy. 'It takes advocates of possibilities to explore the truth sometimes.'

To Meysah's surprise, Lóim held out his hand, and he and Jimmy shook hands.

'You know, I never thought I'd say this, but you're all right, Lóim. Not the bully I thought you'd always be.'

'Yeah, well, you're not so bad yourself, Meysah.' He smiled. 'On the most part,' he added.

'On the most part?' Meysah exclaimed. Lóim shrugged. The two chuckled, smiling at each other.

'Now that we're all friends,' said Jimmy, 'can we get back to figuring out what existed first and what created the world?'

'Magic existed first. It exists in all things,' said Lóim. 'Or so we're taught.'

'But dragons brought magic, and the Mighty Spirit created them, so *she* existed first,' Jimmy argued.

'Unless the dragons are embodiments of the Mighty Spirit,' said Lóim.

'Hey, I think you're onto something,' Jimmy said, pointing at Lóim, who was nodding back emphatically.

Meysah shook his head, chuckling to himself.

Tom let out a breath. 'That could have gone far worse,' he whispered.

'Let's thank the stars,' whispered Ihal, 'but not too loudly.' She and Tom exchanged a laugh.

* * *

In the evening, the group set up a campfire and sat around it. Several of the younger knights had demanded a story. Bahvley had already told them most of his Kiki stories, Tharguen only knew stories about the darks of Mork, and the Kikies had never done this sort of 'ritual', as they called it. That left Vigh and Boreth, who had been around long enough to collect a repertoire of interesting stories, and thus they began.

'It was twenty years ago . . .' started Vigh in a serious and mysterious voice.

'Well, no, it was twenty-five,' corrected Boreth.

'No, twenty!'

'Twenty-five. I remember because it was when my old horse died.'

'Fine, how about you start the story?'

'All right.' Boreth changed his tone to match Vigh's mysterious atmosphere. 'It was twenty-five years ago, and Vigh and I were travelling south to help clean out the rubble from the broken wall. When we got to Lani, one of our friends told us that the broken wall had created a cave in the Free Fields, and that strange wailing was coming from it. Moaning and crying and sighing, as if Morkans were trapped in there, or perhaps Telorians.'

'And no one dared to go near it,' continued Vigh. 'You could hear the strange sounds away from Lani, even. It terrified everyone. But *we* dared to venture to it and *into* it to discover what devilry lay inside. There was no clear way into the cave; we had to dig a hole in the ground and go under the boulders.

Once inside, we could barely see, but our eyes adjusted.' His tone suddenly became more casual. 'Especially Boreth's – he has excellent night vision.' Vigh resumed his foreboding narration, 'We walked quietly through the labyrinth of rocks and boulders. It became stuffy and more difficult to breathe.'

'Especially the place where we had to swim to get under more rocks. And after that, Vigh went one way and I went another, in two different clear paths that led to two more different paths. We both turned back to report this, but it seemed a wall of stone had appeared – a wall that hadn't been there originally and was suddenly there on our way back.'

'Wooh, that's disturbing,' commented Tom.

'We each walked for a while, trying to choose good paths,' said Vigh. 'I went always right, of course; it's the way to go in a labyrinth. Boreth went always left – a good thing, for we met up again. Here the soil was softer, but as we walked, we heard a strange sort of thump, like a person knocking on something, trying to get out, but no one was there.'

'No, the soil thing was after the raining pebbles,' Boreth noted.

'Boreth, that's after. The pebbles are after.'

'I thought it was before. So, I guess not. You see' – Boreth lowered his tone again – 'we were walking and pebbles started to rain down on us. A downpour, and we had to run through, and it didn't stop. The pebbles kept on raining down. When we stood safe from the pebbles, a foot away it still rained pebbles. Then we stepped on something strange and realised what it was when the skull rolled away: a Morkan's skeleton, with pieces of its dark cape still intact.'

'Maybe the whiner was finally dead,' said Jimmy.

'No, because the moaning still went on,' said Vigh, 'and it got louder and louder as we got closer and closer to the source of the terror. And then we saw it.'

Vigh and Boreth paused dramatically.

'Well,' prompted Meysah, 'what was it? A ghost?'

'Several ghosts?' asked Lóim.

Boreth picked up a few rocks from the ground and created a funny-shaped kind of wall. He took it into his hands and blew between the cracks, creating a strange shriek.

'An air hole!' Boreth announced in victory. 'It was the wind of Colouring passing through a few tiny spaces that sounded like moaning when echoing through the cave of fallen boulders.' He and Vigh laughed.

'But the pebbles?' asked Ihal.

'A shower of dust from the slowly still crumbling and eroding wall outside, seeping in through the cracks,' explained Vigh.

'And the mysterious walls?' asked Pete.

'It was night,' Boreth said, 'and everything looked the same. We stopped midway, changing our angles, and there was a wall in front of us, but we were only *facing* the wall instead of facing the path. We took a wrong turn, that's all. But we panicked then and turned back, instead of thinking rationally.' He grinned. 'Vigh and I tend to think in the same way, we know each other so well. That's true partners for you – make the same choices and the same mistakes. Some of us, however, are more advanced.'

'Sure,' said Vigh. They both laughed hard, sharing an inside joke.

'Did this really happen?' asked Mittah sceptically.

'It did! It did!' Both Lords laughed.

'That's what's so funny about it!' said Vigh. 'And then we had to find our way back, feeling silly and still spooked.'

'Though, what's truly strange about it,' said Boreth, 'is that we never found out what the knocking sound had been or where it came from. It stopped. And we had figured everything else out, but that one, we could just never explain.'

'Maybe there actually *was* a ghost,' said Jimmy.

'I don't know if I believe in ghosts,' Jeremy added.

'That's because you never met Bob Tweedle,' said Meysah. 'Either that, or it scares you.'

'Well, I don't know if I'll sleep tonight,' Lóim said jokingly.

'There's a moral to this story,' Boreth said, bringing everyone's attention back. 'Never assume the worst. Fear easily gets in the way; you have to ignore it and be bold. Never let fear stop you. For anything.'

'Just when you think you'll get your fill of thrill,' said Forthil, 'the story ends up funny.'

'What's even funnier is all your Kiki laughs and astonishments!' said Niome. 'It's cute.'

'Well, there are twenty basic Kiki laughs,' said Mië, 'and then there are modifications, variations, personalisations . . . you know?'

'And there are ten basic Kiki cries with *their* own variations and all,' said Mimulus. 'I used to be called the very expert because I was a crybaby as a child.'

The Telorians laughed with each Kiki demonstration of their cries and laughs.

The Telorians continued their journey the next few days in good spirits. As the days went by, however, the Sun got hotter, the air got dryer, the Telorians got thirstier, the Kikies needed to go into their magical jar and by now, everyone was starting to run out of water. The only upside was that it wasn't humid, so the heat wasn't quite as draining as it could have been.

This was all due to a spell Niome would whisper to herself twice a day, morning and night. Had she known the Morkan spell to part the water and open the secret door, she would not have needed to do this, but her skills were still limited and this was the only way she and the other four would get into the secret Morkan tunnels.

Bahvley was hoping it would rain, even if it meant more humidity; perhaps it would mean cooler weather too. However, no clouds appeared in the sky; it was abnormally clear. Many grew worried. When they reached the Stream of Fluidity, they noticed that the water was lower than usual, but still they filled their flasks and drank as much as they needed.

When the host of travellers reached the Ortim River, they saw that the river was so low that one could jump in and touch the bottom without getting more than half their body wet. One could walk right across it to the other side. As they continued on, the water continued to drain.

They arrived at their appointed meeting place across from the road that led to the first forest of the Firlan border on their appointed date, the third day of the second week of Summer.

Perhaps they were early, Bahvley had thought, for the day was young and their Firlanian friends had not yet arrived. Or maybe their friends were fashionably late. So, the Telorians settled down to wait. But after a few days, they began to worry.

Niome spent her time by the edge of the drying river, focusing her energy on it – it was not yet knee-deep – and scanning it with her eyes in an attempt to find the entrance she'd seen in her vision. Summer was drawing to an end, and the rainy period had not yet begun. She did not wish to extend this drought longer than necessary.

Now she sat with the other four as they conferred in hushed tones.

'Evil's drawing near. I can feel it,' Tom said to Mittah. 'I sense it. Something will happen soon.'

'I'm just glad that Meysah and Ihal have reconciled,' replied Mittah. 'This trip would've been horrible had they not.'

'You don't seem to realise what I'm saying,' remarked Tom. 'I'm being seriously serious here.' He jutted his neck out at the double emphasis. 'Something dreadful is about to occur, but I can't pinpoint what it is; I'm not as advanced in magic as I'd like to be. But I'm picking up perplexing energy coming from Niome. You remember what Captain Tharguen said? We have to keep an eye on the Five.'

Tom and Mittah looked over at the Five.

'I don't have a good feeling about them being so close to the river like that,' said Tom. 'Something might happen.'

Tom and Mittah joined their friends and at their suggestion, they all got back to safe lands.

Niome had found the secret entrance and had shown the other four where it was. She had instructed them to say their goodbyes, as it were, for today was all the time they had left to spend with the others.

Meysah went to see Ihal. Even though they had long since reconciled, he still feared that Lóim would take advantage of the fact he'd be gone, so much so that he did not want Lóim near him at all, for it reminded him of his insecurity. Luckily, no fight was started, for he and Lóim could share friendlier banter now, and Lóim left the two alone. Meysah kissed Ihal many times, showering her with his love.

After a while, Meysah went to see Jimmy, who stood alone.

'You're not with Gahli?'

'She needed to talk to Ihal and Mittah for a while.' Jimmy looked at the ground and up again. He had a serious look on his face. 'Meysah, why do we have to do this? Why *are* we doing this? Tell me again, because these are supposed to be happy times.'

'I don't feel eager, either. But we're doing this for the others, to lead the phantoms back here and save the others from them in that way, and to save Darakön. The dragons are perhaps our truest allies.'

'Is that *it*?'

'What do you mean "Is that it?" We're part of the Star. We're saving the world, restoring the Freedom of Life!'

'Yeah, well . . . ' Jimmy bowed his head. 'I wish someone else would've joined you.'

'Jimmy, what are you talking about? You don't mean that, do you? I mean, your dreams are in the process of coming true and—'

'It's a burden on my heart to have to leave everyone else behind without them knowing of this!' Jimmy looked up from the ground at Meysah. 'I know I was meant to join you, and I'll always be by your side, it's just . . .' He shook his head. 'Who shall I ask to look after Gahli? Who shall you ask to look after Ihal? We can't ask the Kikies; they can't come out of their jar. This weather'll kill them.'

'I don't know, Jimmy. I'm worried, too.'

'There you are!' Tom strode up to them. He furrowed his brows. 'What's the worry about?'

Meysah and Jimmy exchanged a quick glance.

'If anything were to happen and we were incapable of looking after Gahli or Ihal,' said Jimmy, 'would you . . . ?' He trailed off.

'Look after them? Sure, anytime. You sense it, too, eh?'

'Sense what?' asked Meysah.

'The danger that approaches us. I can feel it, too. It's the wizard in us that allows us to pick it up when others cannot.'

'Yes, we sense it too,' said Jimmy.

'So tell me, Jimmy, when are you going to tell Gahli how you feel about her?'

When night came, the Five could hardly find sleep, even if they knew they needed this rest. They had spent the rest of the day with the other Telorians, trying to make the most of the time they had left, but it didn't feel like enough.

Vigh lay on his back looking up at the stars. Meysah saw he was awake and went to lie down beside him, flat on his back like his master was.

'Master Vigh, why is this so hard?'

'Because you're in love. You have an emotional attachment. When feelings are involved, it can become more difficult to focus on an already difficult task.'

'I have this lump in my throat, and I . . . it's so hard to go! I'm afraid.'

'I know,' said Vigh, his voice soft with sympathy. 'I know how you feel, Meysah. Afraid that you'll never see her again, afraid that she'll forget about you and go with someone else, afraid that she might die. But the worst is that she'll disappear.'

'You were in love,' stated Meysah, deducing.

'Yes.'

'What happened?'

'I don't know. Shortly after Boreth was found and freed, during the Big War, we left on a mission to uncover information and free many prisoners, and we ambushed many Morkan armies. But when we got back, she was gone.'

'What do you mean by that?'

'Just that: she was gone. She died, I think, but see, nowhere was her body. No one saw her die, yet thousands of Telorians were everywhere. I searched among the dead day and night. I searched in and out of Teloria; I looked everywhere. She had just . . . disappeared. I asked everyone and they all said that she disappeared. Perhaps she was taken, but with all those cells in the Prison Tower, I doubt I would've found her, so I didn't look for her. I doubt by now she'd still be alive.'

'Why didn't you ever talk about her before?'

'Because the grief is still too hard to bear, even if it was a long time ago, for I truly loved her.' Vigh swallowed. 'I have not healed yet. That's why I avoid the topic.' He paused. 'I don't think about her much anymore. I was very distracted when I was in love; I sometimes found it hard to commit to my knightly duties. Now, I prefer not to get involved with anyone, and I haven't had romantic feelings for anyone since.'

'But you could move on and get over this sorrow.'

'There's nothing to get over anymore,' snapped Vigh. 'I've made up my mind. I'm not falling into the trap of falling in love again.'

Meysah hesitated before speaking, for he thought Vigh was sobbing. It seemed to Meysah that Vigh was *not* over his pain, that he wished and longed for love yet could not forget his lost love.

'What was her name?' Meysah asked after several moments.

'Tallelah.' There was a long pause. 'Get some sleep, Meysah. You need it.'

Night passed, and those who were keeping watch over the Five fell asleep. At the first sign of light, when the sky was still dark but marble coloured, Niome rose and woke the other four. They stood aside as she cast a spell on the others so they would sleep longer. She had cast it mildly on those keeping watch, but now it put the rest into a profound slumber.

The Five gathered their things.

'I can't look back,' said Meysah. 'If I do, I'll end up staying.'

'Let's go,' said Boreth, sighing. He felt bad for the boys, but his love was elsewhere. This was not as difficult for him as it was for the younger ones. He turned to go. 'Niome?'

Niome now stood still, looking at all the others as they slept. She had tears in her eyes. She went to Tharguen and kissed his brow.

'I love you,' she whispered.

Then she went to the low bank of the river.

'The sooner we get this done, the sooner it'll all be over,' said Boreth. 'And in no time we'll be back at home, along with everyone else.'

They started down the riverbank and into the low river. They walked a short while, then stopped in front of the hatch on the ground a few feet away from where the water was. It was very well hidden. Niome unlocked all its metal bolts with a spell and lifted it, then peered inside.

'Coast's clear,' she announced. 'There's a ladder. It looks old, so watch your step.'

Jimmy went first, then Vigh, Meysah and Boreth. Niome slipped in last and closed the hatch.

Niome then released her spell. The Five heard the rushing water from the other side of the hatch as a roaring wave began filling the river back up, waking everyone on the bank.

Tharguen bounced up and looked around, immediately noticing the absence of the Five.

'Oh, no. Wake up! *Wake up!!*'

Everyone awoke abruptly. The river was filling as the wind began to blow and clouds began to roll in.

Tharguen ran to the river and watched as it filled up loudly. Many joined him. He searched for Niome, Meysah, Jimmy, Boreth and Vigh, but he could not see them. Niome had just been in his arms. He returned to camp and scolded those who had been keeping watch.

'Calireth! Peyvil! Why did you fall asleep?'

'We don't know! We don't understand.' Calireth was stunned and felt ashamed; it was her first time keeping watch in the night, and she had felt so proud to do it.

'Tharguen!' shouted Bahvley. 'It could've been a spell.'

'A spell? From Mirauk? So he can capture them in the night? Creating a drought for whatever sinister and obscure reason, and now he lets the water fill up when we can no longer save them?! And where have they gone!' Tharguen grasped the Kiki jar and got them out. They watched, deeply saddened by Tharguen's desperation. 'Had the Kikies been out, they could've done something, but Mirauk's spell on the weather would've killed them!' He grabbed his hair, breathing through his teeth before shouting. 'What has he done to them, Bahvley? What has Mirauk done!'

Tharguen had shouted so loud, Bahvley could've sworn Mirauk had heard him from Mork.

'This is indeed ill-favoured news,' said Celor.

'Oh, no!' said Tithil as he looked into the distance. He turned to the others in dismay. 'I don't think our friends will be meeting us.'

'Why not?' asked Bahvley.

'My far-seeing Kiki eyes see smoke and fire!'

'What?' exclaimed Tharguen.

'The forest is on fire, the north tip of it.' Forthil and the other Kikies exchanged a saddened glance.

'So not only does Mirauk dry up the river and capture our dearest and most beloved of friends, but he causes a fire also?!' Tharguen exclaimed in disbelief. His shoulders slumped and he hunched over, shaking with grief. 'He's out to get me, just like Merlik told me. All for spite.'

'This is certainly the worst that events have been,' noted Celor, 'and this fire is certainly the doing of Mirauk himself.' Celor knew Mirauk had taken advantage of the drought; he knew that Niome would not have wanted to cause this. He shut his eyes tightly. 'It takes a lot to infuriate a Kiki. He knows how to push us.'

'That Mirauk knows our wrath,' declared Mië. 'For now he destroys nature. It grieves me to see it suffering thus.'

Tharguen searched for answers, but his mind could not settle down.

'There's only one thing left for us to do,' he said as he stared at the river, 'and that's to go help where we can, if we can. If it's not too late.' He started to gather his things. 'Pack up. Take all your things. Fill up on water. We'll eat as we walk; we need to leave *now*. Dessimë, I'm going to need you to make a lot of that meal-like potion. We may not be so fortunate this time around. We're going to need to eat meagerly, otherwise we'll run out of rations too soon. Who knows what awaits us at the Twisted Forest.'

No one had heard him so determined and militant before. Niome was gone, and in an attempt to hide his desperation he replaced it with resolve.

Tharguen came to stand next to Bahvley, lowering his voice. 'Bahvley,' he said, 'I . . . I think I'm in shock. I – I feel sad, yet I can't bring myself to weep, though that *would* be the healthy thing to do.'

'This misfortune is ours to live, but I have a strong connection with my brother and sister, and I don't feel that they are so unfortunate as we fear they are or as we are feeling right now. Come, they'll probably pop in on us within a few weeks.'

'Oh, be realistic, Bahvley! I'm no child to whom you can lie to reassure. They're gone! And only Mirauk knows where.' Tharguen stalked off.

'Tharguen!' shouted Bahvley.

'Why do you even try, Bahvley?' Tharguen shouted back, throwing up his arms. 'It's no use! The damage is done. Nothing can undo it. They took Niome away.' He began to cry. 'I'm sorry, but you're going to have to spare me of your talk.'

Celor looked at Tharguen. He wished he could tell his friends the truth, but he had given his word to keep their secret. As much as it pained him not to, he knew that telling them would do the opposite of helping and protecting them; it would put all of them and the Five in grave danger.

Bahvley, too, started to weep. He'd been separated from his family before and thought of the grief they had gone through. It was his turn, he supposed. How unfair all this seemed.

* * *

The team travelled hurriedly south and eastwards, and some of the days were thankfully quite rainy. For ten long days, they walked before they came upon the Twisted Rapids. Rapid, indeed, for they had to jump from rock to rock with a rope shot to the other side to hold just in case. Some, like Gahli, slipped on a rock in their haste. If it hadn't been for people like Tom to catch them, they could've been swept away by the fast passing water, swept to the falls and to the Great Ocean.

Tom felt the burden of looking after Gahli and Ihal as he had promised. He surmised that Jimmy and Meysah knew something more than just suspecting an event, but he mentioned nothing of it, knowing that if they could not speak of it, nor could he. Tom knew enough about magic to under-stand at least that.

On the other side of the Rapids, there were marshes where beautiful flowers grew despite their environment. By the next afternoon, they were entering the forest. Many trees near the northern tip of the forest were half burnt, some completely, but where the travellers were, the trees had been spared. The place was quiet; only the songbirds uttered any sounds.

Led by Tharguen and Bahvley, the Telorians and Kikies entered the forest.

Chapter Fifteen:
Masters Of Disquise

The Five could hear the rumbling of the water loud and clear. No water seeped in through the hatch. This place was not just secret and secure, but it had been fashioned with some form of magic, which gave the Five an eerie feeling.

They were at the bottom of the ladder now, surrounded by the metal walls of the space. As they walked a bit, the passageway quickly turned into an earth-walled tunnel. It was lit by torches but very dimly, so dim that it was almost completely dark and their eyes needed a good while to adjust. They huddled close in a corner and kept their eyes closed for a bit, and when they opened them again, they could see a little better. Still, it would take a while more to fully adjust to the new setting.

They heard or saw no one as they snuck through the tunnel quietly and slowly, slinking out of sight if they thought they had.

'Obviously, Morkans aren't very fond of light and see better in darker conditions, these dark and corrupted people,' said Niome. 'Unless it's better lit further near a more common area. A bit like the Morkan caves near Dalvar.'

'Why do you suppose these tunnels exist?' whispered Meysah. 'Where do you suppose they lead?'

'Somewhere,' said Jimmy. 'And they exist for a reason.'

'Yes, how very blunt and obvious of you to notice. Thanks for pointing that out to me.'

'They may lead to Darakön,' said Niome, 'as we discussed before.'

'Darakön,' echoed Vigh. 'Yes, possible, but how so?'

'The Morkans don't like the dragons. They want to get rid of them. The only way is by going under, and they may even still think, given what we discovered in Dûnelor, that the bo—'

'Get back,' said Boreth, 'in here!' Niome left 'books' unsaid.

March, march, march went many feet, and from the dark alcove where the Telorians hid, they could see many tall dim shadows. A voice could be heard above the footsteps.

'We've gotten this far; we won't stop now. I tell you, if that *Captain of yours* has second thoughts, then he'll have to deal with me. I won't change directions and split my team in half to do double the work in double the time. Our goal is to get to this point, and this point only, without wasting time. And our orders come from Mirauk himself.' Then there was the sound of paper being scrunched, probably a map being rolled or folded. 'Tell your troops to continue. They're counting on you to know what to do, and until you get further orders or until your Captain returns, don't stop digging, and don't dig elsewhere. I'm in charge here, not him.'

'Yes, sir.' And they marched off.

'We need to get our hands on that map,' whispered Niome once the Morkans were out of earshot.

They followed the Morkans from far enough behind and hid in an empty and abandoned-looking chamber. Silently, they waited another day or two before having an opportunity to take a good look at the map which was kept in another room nearby.

It was obvious to the Five that the Morkans did not think their secret tunnels could be infiltrated; they had left a copy of the map spread open on a large table. The map assuredly indicated that the tunnels were to continue to Darakön. Niome had been right. The map also gave them a better idea of where they were and where to go next. If they could steal a copy that didn't belong to anyone, they figured, they could follow the tunnels and pinpoint the exact location of the Captain's army and know how to sneak by. But knowing the Captain himself had left it there, they left that copy alone.

They kept on sneaking through the passage unnoticed for what felt like several days, hiding to rest and eat when necessary.

Jimmy looked ahead and saw a chair in the middle of the hallway. He turned to the others and in a funny waving-his-arms-from-the-elbows sort of way, he said to them, 'There's a chair . . . in the hall . . .' He paused at the end of each fragment of phrase, making his hands vibrate in the direction of the chair.

'And what do you want us to do about a chair?' said Meysah. Jimmy gave him a look and started over in the same way.

'There's a chair . . . in the hall . . . so when you go by . . . be sure not to konk it. And I think it has—'

Meysah went to investigate and accidentally knocked it down before Jimmy had time to finish his last sentence, making a loud clamour that seemed to echo through the tunnel halls.

'There are Morkan cloaks on it,' said Jimmy quickly, now at a normal volume.

'Ouch!' cried Meysah as quietly as he possibly could in a delayed reaction. 'Uah, now I'm going to have a bruise.'

'And we're going to have a lot more than just bruises if we don't put these cloaks on fast enough!' said Niome.

They quickly removed their cloaks and put the Morkan cloaks on, rolling up their own and putting them in their bags. What the chair was doing there, they only realised afterwards; it had been leaned up against the wall and there were several more chairs placed this way a little further, most likely waiting to be moved.

'What's going on?' said a Morkan approaching, accompanied by many others. He looked directly at Jimmy. Tall and stern-looking, he had a gaunt face.

'That's . . . what *we* came to investigate,' said Jimmy with slight hesitation at the beginning. 'We've found nothing.' Now he spoke in the same tone the Morkan had used, imitating him.

'All right.' The Morkan observed them all, his stance and tone indicating suspicion. '*Wokh reka kuyokh?*' Again he looked at Jimmy, waiting for an answer.

'I am Lugh,' said Jimmy, a name he had invented on the spot, and he stopped there. He could almost hear Meysah mocking him in his head, *That rhymes with slug!*

'Once again, who are you?' The Morkans studied all of them this time.

Jimmy thought, *Lucky guess*, though he hoped he would not have to learn the entire language like Tharguen had. Those few lessons Tharguen had given them many years back had not been for nothing – at least what Jimmy remembered of them.

'I must say I expected a greeting party, but I did not expect to have to look for you.' Jimmy folded his arms, standing his tallest. 'We were sent out from Mork to look for the Five Telorians and to come here afterwards. Mirauk wanted it five against five, but we've not encountered them yet. A large group of Telorians were set off east, but the Five were not among them.'

'Well, we're still waiting for news from the Nephew Dukes,' the other Morkan said. 'If the Five are not headed to the Twisted Forest, as Mirauk suspected, then we'll have to inform the army that set out after them once they get here. There's still a lot of time until then, though. I'm Gohtek, Captain of the group digging through the tunnels. Let me show you around, Captain Lugh. You'll be glad to know we've progressed significantly.'

'That's very good,' replied Jimmy, clasping his hands behind his back. 'Show us, and we may give further instructions.'

'Aah, I knew there would be more,' Gohtek said, sounding vindicated. 'And to think some of our workers doubted their efficiency and wanted to stop and dig to Firlan because *one* Captain thought Firlan would pose a threat!'

'Well, we won't let insecurities stop us, will we, Captain Gohtek?' said Jimmy with a wry tone.

'Indeed, no,' agreed Gohtek, laughing with Jimmy. 'And who are they?' Gohtek motioned to the others standing behind Jimmy.

Jimmy had to think of Morkan-sounding names, and fast. He took his time talking.

'This . . . is Pateek,' he said, pointing at Meysah, regretting it as soon as he said the name. Meysah was going to complain and tease him for this name, not to mention get back at him for it someday. 'This is Rabrikh.' Vigh. Jimmy realised he would also have to remember all of these names. 'Chekht.'

Boreth. 'And Gabore.' Niome. 'We are honoured to finally be here and help with the progress.'

'I shall give you maps and some luxuries and good meals, and together, we shall keep our army at work.'

'Luxuries!' exclaimed Jimmy.

'Of course,' said Gohtek. 'Why does that surprise you?'

Jimmy was stuck and didn't know what to say.

'Mirauk warned us not to expect a proper welcome here,' Niome said at length, lowering the pitch of her voice. Jimmy sighed and nodded to her subtly in thanks and relief for her aid. 'After all, we did have to find you, as my Captain pointed out earlier.'

'That's because the *other* Captain would not receive anyone well. He has grown infuriated of late. And infuriat*ing*.'

'But he is not here now, so why should it matter?' said Niome. 'Who is this Captain?'

'Young boy, I hope you remember the rules of not identifying those you speak ill of so as not for it to haunt you when you do understand why they are the way they are,' scolded Gohtek.

'Pardon, I'd forgotten.'

'That's all right,' said Jimmy. 'Rare is it that my partners here slip in their manners.' He searched for the name he had given Niome. 'Gabore! . . . Is but a learner amongst us, but a brave and powerful one.'

'He has also let his hair grow long, a rare trait among our people,' said Gohtek. 'Giving a look not as tough as they could be, deceiving those around them of the power they hold. Yes, I see it now. One day he shall ripen and become more like Merlik in looks, I reckon.'

'A compliment?' said Niome.

'Of course,' said Gohtek. 'Come, you are tired and hungry, I see, and have been spending too much time with Telorians, or at least observing them.'

'Yes, how could you tell?' Jimmy said sardonically.

'Your attitudes,' said Gohtek. 'It happens to the best of us. Even happened to me once.'

'Yes, well, they are a bad influence,' said Meysah, sensing an opportunity to probe. 'Them *and* their dragons.'

'And their books!' said Gohtek.

Aha! Meysah's hunch had been right.

'They may lie about them, but we'll get our hands on them, wherever they may be hidden. Unless you believe their stories, Captain.'

'No, no, definitely not,' Jimmy said dryly.

'Well, our famous Captain started having doubts about that, too,' explained Gohtek, 'and wanted to abort all projects, go to Firlan instead. He suspected something odd would become of it all.'

Sensing the Telorians, Jimmy thought. They all looked at each other. *They* were the 'something odd.'

'Luckily,' continued Gohtek, 'we managed to change his mind about that. It's his obsession with Firlan and the Five that aggravates me.'

'Perhaps we shall understand matters better after we've supped,' said Jimmy.

* * *

The Morkans sat them down to a good meal at a comfortable table in a better-lit room. The food smelled good; at least Morkans had good taste in that. How Gohtek thought Jimmy was Captain, the Telorian knight did not understand at first, but later on he figured it was since he had been standing closest to him, had taken the initiative to answer in the same tone when Gohtek had addressed him, and had been the only one to speak. In Mork, such behaviour usually only came from Captains. Additionally, Jimmy had been forthcoming with some information, and Gohtek was obviously eager for news. This had garnered trust, and his imitation skills had helped him be relatable to the Morkan Captain.

Gohtek served them a second portion of the hot meal. Maybe this wasn't so bad after all; if Tharguen did it for fifty years, they could certainly do it for a season or two. They would try to divert the digging away from Darakön as much as possible, and without getting too close to Firlan. Meysah thought of how those working Morkans were like ants, and he shuddered and felt uneasy, considering he didn't like bugs or Morkans.

'Why don't you cast your hoods off?' suggested Gohtek. 'No more need to hide here. I know it can become a habit, though. Even in Mork, it's fun when no one around knows your true identity. Go ahead, we all know who we are here.'

Niome whispered a spell to herself, one she'd said a few times since they had donned the Morkan cloaks, and cast her hood off. She looked at the others, obliging them to do the same. They stared back at her in a *'What are you doing?!'* sort of way, but they followed her lead, albeit hesitantly.

'Well, I see that without his hood, Gabore looks almost grown and not as delicate as I thought. He will soon be very strong. He does have certain resemblances with Merlik. Are you sure you aren't related?'

'I doubt it,' said Niome. 'I only met him once, and he didn't like the looks of me.'

Meysah was the first to understand that Niome had been clever enough to cast a spell on Gohtek, and potentially all the other Morkans in the tunnels as well, so that he would see them as he imagined they would be.

After the meal, Gohtek placed a map on the table and explained its function.

'Do you plan on attacking the dragons by next season?' inquired Vigh.

'Yes, uh, Rabrikh, is it?'

Vigh nodded. 'Unwise. I've been there before, and the last thing you want to do is attack when all the dragons are in their home. You must wait until the Summer. Yes, they will be awake, but if they are asleep and disturbed, you have all of them to deal with. In the Summer, they travel, and far and wide too. That is the most opportune time to attack. It would be the will of his Lordship.'

'Very well.' Gohtek rubbed his chin in thought. 'Yes, good thing he rethought it, and like that, once they're out, we can block the entrance. It makes total sense. But we must get under it before then. Our orders were to get there for the eighth week of Winter, ready with an army, but we can delay it. However, we do have to get to the point of the little northern wood by the seventy-eighth of Colouring.'

'That also can be delayed,' said Jimmy. 'There are other routes that need to be made.'

'All right, but the *Captain* won't be happy. You'll have to tell him yourselves.' Gohtek sighed, looking defeated. 'Well, you might as well know if you haven't already guessed it: Kàtchah. He is a personal rival of mine, and will be arriving on that day.'

Jimmy's heart dropped into his stomach.

'Remind me of today's date,' said Jimmy.

'Why, the last day of Summer.'

Darn! Jimmy thought in his head. *I'm missing the best days of the year when the weather is beautiful.* But he replied, 'Great, let's get to work. Because you see, as it happens, Kàtchah is also a rival of *mine*. I have a feeling we're going to get along very well, you and I, Gohtek.'

Gohtek grinned at Jimmy, nodding his approval.

The Telorians had now officially become spies.

Niome had indeed cast a spell, first on all five of them and subsequently on all the Morkans, for them to truly believe their new identities were authentic. 'Let us hope all will work out,' Niome had said to the other four.

Meysah bugged Jimmy about the interesting names he had given them all, as Jimmy had predicted, saying to him, 'Pateek? Me, a Pateek! Do I look like a Pateek to you?'

'Continue like that and you'll sound like one.'

'Sure, *Lugh-ah!*'

He also bugged Jimmy about how this was his first try at being in charge – of Morkans, not of Telorians, even though he wasn't training anyone.

Boreth and Vigh thought of other things.

'If only there were a way to open the hatch when the river's full and wash out and destroy everything here,' Boreth said to Vigh. 'That would certainly simplify the job.'

They gave not much thought to it yet and later gave the Morkans logical reasons to dig random tunnels. The Morkans obeyed, because they believed their deceiving eyes and they believed that the orders came from Mirauk.

At the same time, the Telorians tried to figure out where the exit was until they realised that there was no exit; there was only one entrance at Ortim. How convenient! The exit would be, for the Morkans, Darakön. However, the Five needed to leave before Kàtchah arrived. The Telorians would have to dig an exit for themselves through which to disappear before Captain Kàtchah arrived. Working towards that goal, they dug a few secret tunnels and exits in a few isolated places and made a copy of their own secret map for each one of them.

On one of the days, a Morkan came up to them.

'I am a messenger sending word from the Dukes, Merlik and Garkhktak.'

'Well, go on!' all five urged.

'The Five Telorians are in Dûnelor. Or at least were last seen there by the Dukes themselves. The Five and many other Telorians have allied them-selves with the Dûnelorians.' The Morkan went on to give an account of what he had been told had happened in Dûnelor with the Dukes. It was interesting to hear the Morkan version of the story.

'Have you told anyone else of this deceiving news?' asked Jimmy.

'No.'

'Good. Tell no one; it will only discourage them.'

'Understood.' And he left.

Now the Telorians could control this situation also. All was going as planned, and they spent their time giving orders and digging on their own time in secret. Of course, they had to discipline certain Morkans. Some had rude attitudes and refused to comply, using the excuse that even if the order came from Mirauk, it hadn't gone through Kàtchah. Some Morkans were very loyal to that Captain, which proved even more the power and influence he had in Mork and the danger he posed to Teloria. Even Gohtek had little power over those loyal to Kàtchah, and where he used violent means to get them to obey, the Telorians used words.

As for Jimmy, he was not experienced with this sort of thing, for he hadn't finished learning yet all there was for an apprentice-knight to learn. He consulted Boreth and the others as often as he could. He was still hesitant but his fear was gone, though he dreaded Morkans withal, especially Kàtchah. After their brief encounter with him, the Morkan Captain had made quite the impression on Jimmy, and Kàtchah's reputation didn't make Jimmy feel any better. Another encounter with him would not be pleasant. That's why Jimmy kept strict note of the date every single day.

There was one particular Morkan, however, who suspected the Five of being deceitful. They needed to find a way to silence him, but they didn't want to kill him. Rumour was, he had voiced that he sensed something was amiss. He obviously had some magical traits within him.

He found Niome alone one day when she was studying the maps.

'Why does something tell me you're not who you seem to be?'

Niome turned around. 'I am but a young—'

'You lie. I see the five of you scheming secretly!'

Maybe there was no point in arguing. She was certainly not fooling this one, but it was worth a try.

'You're confused.'

'No, I'm not, Gabore.' He took his sword and pointed it at her. 'Or is that your real name? All my life, I sought answers to mysteries, learning with the help of magic lore, and now I'm discovering—'

'I see there's no point hiding it,' Niome interjected. 'I am perhaps someone else. What if I were a wizard?'

Niome took a step towards him, showing no heed to the threat and looking straight into his eyes. There was still some distance between her and the sword.

'I have nothing to fear from a mere boy!' said the Morkan.

Meysah entered the room. He saw what was going on and unsheathed his sword, pointing it at the Morkan.

'What's this?' said Meysah. 'How dare you!'

'How dare *you*! Mirauk would never give orders to others for us. He deals with Kàtchah only and directly. That is why Kàtchah is in Mork now and then will be on his way here!'

He whacked Meysah's sword away, moving swiftly, and pushed him to the ground.

Niome, in an instant, felt great protectiveness over her brother. She took the Morkan by the collar and lifted him, pushing him to the wall, and held him there. She looked deep into his eyes. He dropped his sword.

'Watch your tongue, Sikhlah!' she said. 'I may look to you as a mere boy, but what if I were the most powerful wizard of all!'

Meysah looked at her, shaking his head; he didn't want her to reveal their identity and blow their cover. He stood hastily, dusting himself off.

'What if,' Niome went on, 'I were N—'

Meysah pulled Niome away. 'Not the polc you thought,' he finished. 'We have powers you don't have! That is why *we* were sent here. Your skills may have detected that we are not who we seem to be, but we have authority. Don't test our patience.'

He lowered his voice at the end, for he saw that Sikhlah was trembling. Sikhlah took his sword and left.

'What were you thinking?!' Meysah whispered harshly, whirling on his sister.

'He would've been frightened to know who I am,' said Niome.

'Yes, and gotten an army to kill us, or at least try to. As long as we're here and trying to save Darakön and Firlan, we should keep a low profile.'

'Well, being in charge is hardly keeping a low profile,' Niome replied quickly, folding her arms.

'Yes, but looking into Morkans' eyes and deciphering their names is more likely to get us discovered than going along with a ruse,' Meysah replied just as quickly.

Niome shook her head. 'Anyway, whatever led me to it, it has passed, but the damage is done. Let's see if we can try to mitigate it.'

She took her brother by the hand and walked out of the room. As they exited, Meysah grabbed his sword.

They hurried to go find the other three; they heard voices. It was Sikhlah and Gohtek.

'I swear, I saw it in his eyes! He even said to me: "*What if I were the most powerful wizard of all!*"'

'Well, if it *is* Mirauk in disguise, then we better obey. He is testing us. Perhaps one of the others is Kàtchah in disguise. Or perhaps they are simply secret wizards here on behalf of Mirauk. Whichever the case, they are to be treated exceptionally well, *with respect.* You should apologise, Sikhlah. That way you will be left alone and Mirauk won't hold it against you but commend you for such caution.'

Meysah and Niome hurried off.

'They think you're Em,' said Meysah.

'Proves they don't know better, because Em is not the most powerful,' laughed Niome.

'Is that arrogance? Pride? Well, I never thought we could have fun in Mork.'

'We're not in Mork,' Niome said with a wry smile.

When Niome and Meysah found the other three, they explained the situation to them. Shortly after, Sikhlah came to them. They all looked at him sternly.

'Uh . . .' hesitated Sikhlah. 'I want to apologise for my behaviour earlier. I . . . I fear I've lost control.'

'Well, you were only being cautious. That's always commendable.' Niome continued sternly, 'Just watch yourself; know who to trust. And hold your tongue.'

'Yes, and I know now that I can trust you. You can trust me.'

'Can we?' said Meysah.

'Leave us,' Jimmy told Sikhlah, holding his hand up. 'His anger will pass.'

'Yes! Captain . . . Lords.'

Sikhlah bowed and left.

'I think Tharguen was wrong when he said that Morkans weren't all that entertaining,' said Vigh. 'He did guess "Lords" right.'

'At least this dark place isn't too dark,' said Boreth. 'Humour lightens my mood.' He smiled, placing a hand on Jimmy's shoulder. 'We have each other. That's what matters here.'

After the incident with Sikhlah, things were even better. The Morkans did as the Telorians commanded without question and served them as though they were royalty – even those who were loyal to Kàtchah. They really did think Niome was Mirauk. Too bad Bahvley or Tharguen weren't there to see it.

At least Niome was able to cunningly persuade the Morkans that it was no longer necessary to go after Bahvley, though she knew she would not be able to persuade them to change their minds about Tharguen. Nevertheless, if these Morkans were convinced the Five Telorians were important Morkans of high rank, they could convince others. There was no guarantee the ruse was going to last forever, but even if only for a short time, it was worth the effort, just in case. This was progress. This was good.

Chapter Sixteen:
The Forest Dwellers

'We must stick together,' said Tharguen, 'and never go anywhere alone. Go nowhere without every single one of us following. I can't afford to lose any of you! Not one, for you are all too dear to me.'

Many of the Telorians and Kikies tried to find something to answer back, but they could not.

Drizzle fell over the trees. They could see no one in the area with the dead trees, so they walked into the forest proper. The host of travellers had been hoping their Firlanians friends would be nearby, but there was no one to greet them, nor was there anyone to meet them during the next two days wherein they walked deeper into the forest, never stopping, for they were all restless.

After the first day of travel in the forest, the Kikies shrunk into their fairy size for good measure. They hovered close by, alert and ready for anything.

At last, the Telorians rested. They chose to do so during the day, for they wanted a clear view around them while the watchers, tired as they were, kept vigil, alternating turns in a rotation. Tharguen, Tom, Lóim and Fimrel were all watching at one point as they sat together.

'Captain,' whispered Lóim, 'we are being followed.'

'Yes, I sense it,' said Tom.

Tharguen kept his head levelled, fighting the urge to glance about.

'I saw someone – an unfamiliar face,' said Lóim.

'It seems our fate is to be spied upon whenever we walk into new lands,' said Fimrel.

Still, Tharguen said nothing, never looking around. His army had grown wiser since Dûnelor, even Lóim, and more wary. They had learnt very well from the Five how to notice subtle details. Tharguen was proud that some were developing those necessary skills. Vigilance was of the utmost necessity, and Tharguen knew he could depend on his team; their loyalty and discipline had proven to him that much in the first days of training. Now, he was certain he had chosen the right polcs to join him, for he knew he must one day return to Mork, but he also knew that his team would be ready for the day when he would order them to follow.

'What are we to do about it?' asked Lóim. Tharguen thought a moment.

'Well, they haven't hurt us,' said Fimrel. 'Let us hope they won't pull the same trick on us as—'

Tharguen lifted his hand to demand silence, subtly lifting his index finger. 'I've seen them also. They've been following us since before the Kikies shrunk back. In the trees above us.'

'That's since yesterday, Captain,' said Tom.

'Yes. I don't know when they plan on approaching us. Maybe they're waiting for us to do something,' said Tharguen.

'What can we do?' asked Fimrel.

'I've been thinking about it since yesterday,' said Tharguen. 'I was hoping one of you would have an idea.'

Lóim stood, a revelation coming to him. He went and awoke Bahvley, whispering in his ear. Bahvley got up and walked right into the centre of the campsite.

Tharguen wondered about this, for Bahvley had not uttered one word since they had reached the Twisted Forest. Yet perhaps Tharguen thought he understood; his polcs had more of a head on their shoulders than he gave them credit for.

'Wake up!' called Bahvley. 'Get up! We have to prepare, okay? I don't know what awaits us, but we have to find our friends. Everyone must keep their wits sharp. It was enough that we lost the Five because of Mirauk's spell. Hopefully, they're safe, but are we? I am greatly grieved by what has transpired and what is happening now.'

The Kikies reappeared in succession amidst the Telorians.

'Your Majesty, are you sure this is the right place and time for a speech?' asked Celor, who knew perfectly well what Bahvley was up to.

Bahvley, even though he was speaking to get the attention of their following strangers, spoke genuinely and from the heart.

'My dear Kiki friend, there's no better time for a speech, for I am desperate to save Teloria.'

'Then the Tellens of the Twisted Forest shall help,' said a voice.

Everyone looked around.

From the trees emerged many polcs clad in earthy colours, all coming to stand around the group of Telorians and Kikies. None were pointing any weapons at them, though they all bore bows and daggers.

The polc continued, 'For now we know for certain that you *are* the friends of the Firlanians. We are Tellens. Once we were Telorians, but we lost contact with Teloria long ago and have since called ourselves this new name.'

The polc spoke with a strange dialect, mostly making his *R*'s sound hard and deep, inflecting up and down at different times, pronouncing every single vowel and consonant as though dissecting the sounds of each word. He was handsome and young, less than Bahvley's age, yet there was wisdom in his eyes. He approached Bahvley.

'Welcome, Bahvley Fairhaven, King of Teloria. I've heard much of you. Let me introduce meself.

I'm Stëinbøk, only a few weeks ago Prince and now King of the Tellens of the Twisted Forest.'

'I'm sorry to hear, then,' said Bahvley, 'that your King has passed away.'

'He was me father.' Stëinbøk looked around, and his eyes landed on Tharguen. 'You must be Tharguen Sumperale.'

'Yes. You are certainly well-informed. Do you know all our names?'

'The ones of the polcs the Firlanians specified to look for. They said you would be with a good-numbered team. Where are the other five they spoke of? Are they in this crowd of young knights?'

There was dead silence among the Telorians for a short moment that felt like an eternity. Stëinbøk looked about them, searching for those who could have been the Five. His eyes met several of the young knights' eyes. Mittah was closest to him, standing between Gahli and Ihal, and she looked to the side at her friends, who kept their heads bowed, and back at the Tellen King, and he lowered his head in understanding.

'They are captured, we believe,' said Tharguen. 'There was a drought and they were perhaps taken by Morkans, for when we awoke, the river was filling again and there was no sign of them. That was but two weeks ago.'

'We don't believe they drowned,' said Bahvley. 'My bond with my brother and sister is strong, and I sense they yet live, though I've got absolutely no idea what happened exactly or where they went or where they may be now. We were all sleeping when it happened – a spell. Still, if something as terrible as death would've happened, we would've felt it.'

'I understand these five Telorians have special powers together,' said Stëinbøk. 'The Firlanians are quite fond of them.' He paused. 'We suffered from the drought as well. Mirauk decided to start a fire. Luckily, the rain came. We thought for many generations, like our forefathers had thought for many centuries, that we could hide here and be safe, and that if no one knew of our existence, neither would Mirauk, but it has proven ill-favoured. Come, I shall bring you to me shelter. It isn't safe out here. Strange beasts roam in the night and have caused many deaths amongst me people, including me father.' He turned to one of his polcs. 'Hunbøk, take the tail and make sure we don't lose any of our new allies.'

Stëinbøk started off and the Telorians followed. They walked for quite some time before arriving at a large tree abode.

Stëinbøk halted. 'We'll stay here tonight; we'll walk fast tomorrow. We have a few shelters like this along the way, but the only real safe place is at our fortress.' He looked up and whistled, imitating a strange bird sound. Down came a ladder. 'Come quick. Night is falling.'

They all climbed up and installed themselves in the shelter for sleep. It was a tight squeeze, but somehow they all fit in the many rooms of the mini house. Most of the Tellens stayed awake.

In the middle of the night, Tharguen awoke suddenly.

'What is the matter?' asked a Tellen.

'I've been having nightmares,' said Tharguen.

'What about?'

'Mork. Ghastly creatures. Niome . . . she's part of the Five.'

'Many of us don't sleep much anymore, for we're *livin'* a nightmare. We watch and try to get rid of the phantoms from up here; they don't climb. But nothin' seems to be killin' them.'

'What do they do to you? For I believe my friends have seen them, and I have dreamt of them.'

'They appear at night and disappear in the day, and they bite. They have sucked the life out of me friends and left them lyin' pale. Some died; others who had been saved in time could not remember who they were or where they were afterwards. Some only lost a bit of their memory, and others have not fully recovered it.'

'They suck the memories to bring them back to Mirauk,' said Tharguen with disgust.

'We've tried speakin' to them, but they don't answer back. They ignore us.'

'How many of you have they killed?'

'Over a dozen died, and more than your army's number were injured and lost part of their memory. So much damage from so few enemies.'

Tharguen scowled. 'How many are there?'

'Five only.'

'Five,' exhaled Tharguen, as though realising something dreadful. 'They're after the Five, and they won't stop until they get them. We have to kill them before the Five get here . . . if they do.'

'Easy to say, but to be easily done . . . these creatures are impossible to kill.'

The Tellen walked to another part of the shelter, leaving Tharguen to ponder as he tried to get some sleep.

The next day, the Telorians followed the Tellens at a breakneck pace, arriving at another shelter just before nightfall. The Telorians were exhausted, for they had only stopped to rest at lunchtime. They travelled quickly in the days that followed, for the days grew short and they needed to reach the next shelter before dusk. The Tellens knew the peril that awaited the Telorians if ever they lagged.

Two days later, they came to a lake. There they found an injured Tellen.

'Oh, no!' said Huck, fearful.

'They've struck again,' sighed Hunbøk. 'This was one of our guards from the next shelter. He must've come to get water.'

'He must have known he couldn't come at night,' wondered Bahvley.

'He did,' said Ihal. 'Look, a trap. A hole.' The Tellen's foot was stuck in a small hole between tree roots. 'It must've been set by some animals. The phantom must've found him there, unless *they* set the trap.'

The Tellen was pale, very pale.

'I'm afraid he's dead,' said another Tellen. He picked him up. 'We won't leave him here.'

'I can take him, Derfbøk,' said Hunbøk.

'It's fine. You need your strength for now. We'll take turns.'

'This is bad,' said Tharguen, noticing that Hunbøk still had healing wounds as the Tellen rolled up his sleeves. Tharguen closed his eyes. 'Mirauk, what have you conjured this time!'

'What's worse is they carry no weapons,' said Stëinbøk. 'They don't need them.'

'It's dangerous out here,' said Bahvley, 'yet you came to greet us.'

'Someone with experience in these parts needs to protect you and guide you. I took it upon meself.'

'Thank you.'

Stëinbøk smiled meagerly. 'Don't mention it.'

They set off again and arrived at the next shelter in the nick of time. Though they didn't see the phantoms, they heard them whispering, yet no one could understand their words. The journey carried on like this for four more days before they saw the walls of the fortress at last. Night was falling quickly; they were almost there but they would have to run for it, run to get there before the sky became completely dark.

'Night is fallin' early tonight because of the clouds,' said Stëinbøk. 'They are dark clouds; night will be darker than usual tonight. Evil magic is at work these days . . . and nights.'

There was rustling in the bushes up ahead. The Telorians drew their weapons.

'Weapons are of no use,' advised Hunbøk. 'Keep your hands free so you can push them off.'

They all kept on running forward until they saw a dark cloaked figure and another figure fighting it. They stopped in their tracks.

'Bahvley, Your Majesty,' said Huck, 'if you could remember where you saw these creatures and how you got rid of them, now would be a good time.'

'I know,' answered Bahvley, 'yet I can't.'

The dark figure became aware of their presence but still held on to the other polc. The Telorians, who were closest, recognised the other shape. Lóim sprang ahead and pounced on the phantom. It staggered back a long way as though it had not enough energy to fight right now, like an animal weakened by hunger. The others ran to Lóim.

'Don't get yourself killed!' cried Tom.

The phantom retreated, almost as if it knew this wasn't the right time. As for the other polc, he was safe and sound.

'Stars, am I glad to see you!'

'Elmezni!' said Bahvley, clapping the Firlanian on the shoulder.

Everyone was led into the fortress through two sets of gates that were quickly closed behind them, and before the group stood several Firlanians.

'We saw you coming from the tower and came to greet you,' said Elmezni. 'We got scared when night fell and still you weren't here. I took a walk, foolishly, towards you to tell you to hurry.'

'My apologies for not showing up at our meeting time,' said Kchalami, stepping forward.

'What happened to you?' asked Tharguen as he embraced the Firlanian Prince.

'We were . . . delayed by these phantoms, and some of us were struck down or almost – it was too dangerous for us to leave the fortress. We're sorry.'

'I understand. It's all right,' said Bahvley.

The other Firlanians looked around, scanning the Telorians. Worried looks came upon them.

'Where's Niome?' asked Kchalami in a troubled tone.

'And Jimmy and Meysah!' said Elmezni.

'Gone, another way,' said Tharguen sadly.

Bahvley quickly explained what had happened.

'That's not good,' said Kchalami. 'It troubles me greatly.'

The Tellens led the Telorians up to the main floor of the fortress, and before the Telorians settled into some guest rooms, they went to see the other Firlanians. Tellens briefly showed them around, and the Telorians and Kikies left their bags in their new rooms, but as polite as they wanted to be, they were all very anxious to see their friends.

Elmezni led them to one common room where many of them sat by a fireplace, and they exchanged welcoming thoughts. Kchalami brought them to another wing, one filled with beds where the others were, those of them who had been injured.

Krystal walked up to them. She had been taking care of the injured, Firlanian and Tellen alike, Kchalami had explained.

'Thank goodness you're safe,' she said. 'We've been so worried. Many dreadful things have happened of late. We are perhaps a bit trapped in this forest, unless we want to risk our lives. But it's otherwise a nice place to be, and the Tellens are very kind to us.'

'Yes, we know,' Tharguen reassured. 'We've had a Morkan set a spell on us while his polcs captured Niome, Meysah, Vigh, Boreth and Jimmy.'

'Oh!' Krystal bowed her head. 'Indeed, more has happened than I thought.' She looked at her friends. 'Although I have trouble admitting it to myself, Mirauk's gaining power, and that's a fact. If Niome doesn't gain as quickly as he does, his power will surpass hers, but there's still time until then. Now they are elsewhere, and we are here. Yet, hopefully they've escaped or will. But come, here lie Petruni, Saviel, Dinankch and Akchmassiel.'

Krystal led them through the infirmary ward and took them to each bed one by one, where the four injured Firlanians slept. First, they went to Saviel.

'Saviel was struck first,' she said, 'but he's recovered almost fully. He's mostly tired these days, but his memory has returned in full.' She led them next to Petruni as she spoke and did the same with each patient, stopping beside each bed. 'Petruni was next, although not very severely wounded. She still feels weak, though her memory was always intact, for we got to her in time. Dinankch was wounded pretty badly. His memories are just starting to return.'

They came to Akchmassiel, the mighty and adventurous Firlanian Captain many of them had come to admire in their previous encounters with him. He lay motionless, as though he was hardly breathing. He appeared very pale and cold.

'Akchmassiel was struck most recently,' said Krystal. 'He is severely injured. He came close to death. At times, it seems as though he is lingering between consciousness and unconsciousness yet still in delirium; he has not yet fully woken. I fear all his memory has gone. If so, Mirauk will know how to defeat Firlan once the phantoms return to him.'

'That's why we'll do our best to destroy them,' said Bahvley. There was a pause.

'Let Mirauk know how to defeat our forest,' Kchalami seethed through gritted teeth, 'but Stars, let my friend live.' He took Akchmassiel's hand in his. 'You hear me? I expect you to wake up.' He bowed his head.

'It is disgusting how these beasts steal our memories with our blood, and we just know they will take all the information gained this way to Mirauk.' Krystal sighed. 'I was hoping Niome would have a spell that could heal them.'

'I might have one,' said Tom. 'I'll look through my spells, see what I can find.' Krystal smiled.

After seeing the wounded, the Telorians went to bed.

The next day, they told their story in more detail to the Firlanians, who in turn told theirs.

As soon as the Firlanians had entered the forest, they explained, they had been welcomed by the Tellens, who had found it pleasant to receive visitors. They had met the Tellen King, Stëinbøk's father, and he had been glad that his people and their cousins were reconciling the disputes of long-dead ancestors of many centuries past.

All had been merry and fine until one night, there appeared what they thought to be Morkans. Their eagerness to fight had backfired on them, for many Tellens were fatally wounded that night by the phantoms. They spied on the phantoms and tried to destroy them, but the mysterious creatures had proven too strong and crafty.

Only weeks ago, when Akchmassiel had been struck and the Tellen King had died, did the Tellens and Firlanians conclude that there was no way of killing the Morkan phantoms.

Stëinbøk had subsequently taken his father's place as King. Then, the forest had begun to smoke up in the north with the fire caused by Mirauk. They were effectively trapped.

Chapter Seventeen:
The Horns Of Earnestness

For the next week or so, the Tellens tried to devise a plan to trap the phantoms. Bahvley strove to remember where he had seen them before. He knew them. The feeling inside that he got upon seeing them for the first time made him know it – recognition. Be it as it may, he could not remember where, when or what had happened regarding them, let alone how he had gotten out of the trouble he had been in then. Frustratingly, he could not remember a single detail.

Tom sifted through the books he had brought with him and found a few helpful verses. As soon as he had spoken them, the injured Firlanians and Tellens looked less pale and the conscious ones felt slightly more energised. The Kikies also contributed some medicine to help their recovery.

Though Akchmassiel remained lost and pale, at least he was conscious now. Kchlami went to see him, along with Bahvley, Stëinbøk and Laurelmi, who was a very good friend of Akchmassiel's.

'Hello, my friend,' said Kchalami. 'Do you remember who you are?'

'I know I am Akchmassiel.' He put a hand to his forehead, wincing. 'What happened? Are we still in Firlan?' He rubbed his forehead. 'We wanted to go visit the Telorians. It's been a long time since we last saw them.' He looked up at Kchalami. 'I remember a dark figure. I may have had a weird dream.'

Kchalami breathed out in relief. 'Thank the stars,' he whispered.

Bahvley stepped forth. Akchmassiel's eyes widened.

'It was no dream,' the Telorian King said. 'It's been perhaps more than six weeks since you left your home. You were attacked and your memory has been sucked out of you, but at least you remember things up to that point.'

'Then I'm missing a season of my life. You're going to have to fill me in until my memory does come back, *if* it comes back. Maybe I don't remember some things, but my wits are intact.'

'I'm glad to hear it!' said Laurelmi. 'I was worried you wouldn't remember who you were or much of your life. A season is minor compared to that.'

'Laurelmi! You cut your hair.'

'Yes, in order to free myself from the grip of an enemy phantom.' He laughed and continued, 'It was quick thinking and a slash of my sword.'

'Looks good.' Akchmassiel smiled.

Kchalami sat down in the chair beside Akchmassiel's bed. 'You have no idea how relieved I am to see you awake. And I'm glad to see your memory is almost completely intact. You bled out more than the phantom sucked away.'

'You should know by now I'm made strong,' stated Akchmassiel.

'That, you are indeed,' replied Kchalami.

Akchmassiel noticed Stëinbøk standing silently. 'Who's this?'

'I'm Stëinbøk. I am a Tellen and recently became King. We've met before, and you met me father before he died. It was the same night you were injured, causing your memory loss. You tried to save him, but both of you were struck.'

'I'm sorry it was not him who lived, for you must be grieving much.'

'Don't be sorry,' said Stëinbøk. 'He lived a full life and died honourably. Had you not risked your life for me father, you would not have been injured, but you tried to save him, and for that I am ever grateful. I am glad you are well now. We took care of you, and your friends also did everything they could for you. You are in our fortress in the Twisted Forest.'

'Well, sounds like I've missed a lot,' said Akchmassiel.

They all smiled. Kchalami knew he would recover well.

As Tom walked the halls of the sturdy fortress, he felt a great burden on his shoulders, one heavier than he would've liked. He had promised to look out for Gahli and Ihal. Rumours had started about Tom because of this; only a few of the Telorians knew them at this point.

There was something else troubling him, though, something of a greater matter than making sure two friends were safe. Being a trainee wizard, his wits were keener than some, and he was beginning to suspect and deduce. Due to the behaviour of the Five before the incident, Bahvley's attitude towards Niome, and Thagruen's dreams, Tom concluded that not only had the Five known something was going to happen, like he had originally figured, but that their disappearance was *intentional.*

'Can I help you, Tom?' asked Mië, coming from the other direction with the other Kikies.

'I'm looking for Captain Tharguen and His Majesty, Bahvley.'

'They're with the Tellens,' said Tithil.

Tom fidgeted awkwardly.

'Please don't read my mind,' he said.

'Why not?' asked Forthil. 'Though . . . it's already been done. Sorry.' He grimaced. 'It was necessary; we suspected you suspected something.'

'You know, Tom, we won't lie to you,' said Celor, 'because you have the power to keep evil away, to a certain extent. And you have the power to protect others. We've been training to not reach into an-other's mind without permission unless in a critical moment. This *is* critical, for you are the Wizard amongst us now. And about what you suspect, you are correct. And we knew about it; I got Niome's permission to read her mind. Aside from the Five, we are the only ones who know.'

'To protect us, I bet,' said Tom. 'That's why they couldn't say it.'

'You know, you're very astute,' Tithil observed. 'Now that your assumptions have been confirmed, you can't tell anyone. And you must understand that we cannot explain more than you already know. We must not speak of it, not even amongst ourselves.'

Tom nodded and left them.

I worry, thought Celor, as the other Kikies listened to his thoughts. *War is brewing here, war is brewing in Dûnelor, war already broke out in Dalvar, even if it's been suspended at present. War might break out in Firlan, and for sure something's going on where the others are. Who knows when Mork will decide to attack Teloria again. If the Morkans spread, they may discover . . . I wonder when Phynd will return with others.*

It was on the morning of the nineteenth of Colouring when everyone heard a horn out in the distance. It kept sounding until it was answered by another horn of a different tone, one that came from a tower in the Tellen fortress.

Many of the Telorians had been sitting around with the Firlanians in one of the large lounge areas that seemed to be part of the halls. A Tellen ran past.

'What do the horns mean?' asked Bahvley, catching the Tellen's arm.

'It means that the phantoms have struck again and we are to go find the injured to try to save them.'

'How far?'

'Two days away,' explained the Tellen. 'Each shelter has its own horn pattern so we know who is calling. We also can easily follow the sound – helps get us there faster.'

'Lenarbøk,' said another Tellen running by.

'Coming!' answered the other. He turned back to Bahvley.

'How many are going?' asked Bahvley.

'So far, only meself and Vessibøk.'

'Then I'm coming, too.'

Tharguen got up. 'Bahvley, what are you doing? It's dangerous, and we still have no plan to get rid of the phantoms.'

'Maybe, but perhaps if I see one up close, I'll remember where I saw them.'

'Up close? Wasn't the one we saw near the fortress up close enough for you?'

'You know what I mean, Tharguen. I am King; I am capable of making my own decisions.'

'Then I'll go with you. I'm not letting you make this foolish decision on your own.'

'Me too. I'm going,' added Ihal. 'You need protecting, Captain.'

'I can't let you go,' said Tom, blocking her path.

'And why not?' demanded Lóim. 'Are you trying to protect her in order to win her over, now that Meysah's not here?'

'The thought never crossed my mind!' said Tom, a neutral expression upon his face. 'Don't project onto me what you would like to do, Lóim.'

'Come on,' said Gahli, 'we'll all go. This is no time for your petty squabbles.'

Tom opened his mouth to reply but thought better of it as they followed the others in a jog.

'I suppose I'll stay here with everyone else,' said Mittah, 'and help here to keep everyone safe.'

'Well, we're here also,' said Elmezni, 'but I want to join the fight so that Tellen and Telorian *and* Firlanian are well protected and fight together.' He bounced up and hurried out of the room.

'Wait for me!' called out Batel and Krystal at the same time.

Those were the eleven who set off to find the injured, while everyone else remained at the fortress, safe yet fearful.

Stëinbøk and some others joined their guests in the large lounge area. A fire was burning in the fireplace. They sat on the soft cushiony chairs without saying a word, for everyone seemed to be in deep thought, but in truth they were waiting with increasing suspense for the Tellens to say something.

At last, Jeremy broke the silence.

'So, I guess we just wait here, huh?'

'Not exactly,' said Hunbøk. 'There are the beds to prepare, the medicine to brew, and a plan still to devise.'

'Oh, that's true,' said Jeremy.

'For now, we may wait,' said Derfbøk, 'for the beds and medicine take little time to prepare, but what plan are we possibly to figure out? I remember when I was but wee high, me folks and I devised a plan to get rid of some Morkans who had intruded in me tree home. That was in the days when little trouble came here. This new threat, well, these aren't regular Morkans.'

'Maybe a Kiki can read their minds and find out how to kill them?' suggested Pete.

'If only that were so,' said Celor.

'We tried,' said Dessimë. 'It's impossible. Mirauk designed them so that their minds can't be read. They're almost infallible.'

'If only King Bahvley could remember where he saw them and how to kill them,' said Huck.

'Your Majesty Stëinbøk,' said Mittah, 'is being King difficult for you?'

'Mittah!' exclaimed Jeremy.

'Well, Bahvley found it difficult at the beginning also. He can give Stëinbøk advice.' She paused. 'I don't mean to offend.'

'I know,' said Stëinbøk. He smiled. 'Don't worry. I've only been King a few weeks, and yes, it's a bit difficult, but not so much different than being Prince.'

'Did you have a ceremony?'

'No. We gave a brief ceremony for me father's soul, but no crowning ceremony was held.'

'Well, maybe with us all here, eventually, we can have a ceremony for you, with Teloria's blessing,' said Mittah.

'Perhaps.' Stëinbøk looked back at the fire.

'I'm sorry,' said Mittah, wincing internally. 'I don't always think before asking questions that don't necessarily concern me. It's just you're so young, and . . .' She trailed off, again worried she was being inappropriate.

Stëinbøk looked back at her. 'Not that much older than you, probably. But don't worry about offence.' He chuckled. 'If you feel that bad about having asked a more or less appropriate question at a more or less appropriate time, then one day you can make it up to me. In the meantime, I'm glad to be getting to know you all here in my home.'

Mittah nodded shyly. She certainly had made an impression, putting her foot in her mouth; she didn't know what kind of impression, though. The Tellen King smiled back at her, though she could not tell if it was to be polite or if she had made him feel better. Regardless, he certainly seemed glad to be with friends.

'Does every Tellen live in this Fortress?' asked Pete.

'Almost every,' answered Stëinbøk, drawing his attention away from Mittah. 'Some live in houses up in the largest trees. It was never safe to live on the ground. Even before this fortress was built, there were those shelters. Animals of all sorts live in forests.'

'Are you many?' asked Malcolm.

'We are as many as we are,' replied Stëinbøk, 'which is not that many in the end.'

'Just like us,' said Kchalami.

'Indeed, cousin,' Stëinbøk said with a smile.

Any relation between the two peoples had not been mentioned before – only in passing by Kchalami before arriving here. Nothing had been discussed with the Tellens. Many things had been thought by both the Tellens and Firlanians about the reconciliation of the families from long ago, but nothing was yet determined or concluded.

'Cousin?' asked Huck.

'If you remember correctly,' said Kchalami, 'the Firlanians come from the line of Mittèlor, long ago, who banished Bortah and those who desired the Portal after the peaceful Telorians' way was changed. Then, King Firlan Mittèlor went into exile with many of his family and founded Firlan. Thus, we exist and follow the command of our King, my father, Firnamel.'

'The others of the family stayed in Teloria,' said Stëinbøk. 'Those who did not wish to leave their home, yet the same fate came to us. Eventually, after many centuries passed, me ancestors felt bad for stayin' and not followin'. Not knowing where the others had gone, they wound up at the Twisted Forest and founded their own region, deciding to reside here and hide from evil. Only the rare few, ancestors of your friend Fimrel, remained in Teloria.'

'That's right,' said Fimrel. 'It isn't for nothing that I, like few others, have a Firlanian type of name. I'm drawn from the Mittèlor line, too, only many, many, many times removed.'

Everyone nodded and then looked again at Stëinbøk. He continued.

'It was when Mekhtel ruled – he who was a direct descendant of the Mittèlor line, long before his fall, at the beginning of his rule – that many of me people decided to get together. They were originally going to cross the Ortim River and travel to Firlan, but Mekhtel's forces drove them here to the Twisted Forest.

'They hid but were too frightened to go home to Teloria, especially once Malgar became King. Everything here was established and everything was nice, living in warm homes up in the trees, but he gave Tellens a scare. Thus, they decided to reinforce their safety here. So, me ancestors built themselves a fortress that would protect us, or perhaps was it with the intention of isolatin' ourselves. Who knows? It was a long time ago, before me time. But one thing remains certain: we remain Telorians, even if we changed the name in order to distinguish ourselves from Telorians from Teloria proper, the walled Teloria, and we remain the cousins of all Firlanians.'

Stëinbøk smiled at Kchalami. 'We are prepared to help in any battle that concerns our relatives, and our people and their friends. We are glad you came along to break the ice in this time of isolation. By fear, we have seldom ventured away from this forest. We're pleased to have met the Kikies and wish to learn more about them and meet the rest of them. I hear you speak of the Dûnelorians and the Dalvarans; I should very much like to meet these people.'

'I've no doubt you'll have the occasion to,' said Kchalami.

Stëinbøk took a beat. 'I don't know why we never came to help Teloria during the Big War, really. Perhaps still believing that Miruak wouldn't know of our existence if we hid here. Call us cowards, for perhaps it's what we are. Sometimes I thought me *father* cowardly. But now, we're going to make up for those times and be at the very front when we confront Mork.' There was conviction in Stëinbøk's voice.

'We will take counsel from those like your King, as you suggested, Mittah, and from Captain Tharguen, who have both been to Mork, and we will make amends.' Stëinbøk looked at the group of Telorians and Kikies before him. 'I am fascinated by all of you, and I feel truly blessed that you are here at a time when we need allies most. And you know what' – he looked back at Kchalami – 'we will repay you for all you have done and for all that we failed to do in the past. We won't fail you this time, I promise.'

'You never failed us,' said Kchalami. '*We* are the ones who failed you, leaving you behind.'

'And not going to help you when you left,' said Pete, 'us Telorians.'

'To us, it is a miracle that you still live,' said Kchalami, 'and I know that Bahvley would say the same in this matter.'

Stëinbøk and Kchalami shared a stoic expression before both smiled warmly at each other. It seemed to many as though the cousins had reconciled after a fight, even though, as far as the Telorians knew, there had been none. Yet, perhaps there *had* been, when some from the Mittèlor line left with Firlan while others stayed. Perhaps there had been a heated argument that divided the family after Bortah had been banished that had now been resolved once and for all, all these centuries later, and the tension or resentment that had remained was finally gone.

'Don't mind my asking,' began Huck, 'but how come all of your names end in "-bøk"?'

'Not all our names,' laughed Hunbøk, 'but a very pertinent question. You're quite curiously observant, but not enough. Not all our names end that way. Those who end in "-bøk" are those of the close royalty, those whose line is directly related to the Mittèlor brothers. Others are called "-lenk", those are from the second line, or should I say once or twice removed. From the other lines, there are few, so they are grouped to be called "-gon". Call us old-fashioned, but the names of our beautiful wives and sisters end differently from ours, in three groups again: "-fin", "-vøn" and "-ldu".'

'This was to distinguish ourselves more from visitors than from ourselves,' another Tellen explained. 'And to differentiate ourselves from Telorians when we left Teloria. And when that was, we were also a much greater number than this. No one lived here but the animals, but not everyone knew everyone, so if our ancestors met people, they knew by their names if they were one of them or a spy or visitor from somewhere else. We are only but a couple hundred left.'

'Interesting,' said Mittah. 'About the names. A shame about the number.'

Another horn was heard out in the distance.

'What's that?' asked Malcolm.

'The signal to say that someone's been injured,' said Stëinbøk. 'Two in less than a full day's cycle between. They must be gettin' hungry, the phantoms. Every time they strike, a horn is blown. We call them the Horns of Earnestness.' He paused a long time. 'Every day, I wait in fear for the next horn to sound, for the next call that we've lost yet another one of our people, or almost. And before it was these disgustin' . . . beasts, it was regular Morkans who came and tried to destroy us.'

He looked at Kchalami. 'We tried to leave. We wanted to, but to us, the thought of being welcome in Firlan seemed too far away due to the conflict that existed ages ago, and some Tellens snuck by to Teloria only to discover that Morkans were there and Teloria was destroyed, or so we thought. A small team and I travelled near the south of Teloria some years ago. A lot in Teloria had been fixed, but we found no one but Morkans, again. I took a risk in goin'. A shame we thought Teloria had been over-taken.'

'We were all in hiding,' said Eerzin. 'The first time your people went was probably during the Big War, the event that made King Bahvley and Captain Tharguen go to Mork with many of our friends. It explains why you couldn't help us then. I had stayed, for I was not well enough to go with them after a severe injury. That saved my life, as it turns out; they were the only two to survive. But I will let them tell you the details of their experience there.

'I, on the other hand, was sad not to tag along, but today I am glad I did not die trying to retrieve the *Book of Enchantment*. The second time you went to Teloria, everyone was in hiding, for Mork had attacked again. Little did they know that the *Complement Book* had gone with the Five to Mork, where they retrieved the *Book of Enchantment*.'

'I understand now,' said Stëinbøk. 'And then, the Five went to Darakön where the books were destroyed?'

'Yes,' said Kchalami, who had briefly told them the story. 'That was six years ago, when we met them for the first time after living in Firlan for so long. We, too, were isolated. Cousins act alike, I suppose.' He chuckled. 'Anyway, their story is an exceptional one. It's a shame they aren't here to tell it.'

'It's a shame everyone was in hiding when you came,' Mittah told Stëinbøk. 'We Telorians didn't even know if there was anyone who lived in this forest or not, though we hoped there was.'

'Well, perhaps we were not meant to meet until now,' said Stëinbøk.

He smiled warmly. There was such a liveliness about him, as though any tragedy he had lived through had been healed with this conversation. When the Telorians had first met him, he seemed stern, almost ageing with woe, as though his youth was masked. But now that his grief had been expressed and there was no more reason for regret, and no more animosity between the Tellens and Firlanians, he smiled and laughed along with the others – something he had not done in many long years.

Chapter Eighteen:
Blood In The Night

Down to the Fortress Gates the three Firlanians and six Telorians followed Lenarbøk and Vessibøk, grabbing their bags and cloaks from their rooms along the way.

'You don't know the peril you are gettin' yourselves into,' warned Vessibøk.

'Yes, we do,' said Bahvley. 'We're well equipped and well geared. We'll be safe.'

'Then I hope you're prepared to run the whole day.'

They sprinted into the depths of the forest and ran a long time before finally slowing down. They heard another horn in the distance.

'It's coming from a different direction than the other call,' said Gahli.

'Indeed!' said Lenarbøk. 'Someone else has been found injured this mornin'. Or perhaps it is now afternoon. We shall answer the first call and then go to the next.'

'How do you know where it's coming from?' asked Tom.

'When you've lived in the forest as long as we have,' said Lenarbøk, 'your ears become *very* sharp. Also, each horn has its distinct note, and each shelter has its own horn. We know exactly where the calls come from.'

'Good old forest life,' said Elmezni. 'We have similar signals in Firlan.'

'Then perhaps you can take the lead for a while. Me ears are tired for the moment.'

Elmezni smiled and gladly took the lead, guiding the others on paths through the thick bushes and tall trees.

After a while, Elmezni halted. Here the path split, and though the two paths were almost parallel, they still ran in opposite directions. Elmezni didn't know this forest, so he couldn't hope to guess which way to go.

Every now and then, the group heard the two distinct horns, and here the horns sounded nearly at the same time.

'Why do they keep calling out?' asked Lóim.

'For us to follow the sound,' said Vessibøk. 'Which is sometimes faster for us than to remember the location of each shelter with whichever horn. We brought no map, for we know our forest, but this makes it easier for us to find them. They will keep callin' until we reach them.'

He went to the front of the group and waited patiently for the next call, listening carefully. 'This way!' Vessibøk boomed when the call came, pointing at the path that veered westwards. 'We must hasten.' He darted off, the others following close behind. 'The phantoms, when they appear,' he explained as they ran, 'can do so at the other end of the forest, like they can emerge right next to us, and we've already delayed enough while we waited.'

He pushed aside a branch that stuck out into the path, cracking and bending it as he and the others hurried along the path as fast as they could. However, near dusk, some could no longer keep up, and they slackened the pace.

They were near the closest shelter now, and they all reached down into their reserves to push forward and make it before the fall of night.

It soon became dark under the trees. Pale leaves fell.

'The leaves are changing!' said Tom, also noticing the wind that was blowing the first few leaves off.

The moon was up now and had begun to glow as the light of the sun completely vanished. Still, the company sprinted towards the shelter, all using their very last bit of energy. They heard moving shapes but did not see them.

When they reached the shelter, those up high sent down a rope ladder. The group heard no more sounds coming from behind the trees. They climbed up quickly, first Bahvley, then Tharguen, then the five foresters followed by Tom, Gahli, Ihal and Lóim.

'Phew, we made it,' said Lóim as he climbed. Then: 'Uh! Ah!'

Someone was tugging him down as he strove to hold on to the ladder. He kicked the wretched beast, but it would not let go; it was unfailingly strong. Lóim slipped down a level and quickly grabbed the next bar on the ladder. Tom jumped down and pulled the phantom away from Lóim.

'Excuse me,' he said to the creature, 'but you're quite rude!'

It seemed to Tom as though it looked at him with a most puzzled expression before pouncing towards him. But Tom was swift and up the ladder he went, that one moment giving him enough time to lunge upwards away from the phantom and to safety.

The Tellens pulled up the ladder. They were all safe now.

'Congratulations!' said Lenarbøk. 'These creatures are not easily outwitted or thrown aback.'

'Must be my wizard skills,' replied Tom as he plopped down to rest. 'Perhaps it sensed my power . . . though I'm not entirely sure that's a good thing.'

The next day proved to be more promising than the first. The group of rescuers left in the early morning after a good rest and a breakfast that was satisfying enough. They walked at a rapid and con-sistent pace, never losing speed. The day was warm, and the Sun fed golden light on the changing leaves. Even if there were no red or golden browns yet, there were yellows and oranges, and to the Firlanians, this was the height of beauty.

In Firlan, the woods were cast with a spell to last the year without any enduring damage or change, sealing out the frost, even if the trees were not evergreens. Only was it cool for a short while in the dead of Winter. Their trees had large leaves, and from the tower they could see a sparkly white blanket of snow on top of them, whilst those who walked about felt the cool air but were yet in the warmth. This, the Firlanians explained to the Tellens. Never in their lifetime had they seen the true beauty of Colouring and the falling of the leaves.

The day passed pleasantly, and in time they reached the shelter where lay the injured Tellen before night had fallen.

Lenarbøk knelt beside his delirious friend, only a little pale but also cold and shivering like when a fever hits. Lenarbøk took the Tellen's hand.

'Hold on, lad, we'll get you home.'

'I don't understand how this can be,' said Bah-vley, 'when the other was dead.'

'It depends where they're struck,' said Vessibøk. 'These monsters bite on the arms, the legs or the neck, or even the stomach, and they suck their victims' blood out, suckin' their memories and the life out of them. How long they suck determines how badly off the wounded is, and where they strike as well.'

'Luckily for Merilenk, it was his arm at the wrist, and by what he's saying in his delirium, he's only lost track of a few weeks,' said Lenarbøk, relief on his face. 'Some we know lost many long years or even generations.'

'Has anyone ever lost all completely?' asked Ihal.

'Not yet,' said Vessibøk. 'Sometimes we fear they have, but up to date, no one has. And hopefully, no one ever will.'

The night was quiet and passed slowly to some, while to others the cloudy morning left them tired and wanting more sleep. Nevertheless, they had a mission and were on a tight schedule, so they got up and fought off any drowsiness. As Bahvley had put it: 'Once you're up, you're awake, but if you stop for a moment, you'll be sleeping for a day.' It was with this assertion that Bahvley had gotten through many days and weeks with little sleep, or even none at all.

The travellers took turns carrying Merilenk, and by nightfall they had reached another shelter. The next day, they changed course and went more northwards, passing by the small lake that had formed long ago when Zaccher Lake had flooded and formed a stream that trickled down to the dry dip of these woods. Now, dry no more was the dip, instead filled with the enchanted waters that came from the large and deep Zaccher Lake.

Another two days passed before they came to the shelter northeast of the fortress from where the second horn call had come, six days away from the fortress.

Lenarbøk and Vessibøk, who bore Merilenk, went up first. The others followed up the ladder and into one chamber, and then over a wooden bridge-like passage to the next tree where, in a slightly larger chamber, lay Mellavøn, a good friend to many of the royal court.

'What happened?' asked Lenarbøk, his tone filled with grief.

'The ladder broke,' answered a Tellen. 'The cord got cut on one side and she slipped, givin' the phantoms the perfect opportunity to pull her down completely.'

'Where were you?' Lenarbøk growled.

The other Tellen he spoke with bowed his head. 'We reached for her, but . . . they took her away. When we'd jumped down the ladder, they were gone.' He looked over at Mellavøn. 'We searched for her and found her near mornin', brought her back here and called out to the fortress. I'm sorry we were not faster in getting to her or in finding her once she'd been taken away.'

'That wasn't your fault. You did all you could,' Vessibøk said gently.

'What a fate,' said Bahvley.

He took a good look at Mellavøn. Her face was pale, her silky dark hair tangled up, her garments torn and dirty.

'Where was she struck?' asked Vessibøk.

'The stomach,' the other Tellen answered. 'I think they took her away from where we could defend her, struck her, and then left her, for she was alone when we found her.'

'Will she die?' asked Bahvley, looking up at the Tellens.

'Undoubtedly,' replied Lenarbøk, his jaw tight, 'but it will be some time before. Perhaps she'll experience a lot of pain, but there may yet be a chance to save her. She is me good friend, and she is close in kin to Stëinbøk. She is also one of the few to understand magic lore the way Telorians do. We've lost most of our wise ones in the many generations here. She is no wizardess, but the closest thing to one we have, and she is a strong fighter. If she dies, then we are in greater danger than we feared.'

'And that's already a lot of danger,' said Lóim, his voice low. He shared a dismayed look with Bahvley.

'What of Merilenk?' asked the other Tellen.

'He's already recoverin',' said Vessibøk. 'It won't be long before his memory begins to return.'

The next morning, Bahvley took it upon himself to carry Mellavøn. Tharguen had noticed that his friend seemed quite taken with her, yet he was not fully sure of it. The Sun shone brightly that day, though it did not liven the spirits of the younger Telorians, even as Elmezni, Krystal and Batel tried to cheer them up.

Lóim was walking alongside Ihal and Gahli, speaking in hushed tones. Tom, who walked behind them, crept closer, peering over Lóim's shoulder.

Lóim quickened his pace, but Tom kept on creeping closer and closer, and Lóim just knew Tom was listening in.

Lóim spun to face him. 'What's your problem?' he snapped.

'What?'

'You know, your problem! Always listening to hear what I'm saying, butting your nose in where it doesn't belong, always watching my every move, with your hawklike eyes. Why?'

'Uh . . .'

Lóim studied him carefully. 'I see. I see what you're up to. That would explain your odd behaviour ever since the others got washed away by the river.'

'Don't talk about them like that,' objected Tom.

'What are you protecting? What are you hiding? Are you that afraid I'll take advantage of the situation? I'm not an idiot, just a friend to those who are your friends too.'

'Well, if you should know, yes, I am worried you might take advantage of—'

'Why? Don't you know me by now?! I'm arrogant, yes, I admit it, but stupid and insensitive, I am not.'

'Well, sometimes it's hard to tell,' Tom rebuttled, taking a step towards Lóim.

'I can be violent, too.' Lóim got right in Tom's face.

'Hey! Come on!' Tharguen shouted angrily, pulling the two Telorians apart. 'This is not the time, nor the place, for such squabbles. What are you, children? There's enough war going on here. Take a look around you. There's peril here, there was battle in

Dûnelor, and there will be another. Who knows when war will break out again at home. If you want war, perhaps we can send you to fight alongside the Dalvarans!'

Tom and Lóim fell silent. Tharguen glared daggers at them, and the two skulked away from each other, disgruntled. Grumbling to himself, Tharguen continued on whilst keeping an eye on Lóim and Tom, who said no other word to each other for the rest of the trip.

'They've been acting very strange lately,' Gahli told Ihal.

'Too strange,' added Ihal.

'Perhaps they don't know how to act, considering,' suggested Gahli.

'Well whatever it is, it isn't helping.'

'No, it isn't.'

Elmezni sidled up next to Lóim. 'What was *that* all about?' Lóim gave him a sideways glance. 'It's obvious you're preoccupied by something. I promise I won't tell anyone.' Lóim gave no reply. 'I'm the trusted Firlanian friend.'

'We hardly know each other,' Lóim countered.

'Then you know I don't have any preconceived judgements about you,' replied Elmezni, grinning.

Lóim rolled his eyes. 'I suppose it might help to get things off my chest.' Elmezni waited patiently while Lóim mulled over how to express what was going through his mind. 'I think Tom knows something about the Five . . . regarding what happened. I'd like to think I'm observant enough to deduce such things. See, he was spending time with them before their disappearance. I understand if there is magic at work that those who practise magic cannot speak of, but . . . if there is . . . I guess I wish I'd know, too.'

Elmezni furrowed his brow. 'Assuming he does know something, are you perhaps envious Tom was confided in and not you?'

Lóim shrugged. Then: 'I get it, I'm not close with them,' he said coldly.

'How did you feel when you and everyone realised the Five were gone?' asked Elmezni.

'Truth be told, I feel really bad about what happened. I was devastated; I'm not entirely sure why.' He worked his jaw before speaking again. 'I've started looking up to Meysah. I know I used to be mean to him, but even now I'm trying to remember advice he gave me.' Lóim's expression became stoic. 'I've always been proud. I was too proud then to admit it, and I'm too proud now to tell my friends. Despite everything I put him through growing up, Meysah pulled through in Dûnelor, he was there for me. I was injured and . . . I panicked.' He winced in embarrassment.

'To be fair, the first time I got injured from an enemy I panicked, too,' said Elmezni.

Lóim looked at him. 'The polc didn't judge me, didn't laugh at me, didn't tell me I deserved it. He bandaged me, told me to get it together, and went to get help.' He turned to face the front again, his expression softening. 'He's my friend now.' He shook his head. 'Never thought he'd be.' He let out a one-breathed laugh. 'When Meysah and Jimmy returned from Mork, I think that's when I started to respect them.' He smiled. 'Jimmy's really set on his beliefs, but we had a good debate during our travels.' Lóim shook his head again, still smiling.

'It sounds to me like you're just worried about them just as much as the rest of us are,' said Elmezni. Lóim nodded. 'If there *is* something magical polcs know, you know as well as I do there's probably a reason the rest of us don't.'

Lóim shrugged. 'So far I've been able to cope by ignoring the worry.'

'You mean by being stern and acting cold because you're burying it deep inside?' Lóim gave Elmezni a nonplussed look. 'I look up to them too. I have to believe in my heart that they're all right, and that there's a reason for all this.'

'I hope you're right,' said Lóim, his stoicism being replaced by apprehension.

The next several days went by fairly smoothly. Merilenk was coming back to his senses, but he was not completely conscious yet. Bahvley and Lenarbøk took turns carrying Mellavøn, who finally spoke aloud, somewhat aware of what was going on around her. She was at first incomprehensible, but then she started to ask Bahvley questions about what had happened to her. She had not lost all her memory. In fact, it had been barely affected, but the wound was deep and grave, and even after the beast had left her, there had been a lot of blood loss. It was a miracle she hadn't died that night. Perhaps magic sustained her. However, Mellavøn *was* dying, albeit slowly, yet when she opened her eyes to take a look at the Telorian who carried her or walked beside her, she forgot about her pain.

Mellavøn asked Bahvley to tell her about himself and of Teloria. He also told her about Niome and the others, and of the Kikies. Although she knew it far too well, she did not mention that she was dying, for Bahvley kept telling her it would all be fine once she had had some Kiki medicine.

Mellavøn was prepared to die; in truth, a part of her preferred not to live through the great war that was coming. She had taken post at the shelter, risking her life, knowing she might die and being wholly prepared to do so. It was bound to hit her sooner or later, death. Now, she wanted to give people hope and survive long enough to share certain important things to certain important people and inspire them. Perhaps Bahvley knew her fate also and was only saying that for himself, trying to convince himself that there was still a chance that she'd live.

On the last day of travel, night seemed to have fallen too soon, for the travellers were still a good distance away from the fortress. Lenarbøk carried Mellavøn, while Bahvley held her hand reassuringly. They all raced as fast as they could.

As they neared the fortress, Ihal stopped abruptly.

'A puddle,' she said.

'But it hasn't rained in days,' Gahli noted.

Ihal bent down and smelt it. 'Blood.'

They heard a grumbling noise. Everyone exchanged wary glances. Lenarbøk cradled Mellavøn closer to his chest as they all slowly crept closer to the fortress gates. That's when they saw the figure looming before the portcullis, a polc lying at its feet. It seemed to still be sucking his blood.

'It's gotten one of our guards,' whispered Lenarbøk, alarmed. 'He must've come out to let us in.'

'They are obviously cleverer than they seem,' said Tharguen. 'Or is this one their leader?' It seemed to be of a larger build, as far as Tharguen could tell.

'I don't know, but they all look the same to me!' said Tom.

Lenarbøk's eyes darted this way and that, his jaw set. Catching his eye, Elmezni and Batel came to stand protectively in front of him, weapons drawn. Others came to stand on either side of Vessibøk, who carried Merilenk.

Everyone crept nearer to the fortress as quietly as they could, but the phantom knew they approached. It abruptly lifted its head, looking straight at Bahvley as it still hovered over the dead guard. A harsh whispery, monstrous voice spoke to him.

'*Ikonow kuyokh!*'

Tharguen eyed the beast with fear. Then he glanced at Bahvley. The phantom cast off its hood, growling hoarsely. Its canines were slightly longer and pointier than polc teeth and were stained with blood. Its face was sickly pale in the moonlight.

Tharguen could not decide if it looked more beastly or more polken. Then it stood, always keeping its glowing eyes on Bahvley.

'Fairhaven!' it said slowly.

Bahvley began to tremble and felt sick to his stomach. He clutched Tharguen. His breathing became erratic, and then, feeling his legs about to give way, he curled up on the ground in a crouch, like someone who'd just been stabbed. He moaned in pain as he held his wrist. At first he was rocking back and forth, then he became petrified and would not move. Still, his body was shaking, his eyes wide open.

'Bahvley!' cried Tharguen, not yet understanding what was happening to him. He knelt in front of his friend and put his hands on his.

'Tharguen,' Bahvley quavered weakly, 'I was struck – that's why I couldn't remember.'

'What?'

'They killed Liffwai!'

Then Tharguen understood. When Bahvley had passed the Islands of Mork, he had been attacked by these phantoms. Fear took hold of Tharguen's heart.

'You intuitively knew you'd seen them,' Tharguen said carefully. 'This has now been proven to be true. You somehow got away. You intuitively know you destroyed them. This must also be true.'

'They struck me – that's how the Kikies found me.'

'Perhaps the Kikies will have more insight into the situation,' said Krystal as several of the others called out to the guards inside the fortress.

'They struck me,' Bahvley said again.

Tharguen swallowed hard, trying to stave off his panic. 'How did you destroy them, Bahvley? Please remember!'

'I can't! It won't come to mind!'

The phantom laughed at them and started for Bahvley, who was still too scared to move. Tharguen stood quickly and pounced on the monster, pushing it to the ground.

'Maybe no weapon will kill them, but we can sure hold them down!' shouted Tharguen. 'Keep a watch in case the others are near and go inside! Bahvley, MOVE!!!'

The phantom tried to bite Tharguen several times, each time being pushed away by him. But in its fury, the beast grew fierce and turned Tharguen over several times, finally pinning him down on his stomach. He grunted in pain, trying to kick the creature.

'Get your bloody hands off my Captain, you demon!' shouted Lóim.

He, along with Krystal and Tom, pounced on the phantom.

'It gets easily angered,' said Tharguen, still struggling.

'Yeah, well, so do we!' said Tom. 'You hear that, bloodsucker!'

'From what I know of him,' began Tharguen, 'Mirauk gave them his temper.'

Krystal put her arm around the creature's neck in a chokehold, and it growled unpleasantly.

'Keep holding it down!' yelled Krystal. 'Tharguen, you can make your escape.'

Tharguen slipped out from underneath the phantom and got to his feet.

The guards had opened the first set of gates, and Lenarbøk, carrying Mellavøn, Vessibøk, carrying Merilenk, and Bahvley were ushered inside. The other Telorians had to practically carry Bahvley, for he still would not budge.

'Come, Captain!' called Ihal from the gate.

'I'm not going until they go first.' Tharguen turned to the others. 'Let go of the phantom and run inside.'

'But it'll go after you,' objected Lóim.

'It's an order!'

They let go of the phantom and ran to the gates. Tharguen took one last look at the phantom as it tried to follow. He looked it straight in the eyes.

'*Takhwod kuyokh tanwakh morofsûkh?*' demanded Tharguen.

'*Kuyokh iliw difnek tugo sookhen ekhunog!*' replied the phantom as it turned around and walked away, back into the depths of the forest.

Tharguen stood still in confusion. Krystal came back and pulled him in, and the guards closed the gates.

CHAPTER NINETEEN:
Praying To The Stars

The injured three and the dead guard were carried upstairs to the second floor. Lenarbøk led the way to the ward where the Tellens healed their wounded, Mellavøn still in his arms, as Vessibøk, bearing Merilenk, followed close behind along with the others. Tharguen and Krystal helped Bahvley, who was hunched over himself, his feet dragging behind him.

Word spread in an instant that they had returned and were safe inside. Everyone who was awake hurried to greet them but were shocked to see the injured, and the Telorians were frightened to see their King in such a state.

'Make way!' Lenarbøk called. 'They need space, and they'll need water and medicine, lots of it, for they've lost much blood and their bodies need to regenerate.'

Many stepped aside, though several Telorians and Firlanians began to panic upon seeing Bahvley in his condition.

'What happened?!' cried Kchalami. 'Did he lose a lot of blood?'

'No,' said Tharguen, 'he wasn't struck.' And then under his breath: 'Not tonight, anyway.'

Tharguen would have liked to elaborate and tell them that Bahvley had been struck only many, many years ago, but time was precious, and there would be opportunities to explain later.

Dessimë looked at Tharguen, who gave her a quick nod, eyes wide, and she read his mind.

'This will take Kiki medicine,' she said.

By this time, many of the Telorians had become agitated with worry and confusion; many Kikies moved in to calm them down.

Kchalami and Dessimë followed the returned group to the infirmary ward. Lenarbøk laid Mellavøn on a bed, as Vessibøk laid Merilenk in the bed across from her. Tharguen and Krystal helped Bahvley onto the bed beside Mellavøn's, uncurling his stiff limbs.

Krystal massaged Bahvley's back gently. 'You're safe,' she said soothingly. 'You're safe.'

Bahvley began to mumble, 'They killed Liffwai. We struggled all night. We were on a boat. We escaped the Islands of Mork, and they followed us. There were eight of them. How did I get rid of those three? The one downstairs . . . it killed Liffwai. Then it got me. On the arm. My wrist – it hurts to remember it. It was them. They killed Liffwai.'

And he repeated the whole thing over and over again. He was given water, and Dessimë gave him and the other two some medicine that she brewed up from the herbs brought from the Kiki land. The Tellens brought in many blankets for the injured.

'I don't understand!' said Kchalami with much concern for his friend. 'What happened? Could somebody please tell me?!'

'I don't know!' said Krystal, speaking hastily. 'All we know is the phantom spoke to him in the Morkan tongue, and then it said Bahvley's name and Bahvley began to tremble and got into the state in which you see him now.' She drew in a breath.

Kchalami nodded his understanding, his face grave with concern.

At that moment, Stëinbøk walked in hurriedly. His eyes widened in horror. He looked from Mellavøn to Merilenk, then he noticed Bahvley.

'He is in shock,' said Tharguen, who held Bahvley's hand in both of his. 'He has remembered dreadful events from long ago.'

'And the others?' Stëinbøk's voice trembled. Lenarbøk bowed his head as he stood by Mellavøn's side.

'Me Lord,' said Vessibøk, 'Merilenk has been injured least and is slowly regaining consciousness. Mellavøn has been struck at the stomach and has perhaps lost too much blood to recover, but at this time, there's still some hope.'

Stëinbøk walked to the bed where Mellavøn lay and crouched low, placing a hand on her arm.

'Me dear cousin,' he said, 'please hold on. Strong and valiant have you always been, and one of the best of our fighters. What ill fate has fallen upon you that you may be dying when so close was your time of glory and honour?' He stood. 'Ill has been me life since me father died,' he spoke angrily. 'Last season, he was still here! I was not ready for this! Not for his death, nor to take over his kingdom.' He shut his eyes tightly, clenching his jaw.

'Do not blame yourself for what Mirauk has caused you,' said Kchalami, taking a step towards him. 'You have done your best. I have seen it, and young or not, ready or not, you have done well thus far. You have your father's eyes and therefore his vision and courage.'

Stëinbøk tried to smile. He looked up at all who were there. 'I must order me people to return. They've been out there far too long this season, this year. It's cold out. This Winter will be the bitterest and coldest of all; I can feel it. All the signs are there.'

He turned and stormed out. Tharguen hurried after him, stopping him in the hall.

'What are you doing? What do you mean by "order your people to return"?'

'Every Winter is spent in this fortress. Me people don't stay out there to freeze, especially not when there are dark dangers lurkin' out there.' He started walking again, even faster than before. 'This has gone on far too long, and it's high time they all returned.'

'But you can't do that!' objected Tharguen, following Stëinbøk still.

'Why? I'm only doing what has been done all me life. Why would I not follow the same procedure as me father, the one we're all used to?!'

'Because my friends are still out there, and they could arrive here any time!'

'What tells you they'll directly come to the Twisted Forest?'

'I know them. If they were captured by Morkans, they'll find a way to escape. And they *will* escape, for they are the mighty Five of the Star, and when they do, their first thought will be to come and join us here.'

Stëinbøk stopped walking.

'I'm sorry, but I'm afraid I can't help you with that.' He started off again. 'If your friends do come, then they'll have to find the fortress themselves.'

'Are you mad?!' cried Tharguen, stopping. Stëinbok kept on walking. Tharguen jogged to catch up again and took pace beside him. 'No offence, but this is too much to take! You're saying that there won't be anyone to guide them and they will be left to maybe suffer the same fate as many of your people have!'

'Captain, what else am I supposed to do?! I've already lost too many dear to me. I can't leave me people out there to die; I'll have no one left to help me protect these lands.' He paused and lowered his voice. They stood at the foot of the watchtower stair now. 'This Niome – you love her very much, don't you?'

'I would die for her if I had to.' Tharguen felt a pang in his heart, aching for Niome.

'If indeed the Five are as powerful as I have been told, they will be protected and not fall to a cursèd fate as being bitten by the phantoms. They may not even come here this Winter if they are to be protected. Perhaps they're already in safe hands. If the river washed them into Morkan lands . . . it's easy to kill a Morkan. Had they come here now with you, they could've perished. Time and fate are on their side, so worry not. Please trust the stars; *I* trust them.'

'I trust that the spirit of Elina watches over them,' Tharguen said in a low tone. 'It is only unfortunate that we are suffering the fate of not knowing what is going on. Are you sure you absolutely can't have people guarding the forest?'

'I'm certain.'

'Then I'll just have to get out there myself and wait for their arrival,' Tharguen resolved.

'I beg you not to! If you go, I'll go with you.'

'But your people need you here!'

'Me point exactly.'

There was another very long pause as Tharguen came to understand. His heart grew heavy and he prayed that wherever the Five might be, they would stay there, or if they were to travel, they would not come to the Twisted Forest until Springtime.

'You can't ask me to do the impossible,' Stëinbøk said in a half whisper. He turned to the guard who stood nearby. 'Go up and at the first light of the Sun, blow the Horn of Earnestness.'

'Yes, me Lord.' And up he went.

Stëinbøk turned to face Tharguen. 'The biggest and loudest horn, with its own pattern and tune for the return of those in the shelters, different from the simple call to answer another's for help. While each of our horns sounds slightly different, the fortress's main horn is completely different from the rest. Me people will slowly but surely start returnin' home and by the first snowfall, everyone will be safe within these walls. If war breaks out, we'll all be together to defend ourselves properly.' Stëinbøk paused. 'I'm sorry you feel the way you do.'

'No, I'm sorry I had to argue with you. Too much has been going on for me to see clearly anymore,' admitted Tharguen. 'You must do what you must do.'

'Go to your friend. He needs you by his side.' Stëinbøk bowed his head. 'I, too, need someone by me side, but those closest to me are dyin'.'

'Not all,' said Tharguen. 'If there is anything you need . . .'

'Thank you. Same goes for you.'

Tharguen tried to smile, but it would not do. He returned to Bahvley.

Stëinbøk went to the other Telorains, who had gathered in the lounging hall where Celor was explaining to them what had happened. Those who had been already asleep when the rescuers arrived had been woken by the others, if not by the commotion, and they, too, were beginning to worry quite a bit.

Stëinbøk sat with them, and after more explanation from the Kikies, the Telorians and Firlanians had calmed and grown silent.

'Bahvley has been struck with memories of evil things this night and is suffering the trauma of it, for he has never remembered it until now,' said Celor. 'More than a generation has passed since the event. He'll recover shortly but will remember it forever now.'

Celor's eyes grew distant with memories.

'When he arrived in our land,' he went on, 'it was me, Phynd and Capooki who found the boat on the shores. We brought both Bahvley and Liffwai to our homes to heal them. Unfortunately, Liffwai was already dying when we found him and died shortly after, but Bahvley recovered quickly, his inner magic fighting for him. He couldn't remember what had happened since he and Liffwai had escaped the Islands of Mork.

'It was by reading his mind that we slowly learnt the language and understood words rather than thoughts and feelings. We made a burial for Liffwai. We were a little wary, not knowing your people, but being able to read Bahvley's mind, we knew we could trust him.

'Bahvley tried to remember for a long while and then one day let it go, figuring he had knocked his head during a storm. We could not extract the memory; we do not have that power, so we let it be as well, concluding a knock on the head was a plausible cause. If only that had been so. If only it was as simple as that. We can't read thoughts that have been forgotten. If we had such an ability, we would have already destroyed the phantoms.'

Everyone listened to Celor's story of Phynd, Capooki, Bahvley and him. Somehow, the sound of Celor's voice soothed their nerves. Then, everyone bade each other good night, for they needed their rest. They could only wait and see what was to be; no one could guess it and no one could tell them, for there were no prophets among them.

The next day, Bahvley was at last conscious and speaking coherently, though he felt queasy. He repeated his story in full about the attack that took place over a generation ago, but still, he couldn't come to remember what he needed to. His wrist still pained him as though he had had no time to feel the pain back at the Islands of Mork and now it was hitting him twofold.

'A majorly delayed reaction!' he tried to joke.

Bahvley stayed recovering in bed, sleeping a lot, while the others went about their business.

'Maybe we should tell Bahvley what's going on,' Kchalami told Tharguen sometime that day. They both stood in one of the corridors.

'No. He has enough to worry about at present. We don't need to give his heart another burden. Besides, it's lucky enough he didn't hear the horn this morning.'

'But as King of Teloria, he has the right to know that Stëinbøk doesn't plan to fight the phantoms until the warm season and that he is calling in his people.'

'Stëinbøk doesn't plan to fight the phantoms until Bahvley remembers how to destroy them,' corrected Tharguen.

'Still, he should be informed that all the Tellens are returning to the fortress and that no one will be out there this Winter,' Kchalami insisted.

'We've been through this before, Kchalami. Niome will be protected. The Five won't come here until after Winter. It took me some time to understand that, but I get it now. Anyway, what do you mean "as King of Teloria"? This is the land of the Tellens.'

'But the land of the Tellens is technically part of Teloria,' said Kchalami. 'It has never been officially separated from your kingdom. The wall only marks the region – same way Firlan has never been its own full kingdom, just its own region. Part of us is still Telorian, and we'll never deny it.'

He leaned forward, speaking with conviction, 'My father, Firnamel, once said to me that if the King of Teloria, our friend, should counsel him or ever order and command him, he would obey and do as Bahvley bade, for he trusts his judgement and doesn't doubt for one instant that his wisdom will falter.'

Tharguen pursed his lips, leaning an arm on the wall.

'These people, being cousins of mine,' Kchalami continued, 'I'm sure will have the same opinion. If he should just tell them to, I'm sure they can find a compromise. They are still Telorian. These woods are not named after them – unlike Firlan, and *we* still follow Teloria's lead – nor did the Tellens name their lands or their fortress – proof that they are waiting for Teloria to guide them! Right now Bahvley, to them, is the only credible person who represents Teloria and who can oppose Stëinbøk respectfully. He is the only person who can oppose any of us respectfully. He is the *King.*'

Tharguen passed a hand through his hair, turning his head from side to side in uncertainty.

'Bahvley will not overstep his ground,' he said at last. 'He will respect the Tellen King. And besides, you've had a chance to know us' – Tharguen motioned to Kchalami with his hand – 'a chance for your trust in us to grow, whereas the Tellens barely know us at all. How dare we command them in their land. Perhaps later, when trust has been built.'

'Well, then, for Bahvley's sake,' insisted Kchalami.

'I can't and won't let him worry about his sister, brother, master and friends,' Tharguen protested, shaking his head. 'It's too much to ask of him right now. He's still recovering. I know how he would feel in this; he's my best friend. And I am not mixing in my own feelings, for if I had it my way' – he pointed towards the window – 'we would all be out there right now.'

'Then what *should* we do?' asked Kchalami.

'Have Stëinbøk order his people not to mention it to Bahvley, and I'll order my team not to say a word about it either.'

Kchalami let out a heavy sigh. 'I don't agree with you, Tharguen, but I will tell the other Firlanians to keep quiet about it for now.'

'It's all for the better,' said Tharguen, 'though I am not the one who'll feel comfort for quite some time.'

'You and me both, my friend,' said Kchalami, placing a hand on Tharguen's arm, his eyes reflecting Tharguen's concern. 'You and me both.'

Bahvley woke from an unpleasant dream, but he was comforted the moment he turned his head. Mellavøn was lying in the bed closest to his, though he could not tell if she was awake or not. He hadn't the energy yet to sit up.

He turned towards the window; it was night again. He had woken briefly during the day and conversed with Tharguen and Dessimë, but surely others had come to see him while he slept. Bahvley looked at the stars.

'I'm confused. Why are all these dreadful things happening? I need counsel, but you're not there to give it to me.'

'Who are you talking to?'

Bahvley turned around. Mellavøn was awake and had turned her head to look at him.

'The former Chief of Knights, Gorthan, Master of Masters. He died while I was away, tortured by the enemy. Now his star shines in the sky. Rumour has it, he died of his own blade so he could become a star before the Morkans could kill him off for good.'

Mellavøn smiled. 'He must've made quite an impression.'

'He was a mentor and friend, to me and to many of us here.' Bahvley paused. 'How are you doing?'

'I don't know,' she said grimly. 'I don't feel very well.'

'You don't look very well, either,' Bahvley said, saddened. 'But you still look better than before,' he added quickly, catching himself. 'Especially when you smile.'

Mellavøn laughed. She stared, beaming at him. 'How are *you*?'

'Better, I think. I did not think remembering the horrors of my past would cause such trauma to my body. I feel tired.'

'Me too.'

'Hey, maybe next Summer I can bring you to Teloria and show you what a beautiful kingdom it is! You should see it in all its beauty – though the most beautiful sight I ever saw was when I met you.'

Mellavøn laughed weakly. 'I'd want to go, but it won't be possible.'

'I know . . . I was just hoping, dreaming.'

'It's only a matter of time. I'm fightin' it off as much as I possibly can, but I'm almost at me wit's end, and if me body doesn't rebuild its strength soon, I won't have any strength left with which to fight.'

'Then I suppose I'll have to describe it to you, then.'

Bahvley painted a picture of every corner of Teloria with his words, every nook and cranny: from the orange and rose morning skies to the vibrant greens of the grasses and trees, from the frosty Winter air to the hot Summer Sun. He told her about his house and his street, about the Royal Halls. He described every person he knew.

Bahvley recounted these descriptions that day as Mellavøn fell asleep. Then, whenever they both were awake he'd continue, and Mellavøn listened intently, asking many questions. Now she had descriptions to fit the stories Bahvley had told her. She asked him to describe Dûnelor, Firlan and Dalvar, and the land of the Kikies and the Colama Valley. She did not care to hear about Mork, though the stories of the Telorians' victory there intrigued her.

Mellavøn also asked about songs, for the Tellens sang seldom and knew very few tunes. Bahvley told her of many different types of songs that he knew, of funny marches like:

When are the fighters coming home?
They've been gone a little too long.
I don't feel like waiting alone,
Let's gather 'round; for them, we'll sing a song.

Of cute medleys like:

Far in the distance, I can see,
Such splendours that summon me.
My strength, I gather for my trip,
New flavours will be on my lips.

But the one that stuck most in Bahvley's mind that he sang in the end had been written long ago, during the wars against Malgar. It was remembered widely and sung by many. Bahvley had sung it many times while he was away; its words were dear to his heart. It was the same song that Meysah had sung to Vigh in the Dalvaran caves.

When all the world seems to be collapsing,
And nothing can be reached by light;
Just remember we have each other
And the Mighty Spirit watches over you.

Slowly, Bahvley got better and felt more alert. His strength returned, and the initial shock passed. When he was strong enough he went about in the fortress with the others, helping in the infirmary ward, healing the Tellens. Yet, he could still not remember how to kill the phantoms. Still, his companions were relieved he was back to his normal self. Merilenk, too, had recovered well, though his memory had not fully returned.

Mellavøn, however, was weakening every day, and every day Bahvley continued to visit her. He sat by her side and made her laugh and held her hand. The Kikies had told him that laughter was one of the best medicines, but such evil was in these demons that no amount of laughing was going to be able to heal her, not this time. It was similar to Mirauk's curse but through different eyes – or teeth, as it were.

By this time, Bahvley had expressed his feelings for Mellavøn and how sad it made him that she would be gone soon. She, too, had expressed how she felt and let him know that she could not have asked for a better gift than this: to know him for many cherishable days, to know love before her death. This, they'd often repeat to each other.

'It's a shame we've known each other for so short a time. We met but weeks ago and you will leave me so soon, too soon.'

Bahvley sat on the edge of Mellavøn's bed and held her hand close to his heart. Mellavøn spoke seldom now, and when she did it was low, weak and slow, even if she put great effort into it.

'It must be a lot of woe for a King to bear,' said Mellavøn.

'Perhaps,' said Bahvley. 'But the woe will be nothing compared to the joy I've felt. You almost made me forget my troubles, and for a time, I did. You can ask Tharguen; I never stop worrying or being alert. And I suppose Meysah, my brother, takes his anxiety after me. But he's a lot worse when it comes to nerves.' He tried to smile. 'I wish Meysah were here now.' He bowed his head.

'I would have gone with you,' said Mellavøn. 'You know that.'

Bahvley nodded. 'I would have made you my Queen.'

'Perhaps, once I'm gone, I'll see Teloria from above and I'll know of all the wonders you told me. I was strong with magic – maybe not much, but a little. I learnt from me aunt. So maybe I am powerful enough to become a star, and then, from up above, I can look down and see the world and you, and guide you and protect you.'

'Don't talk about such things now.' Bahvley swallowed hard.

'No. I want you to know that I'm not afraid, and I don't feel any pain anymore. It's all gone.'

Bahvley's heart sank. 'Why was there no one to protect *you*? Why did no one guide *you*?!'

'That doesn't matter anymore.'

Bahvley began to sob. He put his warm hand on Mellavøn's cold cheek and bent down, gently pressing his lips to hers. He kissed her for a long time, deepening the kiss with each passing moment. It was their first kiss, and their last.

'Goodbye,' whispered Mellavøn as Bahvley leaned his forehead on hers, his hand still on her cheek. 'I hope your sister succeeds in destroyin' Mirauk, and I wish you a very long and joyful life. Think of it as though I'm going on a trip, and you'll see me when you leave for your last trip. You moved me in the little time I knew you, and I die happy. I held on longer thanks to you.' Tears tricked down her cheeks.

'I love you,' Bahvley whispered.

In a last effort and in her last breath, Mellavøn spoke, 'Bahvley, there are forces beyond your understanding . . . working with Niome.' Then she smiled one last time before her eyes shut forever.

Bahvley kissed her cheek. 'Farewell. I hope you can see Teloria now.'

* * *

Out in the lounge, many sat around together. Krystal and Elmezni were telling stories about Firlan, which interested the Tellens greatly. Stëinbøk mentioned it would be suppertime soon and that he'd enjoy it if they all continued their stories while they supped.

Tharguen took it upon himself to go inform Bahvley, who always hated leaving Mellavøn alone while he went to eat with the others. Sometimes Tharguen even found him eating in her room while chatting with her.

When Tharguen arrived at the infirmary ward room where Mellavøn stayed, he saw that Bahvley knelt by Mellavøn's side, head bowed and sobbing, holding her hand close to his heart.

Tharguen said nothing, nor did he enter. He bowed his head as he stood at the doorway and turned back, feeling chagrin. For Stëinbok, for Bahvley, for all those who were close to Mellavøn and for himself. Though he never knew her the way others did, he had spent brief moments with her and Bahvley. He knew how she had made his friend feel.

Tharguen walked back to the lounge and approached Stëinbøk. The Tellen King's face fell upon seeing Tharguen's expression, and he knew what this meant.

'Hunbøk,' said Stëinbøk, grief in his voice, 'get Hanorlenk.'

Hanorlenk the Second was the Tellen scribe. His grandfather before him had been the official scribe, and now he followed in his footsteps. He was slightly passed polken middle age. While others fought, he protected their history books, their magic books and their books on healing. He could fight if he wanted to, but it was not recommended, for he his role was vital to everyone.

He was the one who would recopy notes or maps from the soldiers, who would write down the name of a newborn and what those who still practised divination could say about this new baby. He was very good at his job. Knights would sometimes write their story themselves in their own words instead of dictating it to him or telling him the main events.

When there had still been prophets, the future of newborns was not the only thing Hanorlenk would scribe down for them but anything they had meditated on or foreseen, and he alone with the prophet knew what was to come. Hanorlenk was not a prophet himself – at least not completely – but he would guard the secrets of a hundred years, being the only one allowed to read the prophecies in advance, the only one wise enough to do so. Now there were no more prophets, but the books on prophecies were still there.

Hanorlenk also wrote down the names of the deceased, indicating their position in the court and their date of death. Unfortunately, these days, there were many deaths to be recorded.

Stëinbøk and Tharguen joined Bahvley and stood next to him. Tharguen put his hand on Bahvley's shoulder.

'I'm sorry,' he said softly. Then he looked at Stëinbøk. 'Terribly sorry.'

Shortly after, Hunbøk, Hanorlenk, Lenarbøk and a few other Tellens arrived. The Telorians, Kikies and Firlanians had been asked not to crowd but to spread word of the event so that the others would know.

Hanorlenk stood with a large book in his hands. Hunbøk held a jar of ink for him with a feather in it. Stëinbøk turned to Hanorlenk.

'Mark: *Mellavøn, daughter of Bidoylenk. Stop.*' He spoke slowly enough for Hanorlenk to write but still at a steady pace. Hanorlenk was able to scribe quickly and legibly. '*After suffering effects from the bite of a dreaded phantom, she died on the fortieth of Colouring, the sixth day of the sixth week, forty-seven-seventy-two. Stop.*'

He paused and took a good look at her. Then he walked to the other side of the bed, for Bahvley was still crouched by her on this side, holding her hand.

'*Too young for death, she will never be forgotten. Stop. She was one of our bravest and most valiant; she knew the magic that many of us have forgotten. Stop. She could fight an entire army of Morkans on her own, and she did. Stop. Let it be known to all that she saved the lives of almost everyone who still lives, and that on many occasions. Stop. Pause.*'

Stëinbøk knelt and took her other hand. He looked at Bahvley. 'Perhaps you would like to mention something?'

'You should write how beautiful she was,' said Bahvley. 'She wanted to come to Teloria with me, you know?'

'Hanorlenk, sign my name,' said Stëinbøk. 'Then write: *She was beautiful and she was loved by . . .*' He stopped and looked at Bahvley. 'This is your part to say.'

'*She was very loved by all, and I dearly loved her.* Stop. *It's a shame Teloria did not know her.* Stop. Sign: *Bahvley Fairhaven, King of Teloria.*'

'You may close the book,' said Stëinbøk. 'Thank you, Hanorlenk.' He stood. 'Tonight's meal will be in her honour!'

A feast was held. Everyone grieved, and they prayed for Mellavøn's soul to find peace. They ate in silence, contemplating this tragedy. Indeed, she had been special to everyone. Stëinbøk knew they would have to carry on, as he had, despite all the losses he was still grieving.

After the meal, a memorial was held for all those who had died that season. They laid Mellavøn's body on a soft pile of hay in the middle of a stone room. As their tradition went, they burnt her body and kept the ashes for magic potions and poultices. This seemed strange to the visitors, but many times had the Tellens drunk a potion made from a powerful warrior's ashes, blended with certain herbs, and were healed from the wound or illness within the day. They had experimented with the herb mixture alone and the effects were not the same. The ashes were magical, and so was the healing.

Such a potion had been made in an attempt to heal Mellavøn, but in the end it could not cure the deep wound the phantoms had caused.

After the ceremony, the Tellens went to grieve on their own. The Telorians, Firlanians and Kikies spent time together and tried to liven things up a little amongst themselves. Those who wanted to be alone, they left alone.

Stëinbøk sat by the fireplace, staring into the fire as the flames rippled and grew, shrunk and moved, watching the fire go from blue to red to yellow.

Derfbøk came to see him.

'Me Lord,' he said. 'Many more of our people have just arrived.'

'I'm sorry, I cannot greet them,' said Stëinbøk. 'I am in no state. Me dear friend and closest blood cousin has just died.'

'They do not expect you to greet them. They've been told the news. You should be comforted to know that they're safe, that no horn has sounded since Merilenk and Mellavøn were brought in. Many more of our people will return tomorrow and many more after tomorrow, and soon, everyone will be home,' he reported in an encouraging tone.

'Thank you, Derfbøk. It comforts me. Make sure our guests are well taken care of. Make sure our true King is doing all right, for I believe this has grieved him more than it has grieved me.'

'I'll do just that.'

Derfbøk left Stëinbøk alone once again and went and did his errand.

Everyone was generally handling the event fairly well. Tharguen had gone to see Bahvley to make sure he was okay; he had hardly spoken a word all evening, and Tharguen feared he would not speak much in the days to come. The Kikies tried to comfort him, and as much as they tried to make him smile, Bahvley simply could not. He was not in a Kiki mood. Nothing else could be done. He needed to deal with this on his own.

Bahvley had a hard time falling asleep. First the memories, then the death. He wished his family were here with him. He wanted Niome by his side, wanted her to have been here to perhaps have pronounced a spell to heal Mellavøn. He wanted Meysah and Jimmy to be here and make him laugh until his stomach hurt, to annoy him and help him forget the pain he felt. He wanted Vigh and Boreth's wise words to comfort him. But they were not here, and it was not so. And then again, perhaps had they been here at the fortress, Bahvley would not have wanted to see them anyway and would still be isolating himself. At least Tharguen was here, and that counted for a lot.

Bahvley finally fell asleep but slept for only a short amount of time. He awoke suddenly from an unpleasant dream. He tossed and turned and wished he could get some counsel from home. He thought of

Henker and Selemil, remembering what they had told him before he left for Dûnelor.

He got out of bed and walked to the window, looking out at the stars.

'So, I finally start to remember after all these years,' he said out loud in a soft voice. 'What a turn. So much has happened I did not expect. And why? You always told me great things would happen to me, but right now, I'm having a hard time taking in all that's been happening. I need a new thought now. I need sweet dreams.

'Henker told me I should ask you for guidance. It's a little bit difficult since you're not here, but if you're watching over me right now, Gorthan, I'll ask only this: protect my people. I could ask you to spare many lives of those for whom it is too late to save. I could ask you to give me better dreams. I could ask you to bring me home and erase my memory of what I have just discovered. But we are all in good hands here where we are, and we'll get through this well. I can deal with these memories. They'll stop haunting me eventually.

'I wonder if you ever had similar thoughts as I when you were young, or if you ever wished you had chosen different paths. I wanted to remember where I had seen those familiar phantoms; now I wish I hadn't. The horror I had forgotten will remain in my mind forever.' He paused and took a deep breath.

'All I ask is that the people of Teloria stay safe and protected. But more so, that Niome, Meysah, Jimmy, Vigh and Boreth stay safe and alive, wherever they may be and whatever may be happening to them. A lot relies on them. They are the most important people in all our lives, in Kaulchèc History, and I ask that you protect them. And Tharguen asks it, too. Keep them safe, keep them in this world. Please, hear me – keep the people I dearly love alive until they decide their time is up.'

Bahvley sighed before walking back to his bed and rolling back under the warm covers. He lay staring at the ceiling for a long time before he fell back asleep.

CHAPTER TWENTY:
Mask Uncovered

As Winter came, it got colder and colder, on top of the fact that it was already frigid under the ground in those dark tunnels where not much was happening except for routine events. The Five found themselves thinking about Bahvley, Tharguen and everyone else from time to time. They had, after all, left them behind to wonder if they were alive and where they were. Niome wondered if they had found the Firlanians, if they were all right and what kind of people the forest dwellers were.

Time was passing by, and Vigh began to worry. He had one main concern: Kàtchah.

'We can only delay so much longer,' he told the others. 'We can't keep the Morkans digging just anywhere forever. And we absolutely can't let them find our secret ways out. We can't disappear out of the blue, but we can't let Kàtchah see us. We may have to create a diversion. Perhaps we can say we need to leave, that we were summoned by Mirauk, and we just tell them to await further orders from Kàtchah. By the time they figure out it was us who misled them, we'll be long gone. Or we can wait until the last moment, try to find out more about what's going on in Mork, what battles Mirauk is planning, and perhaps Kàtchah's arrival will be diversion enough, but . . . we'll be expected to greet him, no?'

'We have to think of something,' said Boreth, 'and we have to think fast. I doubt they'll buy the summons thing though. We never spoke about the possibility of being summoned at any random moment before. It might be taken too suspiciously.'

'But what are we to come up with?' asked Jimmy.

They had spent all their brain energy on creating plausible excuses for the new tunnel plans such that they had no imagination left in them. They couldn't just disappear into oblivion – that too would be too suspicious. Once the Morkans saw that the Telorians were gone, they would investigate, and then Darakön and Firlan would be in grave danger anyway. The Five had to find a way to destroy the tunnels, Meysah had voiced. That was perhaps their best option.

At least they had their secret tunnels from which to escape when the time came. It was unlikely that the Morkans would find these, as the Five had patched everything up to disguise these accessways. There were holes in the walls on the bottom, in corners, hidden by rocks. These led to extra rooms that the Telorians had dug themselves, and it was in those rooms that the secret hatches lay, also covered up. So, even if those first stones were to be removed, it was still not obvious what lay beneath. They had been extremely careful during their digging, being cautious: only digging at night, alone, with the help of magic and in far secluded corners of the tunnels.

Still, they couldn't allow the Morkans to know they were leaving. Otherwise, they'd have a farewell meal and the Morkans would know about the ways out, and that would bring the Morkans too close to Firlan. Plus, it was a danger to themselves, for when Kàtchah would arrive, he'd have his army go after them and stop them. Perhaps Meysah's destruction idea was the best after all. Vigh kept his thoughts on ways to flood the tunnels, but nothing was done about it yet. All any of them knew was that time was passing by, and Jimmy did not look forward to facing the cold of Winter outside.

One morning, as Jimmy was walking through the main tunnel hallway, he came upon a great cape with medals and jewels on it. It seemed to be hanging on a stick, drooping over it imposingly yet majestically. He lifted the cloak and found a sword planted in the ground, also with jewels – dark jewels. It was as though the polc had left it there whilst elsewhere, trusting it was safe to leave it there unguarded. Somehow, Jimmy recognised the garment and weapon, but he couldn't pinpoint where he'd seen them before.

He looked around and saw shadows in the distance. He cast his hood on and turned back. Along the way, he bumped into Gohtek.

'Oh, I've been looking for you, Captain Lugh. Kàtchah has arrived.'

Jimmy swallowed. *If Gohtek is here with* me, thought Jimmy, *who is with Kàtchah? Perhaps his army, maybe a large one besides that.* They would be in grave danger if that army was to be sent after them once they had fled.

'I'll go find the others and tell them the good news,' Jimmy said, trying his best to sound pleased. 'Don't mention anything until we arrive. I want our presence and progress to be a surprise.'

'Understood!'

Jimmy ran to the chamber where the other four were, the room they shared as a bedroom. He was out of breath when he got there.

'He's here! Now!'

'Kàtchah?! How?' They all exclaimed.

'I guess his magic is beyond what I thought,' said Niome. She began to bumble, 'I created a drought to get us in; he probably froze the deep waters under the ice and bore his way in. In my vision, I saw someone separating the waters with a whirlpool, but that was during the warm seasons.'

'That doesn't matter,' Jimmy panicked. 'Who cares *how* he got in. He's *here*.'

'What's the date?' asked Vigh.

'The first day of the eleventh week of Colouring,' said Jimmy, calculating, 'therefore, the seventy-first.' He shook his head vigorously. 'He's a whole week early!'

'We have to disappear!' said Meysah.

'We'll make for Darakön,' Niome instructed, 'to warn the dragons. We shouldn't be too far anyway.'

They grabbed their things, secured their weapons, slipped their bags on their backs under their cloaks and satchels over their shoulders, and prepared to leave. They snuck out of the room and walked to the nearest secret way out. It was through one of the older narrower tunnels, in a far corner.

'You go first,' Niome said to Jimmy and Meysah, 'then you can help me out.'

They agreed and passed through the seemingly small hole into the secret room. Before Niome even had time to bend down, a Morkan arrived.

'Ah, there you are. Evaluating, I see. We should continue digging in this area, I think. It's a suggestion, of course. Anyhow, *they* are waiting.'

'We are right behind you,' said Boreth as he and Vigh started to follow the Morkan.

Niome lingered momentarily, whispering quickly towards the secret passage in the wall.

'Go on. We'll join you when we can; don't wait up. If anything happens and we don't get to you soon, go to the Twisted Forest and we'll meet there, whenever that may be.'

'I don't like this,' Meysah muttered to Jimmy.

'Me neither.'

Meysah looked down at the accessories in his hands. 'It's a good thing we brought scarves and mitts and hats.'

'Sure is. I told you we might be gone longer than we thought. And these little kits, folded as they were, fit in our bag pockets. We barely noticed they were there. Am I a genius or what!'

'Yup. It's also a good thing Niome enchanted some of these for us to help keep warm,' said Meysah.

'Tell me about it!' replied Jimmy.

'Your dislike for cold prepared us for the un-predictable.'

They tried to smile but the two sobered, for too great was their worry. They each bundled up and then went outside through the hatch at the top. Snow blew fiercely, and the wind was bitter. They took a few steps and sank deep into the snow.

'We're not *that* far from Darakön, I think,' said Meysah. 'We can sprint for a few days. We can stand the cold – we can do this.'

'There'll be plenty of fire and warmth there,' said Jimmy, imitating Meysah's impetuous tone. 'It's enough motivation for me! Let's go.'

And they walked through the depths of the snow, heading for the mountains, hoping only to survive until they reached the dragons' lair.

'What's the plan now?' whispered Niome, catching up to the two Lords who had slowed enough to keep a small distance between them and the Morkan leading the way.

'Figure it out,' Boreth whispered back.

'We can't let Kàtchah see us,' said Niome.

'And we can't let anyone discover the secret, so we're going to the next one,' said Boreth. 'It's the only other way.'

'Ssh! The Morkans'll hear,' Vigh warned.

'But . . . the other ways are past where Kàtchah is,' objected Niome.

'Precisely,' said Vigh. 'We're going to go straight for it, meeting him head-on.'

'Face-to-face,' said Boreth. Always right beside the other in any decision were those two, always together. 'He won't expect people such as us to act like Morkans and show ourselves. It'll throw him off.'

'I just have a terrible feeling about the whole thing,' said Niome.

As they arrived near Gohtek and Captain Kàtchah, the Telorians heard them discussing them, or at least discussing their Morkan aliases.

'But Mirauk has not disguised himself since . . .' they heard Kàtchah argue. 'No, it can't be him. If he would've sent anyone out here from Mork, I'd've known of it; I was just there.'

'Remember, Mirauk doesn't tell everybody everything,' said Gohtek. 'There's a lot we do not know. If he chooses not to tell, there's a specific reason which only he knows, but I swear, there is something in the boy's eyes. Sikhlah saw it, and I see it too. It's him. Either that or this young Morkan's a wizard, but magical, he is.'

The three Telorians and the guard reached the Morkan Captains by the end of their exchange. Two others stood with Kàtchah and Gohtek.

Kàtchah looked at the Telorians carefully; they still wore their hoods.

'Hello,' said Kàtchah. 'I understand you've been taking care of the digging.'

'Yes,' replied Vigh.

The other two polcs turned to them as well and nodded politely and courteously.

Niome swallowed hard. She saw the two Lords stir uneasily in front of her.

However, it seemed Niome's spell had been cast on Kàtchah too. Yet she had not cast it again, and now she did not know whether it was her own power or some trick Kàtchah was playing. Still, she would not have him figure them out so easily; she was going to play the game.

Feeling confident, Niome looked Kàtchah in the eyes and used her magic to glimpse his mind. 'We are honoured to see you arrive so soon, Captain Kàtchah. Though I had almost forgotten, you are always early.'

'Few know of my habits,' said Kàtchah, furrowing his brows. 'I am surprised you know of them yourself.'

'What he means is, the honour remains his,' said Gohtek. 'As it is ours.'

'And muchly ours,' nodded Niome. 'A great honour it is to meet with the Dukes.'

'We wanted to see the operation,' said Merlik, continuing his well-mannered speech to her. 'Kàtchah's masterpiece.'

Her last encounter with Kàtchah, as he had ridden on his horse, had left her with a nasty impulse to insult him. As for the Dukes, they probably feared her more than she and the others feared them. She stopped herself from certain impulses brought on by fear and adrenaline. Kàtchah and the Dukes were being polite with her, treating her like an equal, like a fellow Morkan. She had fooled them. Hence, she reminded herself to remain civil with them as long as they were civil with her.

'Where's Captain Lugh?' asked Gohtek. 'He'll have to forgive me for speaking about you and ruining the surprise.'

'Oh, that's fine,' said Boreth. 'There was an argument between a few of our workers that caught his attention. He went to resolve it. He should be arriving shortly.'

'Ah, well, he's always so attentive to every detail that there is in this place,' said Gohtek complimentarily. 'Why, he even pays attention to the desolate corners.'

'Really?' said the Dukes together with Kàtchah.

'Now, if you don't mind,' Niome began, 'we have a little duty that awaits us. You may wait for us in the room down the hall.'

'Certainly,' agreed Kàtchah.

Gohtek was perhaps praising Jimmy, but he was also revealing details that could give them away to Kàtchah and Dukes. If he were to speak about the rest of them, it could bode ill for the Five. The last thing Niome wanted was for Gohtek to mention how he thought she looked like Merlik and bring even more attention to herself. Too easy was this trick, perhaps, and that was what Niome feared the worst.

The Telorians started off past the Morkans who made for the other direction. The two Lords breathed more easily, but Niome held her breath.

Gohtek stopped. They were only a few steps away from each other still.

'Is Pateek with Lugh?' he asked.

'Yes,' said Vigh.

'How many are there?' asked Kàtchah.

'Oh, only five,' said Gohtek. Niome winced.

'You never told me the number!' Kàtchah snapped.

'Why is their number important?' asked Gohtek, confused. The Dukes were eyeing the Telorians warily. 'All that's important is that they were sent out after the Five and reported to us and were to help here.'

Kàtchah thought for a moment, then glanced at his guards, who slowly surrounded the Telorians. By their hesitation, it was clear they still thought the Telorians were Morkans.

The three Telorians slowly began to step away before they could be completely surrounded.

With a jerk of his head, Kàtchah prompted his guards to move faster, and they did what their Captain asked of them, though their expressions remained that of confusion. Even the Dukes were looking at Kàtchah in a puzzled manner.

'Five polcs arrive. What a surprise.' Kàtchah said with sarcasm. 'Then they have you dig in different directions, *away* from Darakön. They are interested in dark corners left alone – why?' He walked to the three Telorians. 'Two young polcs, two older polcs, and a boy whom you believe is a wizard.'

There was a change in his eyes, as though whatever spell had been upon him had now been broken. The Telorians could back up no longer, now surrounded completely, and the Dukes' expressions and postures changed to one of surprise followed by condescension for Garkhktak and disbelief for Merlik.

'My, what fools are we!' whispered Garkhktak.

'Fools! Fools!' shouted Kàtchah, urgently and angrily. He glowered at Gohtek. 'A spell has been cast upon you! These are the Five Telorians!' Kàtchah turned to Niome. 'Very clever of you, Niome Fairhaven.' He cast off her hood.

'Oh, but that's not the last of my tricks,' said Niome, pulling her hand out of her bag.

She pointed the Dragon's Wind at the Morkans and they were pushed away. Gohtek fell onto his back as the Dukes and Kàtchah staggered back. Garkhktak placed a hand on Merlik's shoulder to steady him.

The three Telorians ran as fast as they could, but Kàtchah was swift. He caught up with them and plunged at them, grabbing Boreth's boot. Boreth tripped and knocked Vigh down with him.

'Two birds with one stone!' exclaimed Kàtchah triumphantly. 'A satisfactory catch.' He sneered at the Lords with satisfaction.

Garkhktak stooped over them, his sword pointed down and ready to strike. Merlik kept running, going after Niome.

Gohtek yelled in anger for his foolishness. He bent his bow and aimed it at Niome.

'No! Don't!' shouted Kàtchah as his guards surrounded the Lords, swords pointed at their throats. Kàtchah picked himself up. 'Don't try anything else, Gohtek; it would be foolish. Such magic is not for us to deal with. Let her escape. Mirauk will deal with her.'

All of the Morkans now saw the Telorian Lords as they truly were.

Niome turned the corner, wishing she could do something to save Vigh and Boreth. Suddenly, a firm grip caught her arm and she jerked backwards, turning slightly to regard the polc who had grabbed her.

Merlik looked straight into her eyes.

'Niome Fairhaven,' he sneered. 'I admit, your power surprises me. A disguise of this sort . . . I cannot decide whether to despise you for it or to admire you.'

'Perhaps you already admire me for it,' replied Niome, doing her best to steady her shaking voice.

She pushed him away and began to run. Again, he grabbed her and pulled her in closer, reaching for his weapon. She looked at him sternly. He paused, his breath hitching in his throat, and scowled as he stared into her eyes. Then, as suddenly as he had caught her, he let go, pushing her away briskly.

Niome stared at Merlik in wonderment, but he did not say anything nor do anything else. He merely stared at her, mouth agape, for what seemed a long moment. He looked stunned, but by what, she could not tell.

Niome backed away slowly, and then she ran and veered to the next corner. When she glanced back behind her, she saw that Merlik remained standing still, staring at her until she had gone.

Niome ran to the secret passage at the end of the tunnel, pushed the stone that blocked the way and passed through it. She then put the stone back and got dressed for the chill that awaited her outside. She popped open the trap door and jumped out, lifting her arms and hurling herself up. Snow was blowing everywhere, but it was the snow from the ground; there was not a single cloud in the sky. This meant cold – very cold. Though Niome had seen many days like this, it was even colder than she could have expected, and she knew that this Winter was going to be the coldest ever. She could just feel the chill.

Niome let her eyes adjust to the light, for the snow sparkled and reflected the sunlight. Then she looked into the distance and tried to see Jimmy and Meysah, but they had already gone too far. Even if Niome had run the other way and gone out the same way they had, she would not have seen them, she reckoned. So, she started to hurriedly walk, scarf over her face, her arms close to her body to keep warm.

'Get up!' snapped Kàtchah. 'Merlik warned me that your power had grown.' The two Telorians stood as guards continued to point their weapons at them. 'I hear you've become Lords. Teloria has a King; Bahvley Fairhaven has been found and spotted. We knew he was still alive. All that's left is to know his location. It's unfortunate for the Dûnelorians that they chose to ally themselves with you and break their deal with us.'

'They knew you Morkans would betray them,' said Vigh as guards restrained him. 'They're not stupid.'

'What a lout you are!' Kàtchah looked at his guards. 'Disarm them! Take their bags, swords, shields, bows. Oh, and check their boots for knives, and their sleeves too.'

Once that was done, Kàtchah turned around and his guards and Gohtek followed, shoving Boreth and Vigh along. Merlik encountered them.

'I see you did not catch up with Niome,' said Garkhktak.

'No,' Merlik replied hesitantly. 'She escaped me.'

He looked at the two Lords and gave them a fierce glare before following the others. They threw the two Lords into a room and locked its door. After a while, Kàtchah and Gohtek returned. The door was closed and guarded behind them.

'My workers have been informed about you,' said Gohtek. 'I must say, never has anyone been able to cast such a spell on me before. How could I have been so blind!'

'I still can't figure out where Niome went,' said Kàtchah. 'Merlik says she veered around a corner and then she was gone. He is in shock; he can't explain where she went either. And the other two, where did they go? Speak.'

'Gone, away,' said Boreth as he and Vigh paced about in the room.

'I see,' said Kàtchah. 'You know, I can easily ambush Teloria again, but Mirauk wishes to wait.' The Lords stood still at this. 'Though if I did, you would not come back home in time to warn them. I find it redundantly foolish of you to keep trying. I'm lucky to have you in my grasp. What a disappointment to Mirauk's bloodsuckers! I guess they'll just have to feed on whoever lives in the Twisted Forest.'

Vigh and Boreth looked at each other in shock and disgust. Vigh felt like shouting out in protest that their friends, Bahvley and Tharguen were there, but he held in his breath instead, as fear gripped him.

'So, tell me, why did you come here?' Kàtchah folded his arms.

'To avoid the phantoms,' said Vigh.

'So you did encounter them before they reached the Twisted Forest. Ah, but you don't know what they're capable of, and I won't be the one to tell you, either. I might just let you find out for yourselves, for one day you will. But I know that that's not the reason why you are here.'

'But it *is* the reason why we are here,' said Boreth.

'Don't lie! Why did you come here? And what are you hiding in Darakön?'

'You know,' said Boreth, 'for once, we're actually co-operating. We're telling you the truth, Kàtchah. We know there's no point in lying to you. Niome had a premonition, which is also how she discovered these tunnels existed. It's actually Merlik's fault; she read it in his mind by looking into his eyes, him and his brother. But it's true. We came here to avoid the phantoms!'

'Then why divert all digging plans to other locations?' demanded Gohtek. 'Seems to me you're hiding something, and don't try blaming the Dukes again. Kàtchah's in charge here, but he could easily give his power here away to the Dukes and have them decide the tortures you are to receive. And believe me, they are much crueller than Captain Kàtchah is.'

'We're not hiding anything,' Vigh said calmly.

'You are,' countered Gohtek. 'In Darakön.'

'We're only trying to help the dragons,' explained Vigh. 'You want the truth? Here's the truth: the dragons sleep in the Winter. We weren't going to let you destroy them in masses. They're our allies. Besides, those caves belong to them.'

'And those books are being kept by them, I presume,' said Kàtchah.

'What?!' exclaimed Boreth in a confused, high-pitched tone. 'You think the books are still around?'

'Teloria would be stupid to keep them with a wizard,' said Kàtchah. 'It didn't keep the books safe last time. It would be a lot safer to hide them in Darakön while the Wizardess grows in power and waits until she's ready to go through the Portal. So, where are the books?!'

'Is that what you think? Because that's not it at all!' said Boreth.

'Oh, no? Then what *is* it!'

'No one was meant to go through that Portal. It belongs to the dragons and the dragons alone. I'm sure *he* knows this by now. The dragons took the books and burnt them before our very own eyes.' Boreth, annoyed, became condescending. 'The two books were destroyed, quite some years ago. They don't exist anymore! Do you get that?'

'You lie!' shouted Kàtchah, grabbing Boreth by the collar and lifting him off the ground.

Vigh pushed Kàtchah away from his friend, who fell, and slowly walked towards the Morkan. Much taller than his friend, Vigh appeared imposing. Kàtchah was perhaps taller than Boreth, but not by much, and Vigh was much taller and much more formidable than the tiny-brained Morkan he wanted so much to kill.

Keeping a certain amount of cool in his voice, Vigh spoke through his teeth as he towered over Kàtchah, 'What do you want us to say? You want us to tell you only what you want to hear?'

'Vigh, don't!' Boreth warned, predicting what was going to come. He lifted himself off the ground.

'Do you want us to say that the books are still intact?' continued Vigh. 'Do you want us to say that we're hiding them in Darakön purposely? Huh!' Now he shouted. 'Do you want us to say that we only mentioned the phantoms because you mentioned them first and that all this time, we were trying to protect the books?!'

Kàtchah took his sword and slashed Vigh's upper arm. A small scratch, but enough to make Vigh yelp out in pain, enough to shut him up. Vigh pressed his hand on the bleeding wound.

'May I remind you,' Kàtchah threatened, 'that you are not as strong on your own without the other three.'

He and Gohtek left the room, leaving Vigh and Boreth there alone.

'What an idiot!' seethed Vigh as he held the wound on his arm. 'We tell him the truth and he thinks it's a lie.'

'Maybe we should tell him what he wants to hear,' suggested Boreth. 'It'll only bring him to his downfall, not to mention humiliation, and then perhaps Em will see that Kàtchah is full of folly.' He paused. 'It's difficult not saying his name, especially on Morkan grounds.'

'Whether we tell Kàtchah what he wants to hear or not, he's still going to dig to Darakön.'

'But Jimmy and Meysah and Niome went to warn the dragons. The Morkans won't get past the entrance.'

'Let us hope so,' said Vigh.

At that point, the door opened again. Gohtek threw a bag on the floor.

'Here,' he said. 'Your supper's in there, and bandages for the wound. If it weren't on the Dukes' insistence, there would be no supper.'

'Thank you?' said Boreth suspiciously. Then: 'Thank Merlik and Garkhktak.' He looked at Vigh. 'They're going to love that,' he chuckled in a whisper.

'As our prisoners, we would like to treat you poorly,' said Gohtek, 'but as you are wanted in Mork and in perfect condition, we are forced to treat you slightly more fairly.'

'What do you mean?' asked Vigh, parsing the subtext.

'I mean that once we've broken into Darakön, you will be brought to Mork.' Gohtek shut the door.

'So now *we'll* be sent to Mork,' said Boreth. 'I'm telling you, they never *only* wanted Tharguen. They want us all, Bahvley included.'

'Em wants us intact,' Vigh said ponderously. 'We're valuable to him, and that means he knows he's the only one who can destroy us. He wants to use us for his magical purposes and turn us into drones against our own people, if he can manage it. I think that's one reason why he wants us un-damaged. Plus, he knows if we look at him, we'll be cursed anyway. Either we die, or he lifts the curse off us but we sell him our souls. Or he'll read our minds and discover Teloria's secrets and then kill us himself. That's the way I see it. It's just . . . how ever are we going to get out of here?'

He sat down and opened the bag. There were two flasks of water, some bread and cheese, some dried meats and a bandage for Vigh's wound. Vigh didn't drink much of his water, for he used most of it to clean his wound; who knew what filth was on Kàtchah's sword.

'I wish we had access to our herbs,' said Vigh. He put the bandage on.

Then the two ate silently.

The next day, after lunch, Kàtchah and Gohtek returned to their captives.

'Did you enjoy your meal?' asked Gohtek.

'Why?' Boreth asked in suspicion.

'Because I hope your stomachs are full and you have enough energy to walk around today,' said Gohtek.

'Let me guess,' said Vigh, 'you're going to make us dig.'

'No,' said Kàtchah, 'but continue being smart-mouthed and we'll make you crawl!'

Gohtek threw two maps on the floor at the two Lords' feet.

'We found these in your bags,' said Kàtchah, 'and we noticed a few changes.'

'What's that?' Boreth asked in a surprisingly friendly manner.

'Secret passages to get out of here!' said Gohtek, clearly annoyed by Boreth's nonchalant manner. 'As far as I know, there's only one way out: Darakön, which we haven't gotten to yet.'

'Quite clever of you to dig exits without anyone else knowing about them,' said Kàtchah, walking towards the two Lords. 'Is that how the others got away?'

'I guess so,' replied Vigh.

Kàtchah whacked Vigh's face with the back of his hand, striking his mouth with his jewels. Vigh looked at him angrily and thought, *This polc really doesn't like my face, does he?*

'Is that how they got away?' Kàtchah asked again, more pointedly this time. 'Yes or no?!'

'Yes!' shouted Vigh through his teeth. He put his hand on the corner of his mouth to wipe the blood.

'We searched everywhere for the missing three,' said Gohtek. 'Now I understand better.'

'Where did they go?' asked Kàtchah.

'To warn the dragons of your arrival,' said Boreth.

Kàtchah backhanded Boreth. 'Why are they heading to Darakön? The truth, please!'

'To get the books before you do,' Vigh conceded.

'There,' Kàtchah condescended, as though he were talking to delinquent children, 'that's better. You see, it all goes well when you say the truth. Now, pick up the maps and show us which of the four passages the others took.'

Vigh and Boreth picked up the maps and unrolled them. The four exits had been clearly indicated: one close to the river, quite off east; another closer to Firlan but still quite far from it; a third to the west, south of the second, perhaps almost at the same level; and the last, more north, near the newer tunnels.

The one Jimmy and Meysah had taken was the second exit. Niome had taken the third. Those two were located close to where Kàtchah had intercepted them. Boreth knew there was no point in lying about the exits his friends had taken; the Morkan Captain was smarter than that.

Boreth relinquished the information, pointing at the two exits in question. 'Jimmy and Meysah got out here. Niome got out here.'

'Ah, I see,' said Kàtchah. 'That's close to where we are now. You're going to take us to those two exits and show us where they are.'

'All right,' said Vigh, conceding.

Guards came and surrounded the two Lords. Gohtek and Katchah walked beside them, holding them by the arms. The Dukes, who had been waiting patiently in the hallway, walked behind, weapons at the ready. Vigh and Boreth held the maps in their hands.

Although they knew very well where the passages were, the masters weren't going to let the Morkans know that. They had preemptively discussed this very possibility: they were going to have the Morkans think they needed the maps to find their way. The maps would help, but if Vigh and Boreth were to have a chance at escape, they had a main idea of where to go.

They arrived at the passage Niome had gone through. Vigh kicked the stones that covered it. A few guards passed through before the two Morkan Captains, Boreth, Vigh and the Dukes followed. Boreth pushed the hatch open.

'Okay, close it,' said Gohtek, 'you're letting the cold air in.'

'It is kind of stuffy in here,' said Boreth, smiling at the Morkan mockingly. The other only narrowed his eyes.

After this, they walked to the passage Jimmy and Meysah had exited from.

'Get an army assembled,' Kàtchah told Gohtek. 'We're going to send troops out after them.'

'I won't let my polcs get too close to Darakön and risk sounding the alarm for the dragons,' objected Gohtek.

'If you get your fastest polcs, there won't be any need to worry about that,' said Kàtchah. Vigh and Boreth looked at each other, worried. 'Don't be so surprised,' Kàtchah told them.

Gohtek nodded and gave some orders in the Morkan tongue to some of his polcs.

Merlik and Garkhktak turned to Kàtchah.

'We're going back to Mork,' said Garkhktak. 'Our uncle needs to hear about this and assess. We *will* be back, though, with an army just for these two. In the meantime, take care you don't overstep your ground and spoil Mirauk's prize.'

'Take them now!' Kàtchah suggested with one brisk shooing motion.

'Tempting,' said Garkhktak, 'but you need them still, and they are too powerful for even us. They require an army to ensure they don't escape captivity. They are safer kept here until our return.'

'You should be proud of what you have accomplished here, Kàtchah,' said Merlik, flattering the Morkan Captain's ego. 'It is impressive. I'm glad we had a chance to see it.' He popped open the hatch. He looked at the two Lords. When he spoke again, his tone was dangerous. 'I will see you both soon.'

Out the hatch the two Dukes went into the dead of Winter, securing the hatch behind them.

Kàtchah and Gohtek led Vigh and Boreth back to their cells. Guards stood outside the door; the two Telorians were alone.

'We have to inform the others that Morkans are going after them and that we're prisoners here,' said Vigh. 'We must make them feel the urgency.'

'Do you think Niome has caught up with Jimmy and Meysah yet?' asked Boreth.

'She always was quite rapid,' said Vigh.

'All right, then. But just in case.'

Boreth closed his eyes and whispered,

Eimai stöihughat,
Dan eimai siginelef,
Idenas mehetot Jimmy!

Vigh did the same and sent the message to Niome. This was their call to each other, their spell in Ancient Telorian, for it had existed before. Normally they only thought the spell, barely whispering its words, but in urgent cases like this when they were all in trouble and separated, it was more effective to actually speak it.

* * *

In the wilderness of blizzards, Jimmy and Meysah quickened their pace even more. As difficult as it was to run in the snow, they did anyway for fear that the Morkans would catch up to them. They knew it was possible the Morkans could leave this very day or the next, but they would assume the Morkan soldiers were already on their tail.

The spell the Five shared didn't say everything, of course, but they knew that Vigh and Boreth were in trouble and that they may soon be as well. They were the only ones who could warn the dragons, but perhaps there was Niome also, Meysah thought, hoping his sister was all right. Still, they were closest to Darakön. They didn't know where Niome was, but she would be safe; Meysah sensed that she would be. Thus, adrenaline or no, they kept moving.

Niome was three days away from Firlan when she received the message. She had hoped she could rest in the forest since it would be warm in there, but since she was far behind her brother and Jimmy, she sensed the Morkans were closer. She kept on going at a steady pace, but it seemed to take forever to walk in the white sea all alone. When she got nearer to the forest of Firlan, she could hear the Morkans on the wind from afar. It was true; she had slowed and was tired. It had taken her four and a half days to get where she was.

Even if she couldn't see them, Niome knew the Morkans would be on top of her by nightfall. She hurried to the forest and hid in the trees, far from the open space but close enough to see the team of enemies go by. A group of maybe a dozen Morkans only were they, but still they presented a sizable threat for one person to defend against.

The cold had somehow weakened her powers, rendering her usual spells to keep warm inefficient. She knew that this was Mirauk's doing, though perhaps it was the separation from the others that contributed to her fatigue as well. There was no point in following behind the army. She had only one other option left: to go to Firlan and spend Winter there. She only hoped that Jimmy and Meysah would reach Darakön in time.

TO BE CONTINUED

<u>THANK YOU SO MUCH FOR READING!</u>

*If you enjoyed this book,
please consider taking a few moments
to write a review on Amazon or Goodreads.
It would mean so much.*

*Thank you.
May the stars shine upon you!*

<u>The Journey Continues</u>

*With the Five of the Star separated
from each other and from their allies,
they must find the strength to carry out their
mission, despite their enfeebled states.
Mirauk's phantoms are hunting them,
and as Bahvley strives to remember his forgotten
past, they all face the might of Mirauk's magic
unlike they've ever encountered before.*

MAP OF THE GREAT OCEAN VALLEY

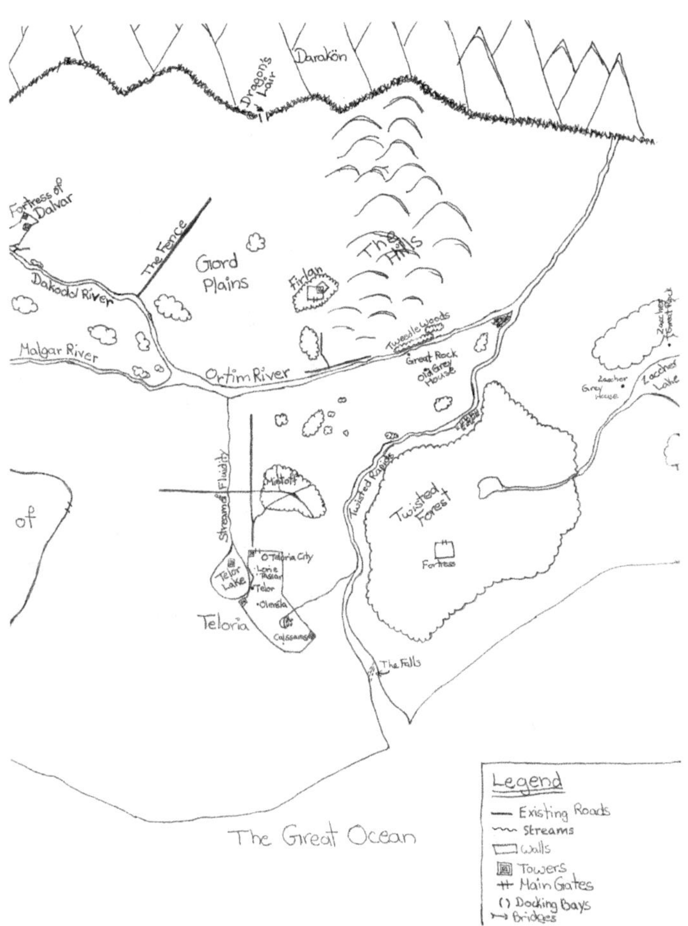

Darakön
Dragon's Lair
Fortress of Dalvar
The Fence
Giord Plains
Firlan
The Hills
Tweedle Woods
Zaacher Grey Rock
Dakodol River
Malgar River
Ortim River
Great Rock Old Grey House
Zaacher Grey House
Zaacher Lake
Twisted Rapids
Twisted Forest
Fortress
Stream of Fluidity
Mintoff
Teloria City
Lorie Thelen
Telor
Olensla
Telor Lake
Teloria
Calissana
The Falls
The Great Ocean
Legend
Existing Roads
Streams
Walls
Towers
Main Gates
Docking Bays
Bridges

About the Author

Celinka Serre is an indie writer and video producer working in freelance and sharing short stories of various genres, as well as anecdotes, on Medium. She

believes in the freedom of creativity and always continues to pursue her dreams. Having begun *Stardust Destinies* at age 19, the novel series is but one of her many projects, being also a writer of fan-fiction, various indie film screenplays, and a few collaborations as well.

<u>Wordpress Website and Blog:</u>
 https://binkyproductions.com/binkyinkwriting
<u>Medium - Stardust Destinies Extras:</u>
 https://medium.com/stardust-destinies
<u>Medium - Main Profile:</u>
 https://medium.com/@binkyinkwriting
<u>Twitter:</u> https://twitter.com/binkyinkwriting

www.ingramcontent.com/pod-product-compliance
Lightning Source LLC
Chambersburg PA
CBHW070801120726
47910CB00001B/255